EXCEPT
For The Bones

Other Alan Bernhardt mysteries by Collin Wilcox

BERNHARDT'S EDGE
SILENT WITNESS

EXCEPT For The Bones

COLLIN WILCOX

TOR

A TOM DOHERTY ASSOCIATES BOOK
NEW YORK

EXCEPT FOR THE BONES

A Tor Book
Published by Tom Doherty Associates, Inc.
49 West 24th Street
New York, N.Y. 10010

Library of Congress Cataloging-in-Publication Data

Wilcox, Collin.
     Except for the bones / Collin Wilcox.
         p.   cm.
     "A Tom Doherty Associates book."
     ISBN 0-312-93162-X
     I. Title.
   PS3573.I395E96 1991
   813'.54—dc20
                                         91-21579
                                           CIP

First edition: November 1991

Printed in the United States of America

0 9 8 7 6 5 4 3 2 1

This book is dedicated to the six of us.

SUNDAY,
July 15th

9:10 P.M., EDT

As he watched her come slowly down the staircase, a provocative upward view that enhanced the flare of faded blue jeans molding flanks and pelvis, Daniels felt himself tightening, involuntarily responding to the way she looked, the way she moved. She was thirty years old. Had she always moved like this, so sensually, so self-sufficiently, so disdainfully? Some women pandered to the male ego, titillated the male libido. Not Carolyn. She challenged men with a thinly veiled contempt for the weakness that made them want her.

Them that had, got.

And Carolyn had.

Meaning that her first impulse would be to throw the envelope in his face. Her reaction, her initial response, was predictable.

But it was her secondary response that would be definitive: the thrust that would follow the feint.

At floor level now, she put her canvas tote bag on the floor and unslung her leather shoulder bag. He'd bought the bag for her in Geneva, less than a month ago. He'd known she would love it. He'd been right.

"The fog's coming in," she said. "Will that be a problem for Bruce?"

"No. I called him when you were in the shower. He said it's clear at Westboro. Taking off in fog is all right. It's the landings that can be a problem."

"I wish you were coming."

"I can't. I've got to be here tomorrow. And you've got to be in New York." He shrugged.

As she strode toward him, her eyes searched his face. She'd sensed

3

a difference, sensed that something had changed. "Shall we go to the airport, then? Is Bruce there now?"

Daniels nodded. "He's there. He's ready, and the airplane's ready."

"So let's go." As she spoke, she came a last, significant step closer. She would kiss him good-bye. She would work her body against his, promises made, promises still to keep.

But this was the final scene, followed by fade-out. Good-bye to Carolyn.

Ultimately, everything ended. Even the sensation of her flesh naked against him, exploring, demanding. Finally exploding, the two of them.

The blank envelope lay on the arm of the sofa, within reach. As boardroom maneuvering must be meticulously choreographed, so must this moment of parting.

He shook his head. "I've got to stay here. You take the Jeep, leave it at the airport. Give Bruce the keys."

"Oh—?" She raised one tawny eyebrow. Did she pluck her eyebrows? Had he ever asked her?

"Oh?" she repeated. Standing motionless, hips loose, shoulders slanted, head cocked, she frowned, studying him carefully. Did women like her live in constant dread of this moment?

Women like her . . .

God, it was a Victorian phrase: "a certain kind of woman." Yet the distinction applied. Some women fucked for hearth and home, some for the money and the mink. Leave love for the poets.

"Carolyn . . ." As he said it, he could hear the equivocation in his own voice. It was a flaw. In both business and love, the offense always won. Take the initiative, take home the prize.

He reached for the envelope, held it out to her. "Here. Take this."

Eyes steady, mouth hardening, body tightening, she used thumb and forefinger to take the envelope. It was a nicely calculated gesture signifying a wry puzzlement, a gathering disdain. Carolyn, in control.

"What's this, Preston? Should I guess?"

"It's a check, Carolyn." He spoke softly, carefully measuring the words, gingerly monitoring the cadence. An hour ago, she'd been doing coke. The coke could set her off, running wild. It had happened at Hilton Head. Only a five-figure check had persuaded the management not to file assault charges.

"A check, eh? Another check?" Yes, she, too, was thinking of Hilton Head. They'd always been so remarkably in sync. "A check for how much?" Beneath the icy words, behind the cold gray eyes, rage was beginning to boil.

"Twenty-five thousand." He was satisfied with his voice, with the tone he could command. His business, after all, was manipulation.

"You son of a bitch." Suddenly she stepped close, swung, struck him on the side of the head, high. And then, as the envelope fluttered to the floor, she was on him. Her body was a wild, writhing knot of fury; her carmine-tipped fingers were talons. Her lips were drawn back to expose her teeth, as if she would tear at his exposed throat. Once she'd asked him for rough sex. He'd laughed at her. Uneasily.

Off balance, he staggered, momentarily recovered, then fell to his knees. Still she clung to him, ripping, tearing. How could he transact business, the man in command, with adhesive patches on his face? Behind his back, they'd snicker.

He rolled away, felt his shoulder strike the coffee table, a huge slab of natural slate. She was on him again. With his left hand he grasped her hair as he struggled to his knees. He jerked her head sharply aside, exposing her face, her jaw. He struck her with all his strength. Instantly, her eyes went blank, her whole body went slack. From an animal crouch, knees flexed, arms going slack now, she suddenly collapsed, fell backward. Her head struck the corner of the coffee table: a melon sound, splitting open.

In the savage silence that followed, only the sound of panting remained.

His panting.

Not hers.

10 P.M., EDT

Ahead, on the right side of the two-lane road, on the shoulder, red and blue and white strobes blinked and blazed: a police car parked behind another car. The police car was white. Was it the state police, or the locals? Was it Constable Joe Farnsworth, doing his duty? Fat, waddling Joe Farnsworth, pistol dangling beneath his paunch, a play-actor's spoof of a policeman. Two summers ago, the bastard had come up behind her, pressed against her, cupped her buttocks in his sausage-fingered hand. Vividly, she remembered the sour smell of his breath on the back of her neck. When she'd turned on him, he'd smiled. She remembered the smile, too: small, cupid's lips pressed between rosy cheeks. Narrow-set, hot little pig eyes. Constable Joe, Carter Landing's bad joke.

But the car had the state police shield painted on the door. Massachusetts' finest: a slim, trim state trooper examining his victim's driver's license in the glare of the patrol car's headlights. The victim was a teenage boy about her age, unsteady on his feet. Driver's license, good-bye.

When Diane had first seen the strobes she'd decelerated, downshifted. Yes, the speedometer needle was on fifty-five. Drunk or sober, sky high or belly-scraping low, she could always drive. She and the BMW—what else was there?

Ahead on the left, Diane's headlights swept over the chain-link fence of the school-bus yard: a half-dozen yellow and black buses, parked for the summer. Followed on the right by the familiar green sign with the white lettering: CARTER'S LANDING, POP. 3,754.

Ten o'clock on a July evening. Cape Cod. Sunday. Foggy. Chilly. Except for The Haven—the summer people, eating and drinking—the town was closed down. Inside the expensive German car with its expensive gadgets glowing in the dark, she was alone. She and the BMW, nothing else. Nothing more, nothing less. Still alone.

Always alone?

Four hours ago—five hours ago—she'd been in New York. If nothing changed in Carter's Landing, everything predictable, locked in, nothing changed in New York, either. Prisons. Herself the jailer of herself. So she'd gotten in the BMW and cranked up the sound and driven down the road, herself outrunning herself, watching the lights of New York disappearing in the mirror. Manhattan. The East Side. Park Avenue. The beautiful people, posing for the beautiful people. Even when they were alone, they posed. Was her mother at their view window now, posing, wineglass in hand, staring out at the East River?

Whenever they fought, her mother's face changed. Beneath the socialite's mask, the features of a fishwife were hidden. Expose the fishwife's face, and the fight was over. Not won, but over.

For both of them.

For her mother, on Park Avenue.

For her, slowing the BMW as she drew abreast of the Village Dry Cleaners.

Like every business establishment in Carter's Landing, all of them dependent on the tourist dollar, the Village Cleaners had the approved Cape Cod saltbox look: weathered gray shingles, white trim, a scrolled Colonial sign illuminated only by small spotlights. Neon was forbidden. But now, at ten o'clock, the sign was not illuminated; the shop was dark. Likewise the living quarters behind the shop were dark.

Signifying, therefore, that while his mother slept, early to bed, Jeff was either cruising or fucking. Or else he was drinking at Tim's Place. The exact sequence was a question of chance. Opportunity plus chance.

She pressed the accelerator, shifted from second to third, felt the car surge.

Yes, she could always drive.

10:10 P.M., EDT

Surprisingly, there was almost no blood.

She'd lost her urine, and the room reeked of feces. But there was almost no blood. There was only enough blood to turn her mass of tawny hair a thick, congealing crimson.

Her wide-open eyes were as inanimate as two stones. Lying on her back beside the limestone slab of the coffee table, her body had already begun to flatten on the bottom. No longer circulating through her body, her blood was settling. *Ultimately*, someone had said, *gravity claims us all.*

Two hours ago, locked together, inciting each other, guiding each other—reveling in each other—they'd made love.

Now, incredibly, she was dead.

He'd drawn the drapes and turned off all the lights, leaving only a single table lamp lit. He was sitting in a chair that faced the ocean. He could hear the sound of surf, that timeless, endless sound. He looked at his watch, but somehow the time didn't relate to reality. It was as if the surface of his consciousness was too fragmented to retain even the most elemental information. His data base was closing down. His—

From a nearby speaker the sound of the telephone suddenly warbled, shattering the silence. A cordless phone, that constant extension of himself, lay on the lamp table beside him. He'd already touched the phone, an automatic response, before he remembered: Carolyn, lying motionless less than ten feet from him. Carolyn, dead.

But why shouldn't he answer the phone? What was the connection?

His recorded message was short, followed by Kane's voice:

"Yeah, this is Bruce. I wanted to check whether you'd left for the airport yet. We shouldn't wait too much longer."

Listening to his pilot's voice, Daniels realized that he was frowning. Always, there was a hint of arrogance in Kane's manner, especially if he was exercising his pilot's safety-related prerogatives. If Kane refused to fly, plans were changed. There was no appeal. Accounting, Daniels knew, for Kane's habitual insolence. A pilot made life-or-death decisions. His life. His death.

Daniels realized that he'd risen to his feet and was moving to his study, to the telephone control panel. It was impossible to talk in the same room with the body.

The simple act of walking helped. He could feel himself surfacing, willing himself to take charge. From this moment on, time would begin to work for him, not against him. The jangle of the telephone had jolted him back to self-command, self-salvation.

He switched on the antique green-shaded brass study lamp, lifted the master phone, touched the button opposite N-50SR, the Beechcraft's identification. Moments later, Kane answered.

Without preamble, Daniels said, "Listen, Bruce, there's been a change of plans."

"Ah—" It was a noncommittal response. "So?"

"So Miss Estes isn't going to go with you tonight."

Silence.

"And—ah—I'm not going, either. I've got to stay here, at least until—until tomorrow." His voice, he knew, was ragged, his delivery uneven. Would Kane notice? Would Kane remember?

"It's just as well. I just talked to Flight Service, and they—"

"But I want you to go anyhow."

"What?" It was a single, flat-sounding monosyllable, Kane's specialty.

"I want you to go to Westboro. I want you to leave an envelope for Jackie, at the registration desk. Then—" Quickly, he calculated: it was a little more than an hour to Westboro, if everything went right. Three hours, probably, round trip. Once more, he looked at his watch. Time: ten-twenty P.M. Plus three hours—he ticked off his fingers. One-thirty, at least. Two o'clock, if Kane had to wait for takeoff clearance.

"Then I want you to come back here. To Barnstable."

"What?"

"That's what I want you to do."

"But, Christ, that could be four hours."

"It can't be helped."

A long, angry silence followed. Then: "That's assuming I can land here. Visibility's down to minimums."

"Do your best." He hesitated. Then, reluctantly: "There's a bonus if you get back tonight. Five hundred."

Another silence, this one for calculation. Finally: "Have you got the envelope for Jackie ready?"

"It will be, by the time you—" Momentarily surrendering to a knife-flick of panic, he broke off. *By the time you get here*, he'd almost said. "By the time you're ready, the envelope'll be there. I'll bring it to the plane. Now. Right now."

"You will?" It was a curious, speculative question. Even though the airport was close by, a precedent was in question. Servants carried envelopes, not the master.

"I want to get out of the house, get some fresh air. I'll be at the airport in a few minutes. If I miss you, I'll leave the envelope at the desk. When you get back, call. Tell the answering machine what time you got in. Then go to bed. I'll call you tomorrow."

On the other end of the line, Kane was chuckling: an insolent chuckle, Kane's little joke. A five-hundred-dollar joke.

Daniels replaced the phone in its cradle, took an envelope and five sheets of blank paper from the desk drawer. Folding the paper, his fingers shook. He sealed the envelope, found a pen, began addressing the envelope. The pen magnified the trembling of his hand. Slowly, as awkwardly as he must have written when he was a child, he began forming the two words: *Jacquelaine Miller.* As he wrote, it seemed that he could hear a prosecutor addressing the jury. The prosecutor would hold up the envelope, for the jury's inspection.

"You'll notice, ladies and gentlemen, how utterly different this childish scrawl is from the defendant's normal handwriting. The cause of this difference, we will show, is acute anxiety resulting from extreme guilt."

10:20 P.M., EDT

As the music hit her she let her body go with it. Manhattan to Carter's Landing to Tim's Place, the last of it, the best of it.

Behind the bar, Polly coolly nodded, then let her eyes wander toward the far wall. Yes, Jeff was there. He was holding a beer bottle, his body moving with the music. He hadn't seen her. Others were looking, though: the townies, looking over the tourist, then looking away. Everywhere on the Cape it was the same: the tourists looking through the townies, the townies spitting behind the tourists' backs. Meaning that money made the difference. Manhattan, Caen, Rodeo Drive, the Cape—it was all the same: the beautiful people posing for each other while the peasants looked on. Last week, at the Barnstable airport, she'd seen Teddy Kennedy. He'd looked chubby and old and angry.

Jeff was sitting at a small round table with two other men and a woman. As she watched, one of the men saw her. He touched Jeff's arm, said something. Quickly, Jeff turned toward her. He was surprised: his standard slow-smiling, lazy-lidded look of sensuous surprise, Elvis without the sideburns.

Carrying the bottle of beer, Jeff rose, said something to the others at the table, walked toward her. Smiling. Strutting.

"Surprise . . ." He raised the bottle, an invitation. "Have you got that ID?"

"I've got better than that, in the car. A lot better."

He moved closer, put his free hand on her waist, drew her close. He could feel her body pulsing, throbbing. An engine, revving up. Tonight, Diane was ready for anything—everything.

But she'd only left the Cape last Thursday, flying back to New York in her stepfather's plane. And now she was back. Would he have gotten involved, if he'd known she would come up so often? How far did she think a bottle of booze and a handful of pills and some New York grass could go? Didn't she ever look in the mirror?

"Okay, gotcha." Taking his time, he finished the beer, wiped his mouth on the back of his hand, put the empty bottle on the bar. "Let's go." He turned her toward the door. As she went through, he turned back, winked. The message: score one more tourist.

10:25 P.M., EDT

Daniels depressed the button that drew the drapes covering the floor-to-ceiling plate-glass windows. Because beyond the window, they waited. All of them.

There were only three elements: Carolyn's body, himself, and the rest of them. The body was the problem. The world was the threat. And he was the fulcrum, the focus. Move the fulcrum, and the equation failed. In prep-school algebra, the illustration had been a teeter-totter, always in balance.

Until now—until this hour—always in balance.

An hour ago his mind had gone numb, leaving him helpless.

Now, an hour later, his mind was racing. But it was a cacophony of confusion: a once-efficient machine gone wild. When he'd been a boy, his father had given him a steam engine, red-painted, with gilt letters and brass piping. The engine's governor, his father explained, was essential. Otherwise, the machine would fly apart.

A smooth, efficient machine. The phrase, he knew, described his mind. The proof was in the statistics, the balance sheet. The proof was in the *Forbes* biography, the cover story.

The slate slab that had been fashioned into a coffee table was further proof. The table had cost more than most men made in a year. It had taken six straining, sweating workmen to carry the slab into the house from a flatbed truck and set it on its base. The base was a section of bristlecone pine, thousands of years old, absurdly rare and therefore valuable. The table was placed in the approximate center of the museum-quality Persian rug that covered most of the oak-planked floor.

And the rug was stained with Carolyn's blood.

10:30 P.M., EDT

"What're these?" Jeff looked down at the two capsules she'd given him.

"Xanax. 'Ludes."

"You think you should do booze and 'ludes and still drive?"

"It's just out to their place." She looked at him, that look she thought was so sexy.

Except that Diane wasn't sexy.

She was rich, and she was wild, and she was willing. But she wasn't sexy.

Whatever it was, Diane didn't have it.

Did she think she had it? Was that why they were there, parked in her BMW, beginning to touch each other, letting it slowly begin, letting the booze and the pills and the grass carry them along?

"Your folks' place, you mean?"

"I mean my stepfather's place. Preston Daniels, tycoon." She spoke with bitterly exaggerated precision.

"We can't go there, though."

"We can most certainly go there." Now the bitterness was bleary, blurred by the backwash of whatever she'd taken. But, still, she spoke like the rest of them. He could clearly hear the sound of the private schools, and hired servants. The voices never changed. Neither did the cars, or the houses, or the clothes—or the airplanes.

Private schools and hired servants . . .

Servants like him, paid to clean up their messes.

He swallowed one of the capsules, swallowed a mouthful of beer. With three other cars—tourists—they were parked in a view area overlooking Nantucket Sound. On the beach below, two figures walked hand in hand along the water's edge. Two dogs, barking, bounding, circled the figures, a man and a woman. Across the dunes, toward town, a forbidden campfire glowed behind the dunes.

Dropping the second capsule in the pocket of his shirt, Jeff touched her bare forearm, let his hand linger. At the touch, she leaned toward him, sighed, rested her head on his shoulder. Whenever he was ready, she was ready.

He moved closer, used his right forefinger to trace her profile, forehead to chin, then down the curve of her jaw to the top of her blouse.

"Hmmm . . ." Languorously, she let her head fall back against the crook of his arm. Her blouse was cut wide and deep. With the little finger of his right hand, he felt the first swell of her breasts.

Summertime at Carter's Landing . . .

Tight jeans and scoop-necked blouses and a BMW that still smelled new. The last time they'd done it, started like this, he'd smelled her musk mingled with the BMW's musk, a turn-on that had made him smile. When she'd asked him about the smile, he'd—

A bright white light suddenly caught them: a cop with his goddamn spotlight, cruising. Joe Farnsworth, fat old Joe, getting his kicks. If Cindy Jensen, thirteen years old, had decided to testify against him, Joe would be on the other side of the badge now.

Slowly, the police car cruised by as the spotlight switched off. But Joe would be back. On a quiet Sunday night in July, with the weekenders gone, Joe would have plenty of time for them.

"Fucking pervert," Diane muttered. "He's played grab-ass with about every girl in town."

"Tell me about it." He popped open a fresh can of beer, drank, wiped his mouth on the back of his hand.

"Give somebody a gun and a badge, and then watch out." As she spoke, she drew away from him, reached for the ignition key.

"Where're we going?"

"We're going to Daniels's place. I already told you that."

"But someone's there."

"No one's there. Believe me, no one's there." She started the car, put it in gear, began to drive. She drove slowly, carefully.

"Two or three hours ago, I was making a delivery out there. I saw a light at your place. And their Cherokee was in the carport."

"Bullshit. He's in Atlanta this weekend. Business. And my mother's in New York. I just left her there."

"Okay. See for yourself." Leaning back in the seat, feeling the soft, easy warmth of the Quaaludes begin to flow, he was aware of his own cool, controlled power: the man with the right words, the right moves, everything covered.

"How long were you in Europe?" he asked. "A month?" Yes, his timing was perfect: low-down and lazy, Bogey on the late show, so calm, so cool.

"A month. Right. Give or take."

"Yeah, well, the reason I asked, your dad—your stepfather, excuse me very much—he's got a girlfriend. Did you know that he's got a girlfriend?"

Bitterly, she laughed. "That's new? Christ, just read the gossip columns, why don't you? Read the fucking National Enquirer."

"But this girlfriend isn't in the *National Enquirer*. This girlfriend is out at your place." Still watching her, he let the words hang there, power plus power, old Bogey, bringing them along. Then, easy and slow and soft: "I'd bet fifty dollars she's at your place. Right now. Right this minute. I bet fifty dollars she and your dad—your stepfather, excuse me very much—I bet they came in Saturday night, in his airplane. And I bet—"

"Jesus—" Suddenly smiling at him, the heat turned up high, she pressed down on the accelerator, sent the car surging ahead.

"Now what?"

"Now what?" It was a hot, tight question. Her smile was wide, her eyes suddenly wild. "Now it's trick-or-treat time, that's what. It's Halloween in July."

He smiled, settled back, let himself go slack. Diane could hit the high spots, no question. Drunk or sober, up or down, there wasn't anything Diane wouldn't do, even before someone dared her.

11:45 P.M., EDT

Suddenly dizzy, nauseated, the bile rising in his throat, Daniels dropped to his knees beside the body, lowered his head, closed his eyes. He must breathe deeply, mind over matter. Because if he lost control, everything ended. Here, now, he was alone: himself struggling to master himself, his only hope.

Please God, himself the master of himself.

Born alone, destined to die alone, those were the givens. But if that was the game, then where was the justice? Because the *Forbes* biography made him more vulnerable, not less. Everyone yearned to see the mighty fall.

So fate had stalked him, finally cornered him here in this empty house. Forced him to kneel beside her body, the penitent to his own terror.

Cautiously, he opened his eyes, raised his head.

Could he do it?

Could he touch that cold flesh again? Could he roll her onto the blanket, cover her carefully, then truss the bundle up with the rope he'd found in the carport, an unexpected boon?

Yes, he could do it. If he could raise his head, clear his throat, blink his eyes back into focus, then he could do it.

Soon it would be midnight. Almost three hours since he'd placed the envelope with the check inside on the arm of the sofa. It was a scene he'd often played before; he'd had no doubt of the outcome. Angry words, a few tears, a brave show of anger before the envelope disappeared into her purse and the exit lines began.

Cautiously, fearful that he might gag, he cleared his throat. Yes, the nausea had passed. Signifying that he could begin.

11:50 P.M., EDT

Ahead, she recognized the turn of the road that would reveal the beach house, see and be seen.

No, not see and be seen. Just see. *I spy*, a game for children.

Meaning that, *I spy*, she must pull off the narrow blacktop road, switch off the headlights, switch off the engine, make sure the transmission was in gear.

All done. To think through it was to do it unconsciously, her mind in control, leaving her body to soar.

I spy time.

Had she said it, or only thought it?

"Why're we parking here?" he asked.

Meaning that she hadn't said it, hadn't said the words aloud. Meaning that she must turn to him, smile, reach across him for the door latch while she said, "It's I spy time. All out." She swung the door open. "Alley-oop."

Alley-oop. It was another phrase from childhood. When her dad lifted

16

her off her feet, swung her high above his head, he always said *Alley-oop.* Laughing. Always laughing.

I spy. Alley-oop. Leftovers from childhood. Were there more? Was life one big leftover?

"I spy," Jeff repeated, mumbling the words. Laughing. Eyes empty. Stoned.

"Come on." She swung her legs out of the car, stumbled, recovered, pushed the door shut. "I spy."

Just ahead, through the knee-high cut grass, a sandy footpath led from the road down to the beach. As she descended, her feet sank into the sand, another childhood memory. But not this sand, not Cape Cod sand. California sand, the beach at San Francisco. She and her father, *Alley-oop.* And her mother, too. Even her mother, then. They'd—

From behind her, Jeff swore softly. Had he stumbled? Was Jeff surefooted? His father was gone, too. Long gone, killed in a motorcycle accident. *Alley-oop.*

On the beach now, walking in deeper sand, she watched the ridge of low dunes to her left. From beyond that ridge, she could see the beach house. Preston Daniels's beach house. All glass and natural cypress and stone, once featured in *Architectural Digest,* a big spread. Yes, now she could see the whole house. Part of it was cantilevered out toward the ocean, built on concrete piers. In the living room, light glowed golden behind drawn drapes. And in the carport, she saw the outline of the Jeep Cherokee. The BMW and the Cherokee were the two cars she most liked to drive.

She was standing motionless in the sand, looking at the house. With a can of beer in each hand, Jeff was standing beside her.

"Here." He handed her a beer. Then: "See, he's in there, just like I said. With his girlfriend, sure as hell."

Still staring at the house, she sipped the beer. Should she go back to the car, pop a Xanax? Should she have locked the car, if the Xanax was in there? Insurance would take care of the BMW. But who would take care of the Xanax?

Trick or treat.

I spy.

Which game were they playing? Why? What was the penalty, what was the prize?

Preston Daniels, surprised. The thought was the prize. *I spy.*

She was walking up toward the house. Opening on the flagstone patio, the front door was on the left side of the house, with the carport beyond. The cantilevered deck faced the ocean. When she reached the patio, she could see into the living area. She could—

The front door was opening. Wearing jeans and a sweater, Daniels was framed in the pale oblong of light. Mr. Perfection: tall, wide shoulders, narrow waist, a movie star's profile. Slowly, cautiously, she dropped to her knees in the sand. Beside her, Jeff was kneeling, too. Could they be seen, silhouetted against the phosphorescence of the surf? There was no moon. Meaning that—

Warily, as if something had alerted him to danger, Daniels was closing the door behind himself. He was standing motionless on the patio, his whole body tense.

Preston Daniels, frightened.

Jeff shifted irritably. "What're we—?"

"*Shhh,*" she hissed.

Daniels was striding across the patio to the carport. Now he disappeared, cut off by the corner of the house.

"Why don't we—"

"*Shhh.* Shut the fuck up, will you? I want to—"

Suddenly Daniels reappeared. Striding quickly, he was carrying a gardening tool—a shovel. With the shovel in his left hand, he went to the tailgate of the Cherokee. He unlocked the tailgate, raised it. The courtesy light came on, revealing the interior of the station wagon, the rear seat folded down. With the handle of the shovel, Daniels struck up at the Jeep's headliner. One blow. Two. With the third blow, the interior went dark. Faintly, metal clanged against metal as Daniels slid the shovel inside the car.

"He broke out the light."

"*Shhh. Wait.*"

Moving erratically now, as if he'd suddenly lost his arrogance, Daniels was striding from the carport to the front door. He opened the door, stepped quickly inside the house. His shadow crossed the curtains drawn across the entryway windows. The shadow moved toward the living room.

"So now what?" About to rise, Jeff gathered himself. "What'd you—"

18

"Wait. Get down." Urgently, she pulled on his forearm. "He—he's acting weird."

"Weird, huh?" Grunting, Jeff sank down beside her, sat on the sand with his back to the beach house, drank from his can of beer. He'd lost interest.

12:01 A.M., EDT

On both knees, Daniels pushed on Carolyn's limp, sickeningly floppy corpse until she lay facedown on the Persian rug. Breathing hard, he felt for her waist.

Her waist?

Or *its* waist?

She'd been dead for almost three hours. When did a dead body become an object, no longer a person?

He locked his hands together beneath her waist, heaved, managed to lift the jackknifed body almost to his shoulder level as he knelt. But her head and her feet still touched the floor; he hadn't the leverage to lift her clear of the floor. Panting now, he shifted his grip, tried again. It was worse, not better. And the rope was slipping, allowing one of her hands to escape the blanket. He lowered the bundle to the floor again, straightened, felt for her head inside the blanket, felt for her shoulders, then her armpits. He crouched, heaved, began pulling her toward the entryway.

Even as a child, he'd never been strong in the upper body. His legs had been strong; in prep school he'd run the fifty-yard dash. But he'd never been able to chin himself more than a few times, and push-ups had always been a problem.

And now—here and now, at age fifty-five—his upper body weakness could cost him. Cost him dearly.

Cost him everything.

19

12:05 A.M., EDT

About to drink from the beer can, the last of it, Diane saw the front door open again. But this time there was no oblong of light. Moments before, the house had suddenly gone dark.

If they came out together, Daniels and his girlfriend, she would run to the BMW, parked just over the dunes. Whichever way they went in the Jeep, she could follow them, trick or treat, I spy. If Jeff moved fast enough, got himself together, he could come. Otherwise, he could walk back to town. He could—

Dimly framed again in the darkened open doorway, Daniels was crouched, dragging some secret burden, just coming into view: a strange, amorphous shape, wrapped, trussed. Responding to something elemental, Diane drew back down the slope of the dune, until only her head showed above the crest. Beside her, Jeff stirred, twisted to face the house.

"What—?"

"Shhh." Roughly, she grasped his shirt, pulled him down. "Shut up," she hissed, her eyes fixed on the patio. Now Daniels was gently lowering his burden until it lay flat on the flagstones. He strode quickly to the front door, closed it, tested it carefully, then returned to the bundle. He bent double, found a grip, braced himself, began dragging the deadweight across the patio toward the carport.

Deadweight . . .

"Jesus," Jeff breathed, "what's that, do you think?"

"It's a—" Her throat closed. Then, in a half-strangled whisper, "I think it's a body. It looks like a dead body."

And, as she spoke, the wrapping parted. Something white protruded: a hand, a forearm, dragging on the flagstones.

"Oh, Jesus," Jeff whispered. "Oh, God." His voice was hushed, awed. Then, differently: "Wow."

12:15 A.M., EDT

The right front wheel struck the shoulder of the road; the BMW tilted sharply. She jerked the steering wheel hard left, lifted her foot from the accelerator.

"Jesus, watch it. Or pull over, let me drive. I know the road. If you don't switch on the headlights, you should let me—"

"Shut up. Just shut up." Ahead, in the darkness, on the narrow, deserted blacktop road that wound inland, she could just make out the shape of the Cherokee as it topped a rise a half mile ahead. The Jeep, too, was running without lights. Preston Daniels, rich and powerful and famous, running without lights, furtive as a thief in the night. With the thought came quick-cut flashes of other images: Preston Daniels, granting interviews. Preston Daniels, at ease in his private airplane.

Preston Daniels, looking at her with that particular smile meant only for her; pitying her, patronizing her.

Despising her.

And now, on the road ahead, he was—

"She must've OD'd," Jeff was saying, his voice tight and strange. "That's what must've happened. I bet she OD'd, and he's freaking out. That's gotta be it. Someone like that, all that money, famous, if she OD'd, what's he going to do? Someone like that, he can't afford to—"

"Shut up, will you? Will you just try and—"

Ahead, atop another low rise in the road, twin red lights winked. Once. Twice. Stoplights. He was slowing, turning to the right now.

"Look—" Also braking, she pointed.

"Jesus." Jeff was sitting straighter in his seat, staring.

"What?"

"That's a dead-end road. A cul-de-sac. Don't turn into it. Go on by."

"A dead end?"

"Yeah—Jesus—I know where he's going. Now I know."

21

"Well?" she demanded, stopping the car and setting the parking brake. "Are you going to tell me?"

"He's going to the landfill. That's all he can get to, down that road."

"What d'you mean, the landfill?"

"They're bringing in dirt and rocks and shit from all over this part of the Cape, and dumping it. They're going to make an overpass, something like that. Every day, the dump trucks come. Pretty soon there's nothing but piles of shit. They bulldoze down the piles, and they start all over again."

"Jesus," she whispered. "That shovel . . ."

"Yeah."

MONDAY,
July 16th

6:20 A.M., EDT

Lying on her back, naked, aware that she dreaded what she would see, what she would feel, yet aware that she must do it, Diane let her eyes come slowly open.

Yes, they were lying side by side in the motel room she'd rented last night. It was the same scene she'd played twice since they'd known each other: awakening in a strange room, remembering the night before as if it had happened to someone else: a different person, in a different place. She'd felt herself blushing as she watched the clerk take his time checking out her credit card and her ID. And when the clerk finally handed over the registration chit, smirking, she hadn't had the stones to ask him the price of the room. Finally he'd told her, the son of a bitch, doing her a favor, she with her gold VISA card, a five-thousand-dollar limit, him with pimples on his face, just another townie. All of them hated the summer people, the tourists. Even Jeff, really. Hating was Jeff's specialty, the thing he did best.

Now she felt the bed shift as Jeff moved. Lying still, she let her eyes close. This morning—here—now—she couldn't talk to him, couldn't look at him, not yet. First she must free herself from the memory of the human hand falling out of the trussed-up bundle being dragged over the patio toward the carport.

The time, she knew, was early; the sun was still low in the sky. It had been almost two o'clock before they'd found the room, undressed, got into bed, began to make love. It had been quick, last night. Quick and rough and meaningless.

Driving toward town last night, back from the road that led to the landfill, they hadn't talked, hadn't said a single word to each other

25

about what they'd done, what they'd seen. She wasn't even sure Jeff had seen the hand, dragging across the flagstones.

He was moving again. Stealing a look, she saw him sitting on the edge of the bed, his back to her. His back was hairy, with tufts at the shoulders. He was shaking his head. But slowly, carefully, as if something might rattle loose. Now he rose, steadied himself, walked to the bathroom. It was a hangover: last night's booze and pills were dropping Jeff hard.

She turned on her right side, found her watch, lying on the table beside the bed. But the numerals were blurred, fuzzy. Had her eyes suddenly gone bad? During Prohibition, she'd once read, people went blind from bad liquor, ethyl alcohol, substituted for grain alcohol. She blinked: once, twice. Yes, the numerals were sharpening: thirty-five minutes after six.

Yesterday at this time she'd been asleep in Manhattan. There was a song from the forties or fifties, a soft, syrupy, sappy ballad, something about the difference a day made: *twenty-four little hours* was the refrain, more retro-chic to go along with old telephones and radios and juke-boxes with bubbles running endlessly through colored neon tubes.

She'd gotten up about nine o'clock yesterday. Her mother had been in the kitchen, drinking coffee and smoking a cigarette. Mail had been scattered on the countertop, and when her mother looked her full in the face, she immediately guessed the truth: her grades had come. Silently, every line of her body registering contempt, her mother had handed over the computer printout: two Ds, one D-minus, one C-minus. There'd been the letter from the dean, too, brief and to the point: probation next year, with a "review of the situation" at the end of her first term.

Using words they'd never used before, they'd fought for almost two hours. Then her father called, from San Francisco. It was interesting, one part of her observed, that both parents had gotten her grades at the same time, the same day. And, God, how predictable it was, the difference in their reactions. Her father had been disappointed, let down, at a gentlemanly loss. Her mother had been flat-out furious.

So she'd left. She'd crammed a change of underwear and her diaphragm and her stash and a half-finished paperback into a tote bag, stuffed her wallet in her purse, and slammed out of the apartment. She'd gotten in her car and started to drive. After a few miles she'd realized that she was going toward Massachusetts, meaning that she was going to the Cape. It was, after all, the only place that meant anything to her. If she found Jeff, fine. If she didn't, fine. There was always the booze and the pills. Xanax. Nirvana in a capsule.

And then, trick or treat, Halloween in July, the whole world had tipped, tilted toward her.

So that, treat and not trick, she was in command. Completely, accidentally, incredibly in command. Money was only money, grades were just grades. But the law was the law, never mind the benefit balls or the dinners with senators or *Forbes* magazine. It all came down to the law, a tooth for a tooth, kill or be killed.

Diane Cutler. Goddess for a day. Whatever power Preston Daniels had, she could cancel it out. Fuck with Diane Cutler and she'd press the button. All fall down.

But where was the pleasure; which way was the high? They hated each other, she and Preston Daniels. Sometimes it seemed that her hatred for him was the center of her life, all that kept her focused.

So why, now, was the void still there? Her finger was on the button, her foot was on his throat. So why did—?

The toilet was flushing, the bathroom door was coming open.

"You, too, eh?" He looked down at the floor, found his shorts, sat on the edge of the bed, began pulling the shorts over his knees, his buttocks. Jeff was only twenty-two, but already a roll of fat circled his waist. "You can't sleep either?"

She made no reply.

"I've got to drive into Boston. One of the pants pressers broke down Saturday. It's a steam coupling."

Silently she nodded, watched him dress. If he cared anything about her, really cared, he'd come to her, kiss her, caress her. He'd want to make love to her in the light of morning, not always in the dark, not always stoned. He'd tell her how beautiful she was, naked.

He rose from the bed, went to the window, adjusted the blinds. "The fog's in."

"Is that a fact?"

Would he hear the sarcasm, pick up on the contempt? Last night, they'd seen something terrible. In bed, desperate, stoned, they'd clung to each other, turned each other inside-out. Yet now he was standing across the room, looking out the window, telling her the fog was in. He was dressed in black jeans and saddle-buckled black boots and a plaid work shirt, a biker without a bike, the story of Jeff's life.

He turned away from the window, looked at her, frowning, his thick eyebrows almost meeting above dark, grudging eyes. "What's that supposed to mean?"

"What's *what* supposed to mean?"

"You know what I mean."

She sighed, pushed herself up against the headboard, covered herself. In daylight, she knew, her breasts wouldn't turn him on. He'd look, then look away. "Why do I get the feeling that this conversation isn't going anywhere?"

He moved away from the window, came toward her. But, a few feet from the bed, he stopped, stood looking down at her.

"So what'll we do?" he asked. "About last night, about what we saw."

Suddenly she realized that she was looking away. Suddenly she couldn't meet his gaze. Why?

"We gotta talk," he said. "It's crazy, not talking about it."

"Don't worry. Go to Boston. Don't worry."

"Don't *worry*?" Suddenly his voice rose, a loud, plaintive lament. Followed, instantly, by a quick, cautious look at the wall. Could they be overheard? "Christ—" Voice low, he stepped closer to the bed. "Christ, someone *died* out there. We should do something."

"Not 'we,' " she answered. "*Me*. I've got to do something. Not 'we.' You go to Boston."

"Oh, yeah?" It was a hostile, petulant rejoinder: a boy on the school yard, taunting another boy, picking a fight. The two words were always the same: *Oh, yeah?*

"I saw it too," he was saying, still speaking in a low, tight voice— hissing, almost. "I saw everything, just like you did. I've got the same rights."

"The same rights?" She shook her head. "What're you talking about, you've got rights? What rights?"

"What're you saying? You just going to forget it? Is that what you're saying? Someone—Christ—someone gets killed, gets buried somewhere out in that landfill, for Christ's sake, and you aren't going to do anything? Is that what you're saying?"

"You go to Boston. I'm going back to sleep. When I wake up, I'll think about it."

"And then what? After you think about it, then what?"

"Look, Jeff—forget it, all right? It's got nothing to do with you."

He was standing with his booted feet spread wide, hands in the pockets of his not-quite-clean jeans, another muscle-bound biker imitation. Now, she knew, he would run through his tough-guy sequence: two or three disgusted shakes of the head, followed by a hunching of the shoulders. "No, *you* look, Diane. You look, and you listen. And you better listen good, because I'm only going to say it once. Now—" Another bully-boy pause, for emphasis. "Now, neither of us knows what happened last night. But both of us saw Preston Daniels, Mr. Big himself, stuffing someone in his Cherokee and driving out to the landfill. And, surprise, it turns out that we're the only ones to see him do it. There was just me and you and Preston Daniels—plus whoever was wrapped in that blanket, or whatever it was. Now—" Another pause. "Now, it's pretty plain that whatever plans you got, they don't include me. Which means that, as of now, as of right this minute, whatever plans I've got—well—that's my business. Right?" He turned, went to the door, opened it, and left.

9 A.M., EDT

Daniels placed the spray can of cleaning solvent on the coffee table, placed the sponge and towels beside the spray can, stood motionless, staring down at the assortment.

A slab of stone . . .

Clearly, he could visualize the tabloid headline: TWO-TON COFFEE TABLE IS BILLIONAIRE'S UNDOING.

And the lead paragraph: *"Unable to remove the rug stained with the telltale blood of his mistress, unable to clean the rug without leaving telltale stains on the polished oak floor beneath the rug, Preston Daniels was arrested yesterday for the murder of Carolyn Estes, who was known to have spent at least two love-nest weekends with Daniels on Cape Cod."*

A plastic drop cloth, the kind painters use . . . If he could find a store open, he could buy a drop cloth, put it under the rug, protect the floor. There was a hardware store in the village. When did it open? Was it open now? Could he—?

The telephone, warbling.

Should he answer?

Yes, he must answer. There were decisions to be made, contracts to sign. Monday morning, nine o'clock. On his desk, Jackie would have already placed a digest of his appointments for the day, all neatly typed. So he must talk to Jackie, the only associate who had his private Cape Cod number. Only Jackie, the one person he could really trust.

"Yes. Hello?"

"Preston?" Just two puzzled syllables. But with it went all hope, everything gone, lost. Millicent, calling from New York.

WIFE EXPOSES BILLIONAIRE'S LIES, SUES FOR DIVORCE.

"Millicent?" It was, he knew, a silly-sounding, ineffectual response. But why was she calling? How could she have—?

"I thought you were in Atlanta." Her voice was cool, measured, cautious. Millicent, reflexively suspicious. Speculating.

"I—the conference blew up. One of the principals—his name is Powell, I don't think you know him—he had chest pains after lunch yesterday. So I decided to come up here, unwind. I should've called you. Actually, I was headed for New York, but the weather turned bad. Bruce found out that Barnstable was clear, so we just came over the top of the New York TCA."

Was he saying too much, explaining too much—protesting too much? Was he—?

"Is Diane there?"

"Diane?" Thank God, he could ask the question straightforwardly, truly surprised, no calculation required, the luxury of innocence. "No, she's not here. Why?"

"Oh—" In the single word he could hear it: the constant mother-and-daughter refrain, that long-running third-rate tragedy. Or was it a farce?

"Oh—" came the drearily predictable follow-up, the lamentation that never ended. "—we had a fight yesterday. Her grades came, from Swarthmore. Actually, they came in Saturday's mail, but Dolores misplaced part of the mail, the usual. I think we're going to have to let her go. I just don't see any other way. We should talk about it, tonight. We—"

"Millie. Let Chester handle it. That's his job, to keep things running smoothly. Tell him to fire her, and hire someone else. Christ, Chester's paid good money, to—"

"Could Diane be in the village, do you think? She left about three, yesterday. Slammed out, the usual. She's on probation at Swarthmore next year."

"Well, she'll—"

"Where else would she go, if she didn't go to the Cape?"

"Listen, Millie, I've got to—"

The phone warbled, another line. Thank God, reprieve.

"Listen, Millie, that's Jackie, I'm sure. And I'm running late."

"We've got the dinner at the museum tonight. I'm introducing Dr. Granger, you know. So we'll be at the head table."

"I'll be home by six."

"And if you see Diane—" Heavily, she let it go unfinished.

"I'll talk to her. Yes."

"Thank you."

"Gotta go. Love you." It was their standard wind-up line, now even more meaningless, more grotesque. Millicent, worrying about a college report card. Him, struggling for survival, fighting for freedom itself. At the thought, the instant's image of a barred prison door suddenly seared his consciousness.

Automatically, he pressed the call-waiting button. "Yes?"

"Mr. Daniels. Are you weathered in?" It was Jackie, tactfully giving him room to maneuver. Did Jackie know about Carolyn? Did she suspect? Yes, almost certainly Jackie suspected. She and Kane, his accomplices. Price tag: a hundred fifty thousand for Jackie, seventy-five for Kane. Checkbook loyalty. Was there any other kind?

"No—no," he answered, "it's not the weather. But there's—Bruce says there's a radio problem on the airplane. A backup radio, nothing serious. But it'll be two hours, probably, before I can get out of here.

31

You'd better reschedule everything for a two o'clock start, and I'll keep you updated. Anyone I should call in the meantime?"

"Kent Williams, on his refinancing package?"

"I should, Jackie. But I'm going to ask you to do it. If he can't stay in New York beyond, say, four o'clock, then tell him I'll come out to Los Angeles in the next two days. Tell him we've only got the last inch to go, assuming the interest rates behave. Charm him."

"I'll try—" She made no effort to disguise her disapproval. So it was happening. Beginning with the change in Jackie's voice, it was already happening. Henceforth, she would be watching. Covertly watching. A hundred fifty thousand, after all, was finite; it only bought so much.

"I'm sorry, Jackie. I've—there's something I've got to handle, up here. A family problem." He considered, then decided to say, "It's Diane. I just got off the phone with Millie."

"Ah—" Now her inflection suggested a reprieve, a reservation of judgment.

When was the last time he'd apologized—to anyone?

"Okay?" he asked. It was, essentially, another apology, a muted plea.

"Sure. See you about two." She hesitated. "Good luck."

"Yes. Thanks."

10 A.M., EDT

As Kane switched off the Buick's ignition and set the hand brake he saw Steve, the line boy, waving to him through the window of the airport office, then holding his hand to his ear: a telephone call. Without doubt, Daniels.

Pocketing his car keys and checking another pocket for the keys to the airplane, Kane nodded, hurried into the office. As he picked up the telephone Kane turned to look at the flight line. Yes, it was there, parked between a Lear Jet and a Falcon: Daniels's Beechcraft Super King Air, one of the best, most stable, most trouble-free airplanes he'd ever flown. For Daniels, nothing less was acceptable.

"Hello?"

"You're back. Any problems?" Daniels asked.

"No. The weather wasn't the best. But it wasn't the worst, either."

"On the tape, you didn't give the hour you came back."

"It was almost three o'clock." He gave it a disapproving sound. The status of pilots, after all, differed from other employees. On the pilot's skill, everything depended.

"Can we be ready to go at noon?" Daniels was asking.

"I'll have to check the weather and the notams, but it should be all right. If not, I'll call you."

"Is La Guardia possible?"

"Probably not. By the time I got the flight plan cleared, we could've already landed at Westboro."

"You can plan on picking me up here at—" Daniels broke off. Then: "No, I'll drive out to the airport. I'll take the Cherokee."

"Will you and—" Meaningfully, Kane let a beat pass. Which would profit him the most: "Miss Estes," the approved greeting—or "Carolyn," the high-risk choice? If he ever caught Carolyn just right, a few drinks downwind, stranded by Daniels in just the right circumstances, he knew he could have her. Once, joking, they'd talked about the mile-high club, he and Carolyn. Get in the Beechcraft, fly out over the ocean, put the goddamn airplane on autopilot. Meaning that he and Preston Daniels would be partners in—

"It'll be me. Just me." Abruptly, the line went dead. As Kane cradled the telephone, he heard someone calling his name. Still warmed by the fantasy—he and Carolyn and the Beechcraft over the ocean, naked on Daniels's own couch—he was smiling as he turned to face Steve, the line boy.

"Here." Steve extended a plain white envelope. "This is for Mr. Daniels. Can I give it to you?"

"Sure." He looked down at the flimsy envelope with "Mr. Daniels" printed in adolescent block letters. Inside, he could feel a single sheet of paper. "Who's it from?"

"A guy named Jeff Weston left it. He and his mother run the dry cleaners in Carter's Landing. I don't know whether it's from him, or whether he just dropped it off."

Kane shrugged, and slipped the envelope into the outside pocket of his chart case. Then: "Put some Jet A in the Beechcraft. Fifty gallons in each side."

"Now?"

"Of course, now."

10:30 A.M., EDT

In successive folds, he began turning back the Persian rug, working from one edge toward the stone slab table. First the rug, then the pad.

An hour remained. Only an hour before he must close up the house, draw the drapes, lock the door, set the alarm, test it, get in the Cherokee, drive to the airport. The hardware store hadn't opened until ten minutes after ten o'clock. When the proprietor had finally arrived, ten minutes late, he'd—

Yes, there it was: the polyfoam rug pad, stained with her urine. He gritted his teeth, drew a last long, deep breath, then folded the rug one final time, draping it over the coffee table. Revealing—yes—the bloodstains on the pad, already darkening. He stepped clear, grasped the pad, doubled it back over the rug—

—revealing two corresponding stains, darkening the oak floor beneath the pad: one stain the blood, one the urine.

Quickly, he unwrapped the flimsy plastic drop cloth he'd bought at the hardware store. He folded the drop cloth, refolded it, covered the stains on the floor. A moment later the pad was back in place, and the rug, covering it. He reached for the bottle of 409 Spray Cleaner and began spraying the two stains.

10:40 A.M., EDT

Diane dropped the key on the counter, left the motel office, walked to the BMW. Overhead, the last of the fog was burning off. As the sun grew brighter, the memories of last night's shadowy menace were fading. The booze, the pills—the shape wrapped in the blanket—how much was real, how much unreal? How much imagined?

During spring break, only a few months ago, she'd thought she was in love with Jeff. Now they were strangers. When he'd left the motel room she'd showered, let the hot water cascade over her for a long, long time. Millions of years ago, life had moved out of the sea to the seashore, freshman zoology. Was that why water could comfort, could heal?

Was that why some returned to the water one last time?

San Francisco, some said, was the last stop for suicides. There was only the ocean left. The ocean, and the bridge. Always the Golden Gate Bridge, one final touch of class, never the Bay Bridge. Sometimes the bodies were never recovered. Sometimes the sharks got to them before the bodies could fill with gas and bloat, rising to the surface.

She opened the BMW's door, got in behind the wheel, closed her eyes, let her head fall back against the seat.

Preston Daniels, tycoon.

Preston Daniels, murderer.

He'd brought his girlfriend to Carter's Landing the night before last. And last night he'd killed her.

And only she knew. She and Jeff Weston, the man she'd once thought she loved, a stranger now. Leaving only her. Here. Now. Alone. Once more—still—alone, unaccountably numbed by the incarnation of her boldest fantasies: confronting Preston Daniels, destroying him. How many times had she lain sleepless in the night, imagining herself confronting both Daniels and her mother? She'd sometimes made herself sob, imagining the scene: the tragic adolescent at bay, desperate and yet fearless, vulnerable and yet invincible, herself the creator of herself.

The scenes always began differently—but the ending never varied. She'd found proof of Daniels's infidelities: pictures, taken with her own telephoto lens, recordings, made with her own tape recorder. Out of pride, her mother would have no choice. She would call her lawyer. Then she would call her travel agent. She would reserve two tickets, first class, on the next flight to San Francisco.

They'd been married three years, Daniels and her mother. Before that, her mother and father had been married for fifteen years. When they told her they were divorcing, they'd taken her for lunch to the Saint Francis. She'd had her fourteenth birthday only the week before. She'd fantasized that her parents had planned to invite her to lunch and give her a very special present, something that had arrived late.

And then, after the waiter brought the main course, they'd told her. It had been her father, really. Her mother had just sat across the table, expressionless, watching her. They weren't in love anymore, her father had said. His face had been stricken, his voice choked. Yes, of course, she and her mother would live in San Francisco.

But a year later, they were living in New York. She'd been fifteen and a half. At the thought, she grimaced. She'd still been so young that she counted her age in half-years.

And now she was eighteen. Incredibly, the fantasies were materializing. One word from her—one call to the police—and they would pay.

11:50 A.M., EDT

Daniels handed his attaché case and his jacket to Kane, then climbed the air stairs to the Beechcraft's cabin.

"All set?" He was satisfied with his voice: calm and crisp, in control. In part, he knew, it was the clothes: pinstripes, white shirt, a club tie, shoes from Savile Row. The uniform. As he'd taken off his jeans and sweatshirt and running shoes and began dressing for New York, he'd felt confidence returning.

"All set." Kane pulled up the air stairs, latched the door closed, carefully tested the closure. "Are you going to sit up front?"

Daniels shook his head. "No, thanks. Things to do." He put his attaché case on the floor beside the small conference table, sank into the forward-facing chair beside the table, and fastened his seat belt. An envelope addressed to him in crude block letters lay on the table. He gestured to the letter. "What's that?"

"A kid from town left it at the airport office for you, apparently. His mother runs the dry-cleaning shop. Or so I understand." Then: "Ready to go?"

Daniels nodded. "Ready." He watched Kane go forward and slip into the pilot's seat. Kane settled himself, buckled up, propped the preflight checklist on the glare shield; began flicking switches, adjusting dials, testing controls, methodically bringing the twin turboprop to life. As the energizer began to whine and the starboard propeller began to rotate, Daniels slit open the envelope. It was a dime-store envelope and contained a single sheet of cheap paper:

> *Mr. Daniels:*
>
> *I saw you at your house last night about midnight. I saw what you did. I also saw where you went in your Cherokee, if you know what I mean. I will wait and talk to you before I talk to the police, but I cannot wait long. There was someone with me who saw the whole thing too. So don't do anything foolish.*
>
>
>
> *Sincerely yours*
> *Jeff Weston*
> *(508) 645-1862*
>
>
> *P.S. I know how famous you are, so you could call yourself Mr. Davis, when you telephone me.*

As he finished the letter the whine of the engines rose, the airplane began to move. Daniels returned the letter to its envelope. He reached for his attaché case. It contained documents that, if compromised, could cost a fortune.

The letter, revealed, could cost him everything.

12:10 P.M., EDT

It was as if the car were responding to some surreal internal guidance, as if it were carrying her along Route 195 independent of her own volition. They were going to New York, she and the BMW. They were going home. No, not home. They were going to 720 Park Avenue, where her mother and Preston Daniels and two servants lived—and where she, too, had a room.

But home was San Francisco. Home was the house on Sacramento Street, and her room that overlooked the rear garden.

Except that the house on Sacramento had been sold soon after she and her mother moved to New York. He'd had to sell the house, her father had tried to explain, because her mother's father had loaned them the money for the down payment. And he wanted his money back.

Always, it came down to her mother. Her mother had wanted a divorce so she could marry Daniels. Because of her mother, strangers now lived in the house on Sacramento Street.

And because of her mother, she and the BMW were traveling west on Route 195, bound for New York.

A few words from an emperor, she'd once read, could change the fate of the world.

A few words from her, and the emperor would topple from his throne, all fall down.

The emperor and his wife. All fall down.

12:30 P.M., EDT

Daniels opened his wallet, withdrew a small slip of folded paper that occupied its own pocket in the wallet. Half of one side of the paper was covered with a handwritten series of letters and numbers, meaningless to anyone but him. Ballpoint pen in hand, he unfolded the slip of paper, spread it on the table beside Jeff Weston's letter. Adjusting the pen, he considered for a moment, then carefully printed *JW 645-1862 BM.*

BM, designating blackmail.

He folded the slip of paper, put it in the wallet. Now he began tearing the letter into very small pieces, which he put in a compartment of the attaché case. He closed the case, locked it, placed it on the floor of the airplane. Soon, they would land at Westboro. Even if he could concentrate, there was no time now to work. Instead, he must focus on controlling his consciousness, preparing himself to make the next decision—and the next.

Three years ago, he'd printed *BM* on another slip of paper. It had happened less than a month before his marriage to Millicent. The man—Gordon Betts—had once driven for him, and had been fired for drinking. A college dropout with a high IQ, Betts had been knowledgeable about investments. He'd also been a talented, resourceful eavesdropper who'd remembered snatches of overheard conversations, and played the market accordingly.

Betts was also knowledgeable about the penalties for insider trading. Since he was being fired, he'd said, with nothing to lose, why shouldn't he tell the authorities what he knew about Daniels's "little shortcuts"? And he'd smiled: that fresh-faced, all-American smile.

At about that time Daniels had learned that Bruce Kane had once been arrested for flying drugs into the country. There'd been juvenile offenses, too, and one arrest for aggravated assault, part of a consistent pattern of violence. But Kane had never been convicted, and he'd been allowed to volunteer for Vietnam, where he'd learned to fly. He was a natural pilot. And a natural soldier, too: a born killer.

At first Daniels had considered firing Kane: there were, after all, scores of corporate pilots available. Then he'd realized that one problem could cancel out the other. The conversation with Kane had taken almost two hours out of a busy day. But never had he concluded a more effective, more subtle negotiation. He'd begun by expressing a desire to help in Kane's "rehabilitation." Two hours later, they'd had a straight business deal: for a five-thousand-dollar cash bonus, Kane would work Betts over, threatening to kill him if he tried blackmail again.

Three days later, Kane called him on his private line to say that "the problem" was taken care of. Later he'd learned that Betts had been in intensive care for three days.

He heard the note of the engines change, felt the angle of the floor shift. They were letting down for the landing at Westboro. He locked his chair to face backward and fastened his seat belt securely. Then he reached for the air-to-ground telephone, touch-toned Jackie's private number.

"This is Jackie Miller." As always, she spoke crisply, concisely. Without Jackie—someone like Jackie—he would never have done it: gone so far, so fast.

"Yes. Jackie. How're we doing?"

"Chester should be arriving at the airport just about now. Are you down yet?"

"We're on the approach, should be down in ten minutes. I want you to contact Chester. Tell him I'll meet him outside the terminal, at the curb. I don't want him to drive out on the ramp."

"Right." In her voice he caught a hint of puzzlement. A limo on the ramp to meet an arriving CEO was, after all, de rigueur.

"What's my day look like?"

"I've got Kent Williams scheduled for two-thirty." She let a delicately timed beat pass. Then: "He's coming here."

Appreciatively, he smiled. Originally, the meeting had been planned for Williams's hotel. As always, Jackie had anticipated, taken the initiative, given him the gift of time. God, how it steadied him, hearing her calm, measured voice. He tried to express his appreciation in the warmth of his own voice as he said, "You charmed him, Jackie." She made no reply. It was a complacent, self-confident silence. Yes, Jackie had it. And, yes, Jackie knew it. "I was going to offer Mr. Williams a

40

ride out to Los Angeles in the Beechcraft," she said. "Shall I? You won't need it for four days. At least—" A delicate pause.

Delicate? Why?

"At least," she continued, "not for business. Not that I can see."

Had her inflection changed?

Did the change signify some secret agenda, some preliminary positioning, perhaps to distance herself from him—from what could happen? Had Jeff Weston called the police? Was it possible that the police had called from the Cape? Was there a message waiting for him? A slip of paper instructing him to call Joe Farnsworth, the overweight, ineffectual chief of Carter's Landing's police department?

If it happened, that's how it would begin: with a telephone message. Good or bad, it all began with a telephone message.

"I'll have to talk to Bruce. Don't mention a ride to Kent."

"Yes sir."

He said good-bye, cradled the telephone. He was aware that Kane was gradually reducing power, beginning the approach. Off to the port side, Long Island Sound was materializing through a thin layer of haze. It was a perfect day for flying. In the cockpit, Kane was busy at the controls, bringing the plane steadily down. In New York, midtown, Jackie was coping with the unexpected change in scheduling. Uptown, Millicent would be with her hairdresser or dress designer, girding for her role in the museum banquet, a milestone that would surely lead to the chairmanship of the museum board, her most coveted prize.

While, on the Cape, Carolyn slept in a shallow grave.

As a favor, his civic duty, he'd helped with the financing of the overpass that would someday cover the landfill. He knew, therefore, that someday her body would rest beneath uncounted tons of concrete.

But he also knew that, as the trucks came to dump their loads and the bulldozers leveled the mounds left by the trucks, the blade of a bulldozer could uncover the body. It was a possibility, a short-run gamble. Long run, though, the concrete would set him free.

But never, he knew, would he be free from last night's images: Carolyn, lying dead in her own blood. Carolyn, wrapped in the makeshift shroud. Carolyn, her body moving with the motion of the Cherokee—as if she were alive, and struggling weakly against the rope that bound her.

Carolyn—tumbling into the grave that had taken him more than an hour to dig, even in the soft, newly dumped dirt of the fill.

And, the final image: a hand or a foot or a head, turned up by the bulldozer blade.

Carolyn, rising . . .

1:10 P.M., EDT

"Where's Chester?" Kane asked as he came down the Beechcraft's air stairs to stand beside Daniels on the tarmac. Kane wore khaki trousers, a light cotton sports shirt, scuffed running shoes. He was medium height, medium stature. The short sleeves of the sports shirt revealed thick, muscular arms. He habitually carried his hands away from his body, as if he were prepared to move quickly, decisively. His sandy hair was thinning fast on top. His gray eyes were flat, revealing nothing. His manner was both watchful and self-sufficient. His face was closed. A white scar ran across his forehead, an inch above his dark, thick eyebrows. His mouth was small, his lips slightly misshapen.

"Chester's picking me up outside." Daniels gestured to a pair of airport line attendants waiting beside their motorized tug for instructions from Kane. "Get the airplane taken care of, then meet me in the—" About to say "the lounge," he broke off. Then: "I'll meet you in the bar. There's something I want to talk to you about."

"When'll we be flying again?"

"The airplane might be going to Los Angeles tomorrow, but if that happens, you'll have to get someone else to fly it."

"Oh?" The question registered both puzzlement and bold displeasure. Kane didn't like others flying the King Air. "Why's that?"

"Because there's—ah—something I want you to do for me, back on the Cape."

Kane frowned. "The Cape?"

"Finish up here," Daniels ordered curtly. "Then meet me in the bar.

Be as quick as you can." He turned abruptly. Carrying the attaché case, he walked across the tarmac toward the terminal.

1:20 P.M., EDT

Impatiently, Daniels waited for the waitress to bring the beer Kane had ordered. Then he began speaking. The words were clipped and the tempo staccato, the approved mode for the commander delivering his battle plan:

"I don't have much time, so I'm going to come right to the point. What I want to talk to you about is Carolyn—Miss Estes. You probably didn't notice it Saturday when we flew up to the Cape, but she was in a pretty strange mood. She was—" The word was out before the terrible realization registered: he'd said *was*. Past tense. But if he corrected himself he compounded the blunder. So, smooth-talking, the maestro of deal-making, he heard himself saying: "She's pretty heavily into cocaine. You probably don't know that, but she is. And the past couple of days—" Projecting a wry puzzlement, he shook his head. "The past couple of days, she was really running wild. That's, ah—" He broke off. Then, the ultimate gamble, he said, "That's what happened last night. That's the reason we didn't go back to New York with you last night."

"Ah." Thoughtfully sipping the beer, Kane was nodding. "I was wondering, yeah." The other man was reacting well within himself. Watching. Waiting. And, plainly, speculating.

"What happened last night," Daniels said, "she got coked up. Really coked up. About eight o'clock, I think it was. And—well—she started an argument. A fight, really. I mean, she started hitting me. So—" He raised his pinstriped shoulders, a carefully calculated shrug. "So I hit her back. So, Christ, the next thing I know, she's out the door. She had a set of keys to the Jeep, and she was going to take the goddamn car. And—well . . ." He was pleased with the pause, with the timing, the tempo. Yes, it would work out. He could feel it, sense it. "Well, I stopped her. I clobbered her. I didn't have a choice, unless I wanted her to get into that Jeep, which I didn't. So, Christ, the next thing I know, she's taken off."

Kane frowned. "She took off? Where?"

"The last I saw of her, she was walking across the dunes, toward Carter's Landing. That was about eight-thirty, I guess. Of course, I expected her to come back, but she never did."

"So she stayed in Carter's Landing last night . . ." It was a speculative comment, dubiously delivered.

Once more, Daniels shrugged. "For all I know, she could've taken a cab, and gone to New York. I wouldn't doubt it."

"So why're you telling me about it?"

A final pause—one last handhold, surrendered. Then: "It's about that letter you gave me. That hand-delivered letter."

Kane made no reply. Instead, he lifted his glass, drank the beer, watched Daniels over the foam-flecked rim of his glass.

"It was from someone named Jeff Weston. I've got his phone number. He was—I guess he saw what happened. Maybe he thought I was—" Suddenly his throat closed. But only for a moment. "He might've thought I really hurt Carolyn. Seriously. All the noise she was making—shouting and screaming—I can understand how he'd think that. So now he wants to—he wants me to call him. It's—obviously, it's blackmail. So what I want, what I'd like you to do, is—" How should he say it? Did he need to say it? Cautiously, covertly, he searched the other man's face.

No, he didn't need to say it. All he had to do was wait for Kane to finish his beer, place the glass on the table, and say, "Is it like that driver you had—Gordon Betts? Is that the way you want it handled?"

Conscious of the sudden lightness, of the overwhelming rush of relief, he nodded—once, then once again.

"Same terms?" Kane asked.

"Better."

"Better?"

"Better. Much better."

4:30 P.M., EDT

As she slid her key in the lock and turned the knob, she felt it beginning: the leaden void at the center of herself, the heaviness dragging at her arms, her legs, even the muscles of her neck. If this was home, it was the burden that never ended.

"Diane?" It was her mother's voice, from down the hallway, from her bedroom, her dressing room. Yes, the timing was right. At four-thirty on a given afternoon, her mother would be dressing to go out. Millicent Crowley Cutler Daniels, exactly forty years old. Gown by Randolph, probably; coiffed by François, probably. And, soon, face by whichever trendy plastic surgeon charged the most. For now, just the face. For now, the boobs and the butt were still doing their jobs, thanks to the daily workouts, and the massages, and the good genes.

Did they still make love, Millicent and Preston Daniels? Did they sweat and grunt and rut on each other, in company with the rest of the race? She'd used to imagine them, locked together. Now she didn't bother.

"Diane—is that you?"

"It's me." She stood motionless in the entrance to the hallway leading to the bedrooms. Her bedroom was at the far end of the hallway, the last one on the right. Escape was therefore cut off. Little girl lost.

As, yes, her mother was stepping out of her dressing room. The emerald-green cocktail gown was perfect with the eyes and the hair and the gold sash and gold slippers and the emerald pendant. The face was perfect, too. Affluence on parade, the ultimate personification of the wife as trophy. Without her—or someone like her—the Preston Daniels image would be irreparably flawed.

"So you're back."

She lowered her leather tote back to the hallway floor, crossed her arms, tossed back her hair, raised her chin. Saying defiantly: "I'm back. Yes."

Standing stiff and perfect as a mannequin, hands clasped at her waist, the approved finishing-school posture, her mother spoke in a voice that matched her pose:

"Where'd you go this time, Diane?"

She had no answer. Incredibly, all during the long drive down from the Cape, she'd been unable to decide how to answer. Each plan canceled out the plan just made; doubt had preyed on certainty. One minute she'd felt like the winner, the avenger, the conqueror of Preston Daniels. The next minute—the next instant—she'd felt like the hunted one, the prey.

Who was her target—her victim? Was it Daniels? Or was it really her mother? Were they the same target? Must she destroy them both? Did she really want to destroy her mother? Could she?

Finally she'd turned up the sound system and surrendered herself to the beat of the music and the pulse of the car's power. Later—here, now—she would lock her door, go to the bookcase and reach behind the books and take out the clear plastic envelope, her stash.

Home was where the stash was.

Did her mother realize that if she'd taken the clear plastic envelope to the Cape, risked taking it, she might never have come home?

"Well?" Still in her finishing-school posture, her mother was now looking at her tiny gold watch. Price: five thousand. Tiffany's, of course. "Was it the Cape? Did you go to the Cape?"

Meaning that here—now—all the time had gone. The hours had been consumed by the minutes, the minutes by the seconds. Because if she said she'd been at the Cape, then she would go on. She would say more—and more. Until one was the victor, the other the vanquished. This time, there'd be no doubt.

Honesty, she'd learned, was the cruelest weapon. Answer the question—reveal the wound—and the victim was the winner, loser take all.

She drew a deep breath. Then, watching her mother's face carefully, she said, "Yes, I went to the Cape. I got there about ten o'clock."

"But you didn't stay at the beach house." It was a bitter statement, laced with contempt.

Once more, she made no response. Why? This was her chance, her opening. A final thrust, and she'd win. Why couldn't she do it?

"Answer me." The command echoed and reechoed, torn from deepest, earliest memory, a well of endless bitterness.

Releasing her. Finally releasing her.

"No," she answered, "I didn't stay at the beach house. I stayed at a motel. I forget the name. But it'll show up on the credit card statement."

"You slammed out of here, and drove up to the Cape, and went to a motel with that—that—" Wordlessly, her mother began to shake her head. Her calm, cool expression was disintegrating. Her impeccably drawn features, a miracle of makeup, were distorting.

"His name is Jeff Weston."

They were close, now. So close they could touch each other. So close that her mother's whisper stung like a scream of rage: "Thank you. Thank you very much."

Freeing her to strike out again: "Would you like to know why we stayed at a motel, instead of the beach house?"

"I imagine it was because your father told you not to—"

"He's not my father, Goddammit. He's your husband. He's your rich, handsome, successful husband. But he's sure as hell not my father."

"He's also the one who sends you to college, and who bought your car, and who pays your bills. *All* your bills."

"He doesn't pay for college, and you know it. Dad pays."

"He pays the tuition. But he doesn't pay for—"

"Forget it. Just forget it, all right?" Breathing heavily, aware that she was losing control, she moved forward an angry half step. Saying: "Excuse me. I was going to my room. Do you mind?"

"Don't take that tone with me, Diane. You might be eighteen, but as long as you're living here I'll thank you to—"

"Listen, Mother—" She broke off, struggled for control. Then: "Listen, if that's what's bothering you, then maybe you shouldn't sweat it. Because I don't think I want to go back to Swarthmore. When I think about it, I hate the place. From the first week, I hated the place. So why don't I just leave? Why don't I go out to San Francisco and see Dad? What about that?"

Now the flesh around her mother's perfectly outlined mouth had gone pale. When someone got angry enough, she'd read, or got scared enough, then the blood went to the solar plexus.

"This isn't something we can discuss now, Diane. It's almost five o'clock. And we've got to—"

"Don't tell me. You've got to go to a party. You and Preston. You can't stop to talk. Tomorrow, maybe, we can talk. Should we make an appointment, Mother? Should we?"

"I'm giving a speech, as it so happens, at the museum. A very important speech."

"Oh." Viciously mocking, she struck a pose. "Oh. How nice. How jolly for you."

"Listen, Diane—your father's coming. And I—"

"Oh. Well. If he's coming, then I think I'll leave. I think I'll get a few things together, and leave." She stepped forward again, struck her mother's shoulder with her shoulder. It was the first time they'd ever made angry contact. Or, in recent memory, any contact. "Excuse me. I want to go to my room. Do you mind?"

"*Diane.*" Just the one word. All that hate—eighteen years—all of it distilled in the one word. Here. Now. Everything.

"*Forget it.*" At her own door now, she flung the words over her shoulder. She went into the room, slammed the door, locked it. Wiping at her eyes with the heels of her hands, she went to the bookcase, reached up, withdrew the plastic envelope.

She'd never taken the whole stash with her before. It was a terrible risk, taking the whole stash. But she'd never felt like this before. Never.

She checked the closure of the envelope, thrust it into the leather tote bag, at the bottom. She went to the bureau, opened a drawer, took out underwear and blouses, jammed them into the bag, together with a pair of jeans. She'd always been amazed, how much the tote bag could carry. She went to the door. Then, with her hand on the knob, she hesitated, turned back, let her eyes linger a last time on the room, with all her things. Over the desk, she'd tacked a movie poster: James Dean, squinting against smoke curling up from a dangling cigarette, her favorite poster. It was an original, a collector's item. She went to the desk, ripped the poster down, tore it up, went to the unmade bed, scattered the pieces on the bed. Eyes stinging, she stood motionless for a long, final moment, looking down at the bed. Then she went to the door, picked up the tote bag, opened the door. A half-dozen steps down the hallway revealed that, yes, her mother had left her door open. It was an assertion of authority; a closed door would have signified defeat, retreat. Holding the tote bag, she went to the doorway. Facing the mirror, her mother was seated at her dressing table. She was

48

working on her eye makeup. Had tears damaged the makeup? Was it possible that her mother could actually cry?

Diane stood silently for another moment, watching. Then, quietly, she said, "On your way to the party, ask Preston what he did last night. Ask him where he was, what he was doing, about midnight."

She turned, walked down the corridor to the front door. One last time.

4:50 P.M., EDT

"Yes, sir?" Behind the counter, the sales clerk smiled. He was a tall, gaunt man with washed-out eyes and a pinched, uncertain mouth. His face was gray-stubbled. Resting on the counter, his blue-veined hands were knob-knuckled.

"Do you have any short lengths of iron pipe?" Kane asked.

"We sure do. What diameter? What length?"

"An inch, three quarters, it doesn't matter. About eighteen inches long."

The clerk nodded. "How about an inch? We've got that in stock."

"Fine."

5:20 P.M., EDT

After locking the tote bag in the BMW's trunk, Diane slid into the driver's seat, shut the door, sat motionless, staring at the concrete wall of the parking garage. As she'd ridden down in the elevator, fighting tears, she'd remembered the things she should have brought: her favorite bomber jacket, her snapshot album, her Madonna tapes, the serape that went so well with blue jeans. Her big saddle-leather purse was beside her on the seat. She opened the purse, checked inside. Yes, she had her wallet.

Was she really going to San Francisco?

Would Daniels cancel her credit card, if she went?

Once she'd gotten five hundred dollars in cash, on her credit card. She could do it again. And again—five, ten times. Right now. Then, if Daniels canceled her credit, she'd still have enough money to get to San Francisco. She wouldn't stay with her father and his family, wouldn't make that mistake. Instead, she'd tell her father that she was going to work in San Francisco. He would stake her to an apartment, first and last month's rent—a fraction of what Swarthmore cost for a year. She would be a waitress at a health food restaurant. She would get a dog, take him running on the beach. She would—

Behind her, shapes were shifting, the light was changing. In the mirror she saw a familiar shape: Daniels's black town car, with the tinted windows in back. Instinctively, she thrust her key in the BMW's ignition, about to start the engine. But the town car had stopped, blocking her way out. In the mirror, she saw the black car's rear door swing open. Carrying his attaché case, that permanent extension of himself, Daniels was getting out of the town car, striding to the passenger's side of the BMW. Unaware that she'd meant to do it, she swung her own door open, got out of the car. Was she escaping? No, she couldn't leave the BMW, not with her stash in its trunk. Across the roof of the BMW, she faced her stepfather. The town car was moving away, leaving them alone.

"Where're you going?" Daniels's voice was flat, his CEO's voice. But his eyes were different. Here—now—his eyes were different. It was as if, for the first time, he was really looking at her. Really seeing her.

"You can ask my mother where I'm going. She'll tell you. On the way to the party, when you're having your little chitchat, she'll tell you where I'm going."

"What little chitchat is that?"

"You'll find out. It's about last night. I told her to ask you about last night."

Still facing each other across the roof of the car, she saw his eyes change again: murderous eyes, cold and steady and deadly, boring in, impaling her. Thank God for the car, her shield.

His voice was hardly more than a whisper: "Where were you last night, Diane?"

"I—" Her throat closed. She couldn't speak, couldn't reply.

"Were you on the Cape last night?"

She was shaking her head, involuntarily backing away. But her buttocks touched a car in the next parking stall. If he came for her, she would move in the opposite direction, keeping the BMW between them. When she was a child, it had been her first hint of power, keeping the dining room table between her and her mother, avoiding a spanking.

But Daniels wasn't coming for her. Instead, still speaking very softly, he asked, "Were you with Jeff Weston last night, on the Cape?"

"I—I—" Even if she could speak, she couldn't have found the words. God, it had started as a spaced-out prank, trick or treat, Halloween in July. Did he know that? Should she tell him?

"You *were* there." It wasn't a question; it was a calm, calculated statement. He knew. Looking at her face, he knew.

She saw him draw a deep, decisive breath, then glance down at his watch. Preston Daniels and his watch, the inseparable duo. How much was a minute of his time worth? It was a problem for a computer. His net worth, someone had said, was more than some small countries.

When he spoke, his voice was dispassionate: "I've got to change. I'm running late." He let a beat pass, his eyes locked with hers. Then, very softly: "We'll talk later. In the meantime, don't talk about this. To anyone."

Without waiting for a reply, he picked up his attaché case, turned his back on her, walked quickly, decisively, to the elevator.

6 P.M., EDT

She opened her address book on the scarred shelf of the phone booth, punched zero, punched the area code and the number, then punched in her credit card number. Along with the BMW and a sound system and a closetful of clothes, Daniels had given her a private phone and a calling card.

On the Cape, the phone was ringing.

Where were they now, her mother and Daniels? Were they in the town car, on their way to the museum? Had Daniels—

"Cape Cleaners." It was Mrs. Weston's voice.

"May I speak to Jeff, please?"

"He's out on deliveries, and we're just closing here. Who's this speaking?" It was a suspicious-sounding question. She could imagine Mrs. Weston, petulantly frowning, with the phone on its long cord propped in the hollow of her shoulder as she waited on a customer, or sorted through tags.

"When'll he be back, do you think?"

"Who's this, please?"

"I'm a friend of his. Just a friend. I'll call back. Thanks." She broke the connection, tucked the address book in her purse, stepped out of the oven-hot phone booth; momentarily leaned against the glass sides of the booth, eyes closed. She could hardly remember leaving the parking garage, fighting her way through the midtown rush-hour traffic and up to the New England Expressway, where she'd finally found a service station with a pay phone that worked. Then she'd taken two Valiums, just enough to steady her. Then, already feeling better, she'd made the call.

But now, instead of driving west to California, she must drive north, to the Cape. Because only when she'd talked to Jeff, only when he'd told her what happened, could she leave for San Francisco.

9:15 P.M., EDT

Ahead, the panel truck was turning off the blacktop road and into a narrow, cypress-lined lane, no more than two tracks in the sand. Now the truck's brake lights winked. The truck came to a stop, the lights went out, the engine died. Was Weston making yet another delivery, this late? How many cottages could there be in the lane? Three? Four?

Kane drove slowly beyond the entrance to the lane, turned off onto the shoulder of the blacktop road, switched off the engine, let the Buick coast to a stop, lights out. As far as he could see in either direction, from one low rise to another, the blacktop road was deserted. Overhead, shreds of low-lying cloud cover crossed in front of a pale half-moon.

Wrapped in black friction tape, the pipe was on the car's floor, on the passenger's side. But first he must decide about the keys. Should he leave them in the ignition? It would save a few seconds, afterward. Yes, he would leave the keys. Here, now, during the next few minutes, the risk that the car would be stolen was nonexistent.

He'd unscrewed the Buick's courtesy light, so when he swung the door open there was only darkness. He stooped, got the pipe, hefted it, held it in his hand while he carefully closed the door. Across the dunes, in the direction of the ocean, the lights of a few scattered cottages shone. To the east, toward the airport, a corporate jet was turning onto the ILS approach for Barnstable. The blacktop road was still deserted. He turned to face the row of cypress trees that defined the nearby lane—and concealed the panel truck with CAPE CLEANERS printed on either side. From the lane, he could hear voices. Could one voice be Jeff Weston's?

At eight o'clock—more than an hour ago—driving at random, he'd first seen the panel truck at Tim's Place, the bar on Route 28 frequented by locals. If he'd been ready, he could have done it then, in the dimly lit parking lot at Tim's Place. It would have made sense: a barroom argument settled in the parking lot. Two men struggling silently, viciously, until one of them picked up a tire iron.

But he hadn't been ready then, hadn't prepared himself.

Slowly, his footfalls muted by the sand on the road's shoulder, he drew closer to the lane—closer to the van. Now, once again, he heard voices, one of them a man's. Weston's. During the past two years, flying Daniels to the Cape, spending time at Carter's Landing, at the house on Sycamore that Daniels kept for his hired help, he'd occasionally seen Weston at the dry-cleaning shop. And, yes, he'd once seen Diane and Weston together, riding without helmets on a chopper, a wise-ass biker and his wild-haired girlfriend, riding out to—

"Good night," the male voice called out. "And thanks. I'll ask about the slacks."

Weston. Unmistakably, it was Weston. Coming closer—suddenly closer.

Quickly, Kane strode forward. The rear of the van came into view, then the whole van—then Weston, standing beside the van, reaching forward to pull his driver's door open.

"Weston." He spoke softly, cautiously, just loud enough for the other man to hear. "Shhh." Holding the pipe with his right hand, concealed behind his leg, he raised the forefinger of his left hand to his lips. Repeating: "Shhh."

"Wh—what?" Startled, instinctively crouching, on guard, Weston turned toward him, hands raised.

"Be quiet." As if they were fellow conspirators, he spoke urgently, sibilantly. In the moonlight, he saw Weston's face change as he straightened slightly, relaxing out of the self-defensive crouch. Weston had recognized him.

"You're Daniels's pilot."

"Right." He gestured back toward the road. "Come here. I want to talk with you." Careful to keep the pipe concealed, Kane turned, strode back to the blacktop road, walked halfway to the parked Buick. He turned to face Weston, who was cautiously following him. From the east came the sound of an engine. Headlight beams were glowing from behind a low hill, then topping the rise, lowering, coming toward them, fast. As if they were reacting to the same unspoken command, both men turned away from the road, averted their faces. For this roadside meeting there must be no witnesses—no one to remember, to identify them.

Facing Weston again, still holding the pipe concealed, Kane spoke conversationally: "Mr. Daniels wants you to know that he got your note. That's why I've come. I want to talk to you about that note."

"Ah." As if he were relieved, reassured, Weston nodded. "Yeah. Good."

"He wants me to tell you—" As he said it, Kane brought his right hand away from his side, brought the pipe up enough for Weston to see. "He wants me to tell you that this is just for openers, just the first installment. First a pipe. Then, if you keep fucking with him, it'll be a gun. And you'll be dead. Have you got that? Do you understand what I'm saying, you miserable piece of—"

Weston lunged forward, swung his right fist, struck Kane high on the head, a glancing blow. Kane crouched, swung the pipe, felt the pipe strike the top of Weston's hip, enough to throw him off balance. But, recovering, Weston threw himself forward, a wild, desperate tackle. Kane stepped back, brought up his knee into the other man's chest, broke Weston's grip on his legs. As Weston staggered, off balance, the pipe came crashing down, once striking the left collarbone, once striking the shoulder, once striking the base of the neck. Suddenly Weston's knees buckled. As he fell, the final blow struck just below the left ear. Weston fell on his right side, facing the road. He tried to speak, but could only gurgle. Blood was pouring from his mouth.

Kane straightened from his crouch, stepped back. Dropping the pipe in the sand beside the road, he examined his hands for blood. There was nothing. From the west, another car was approaching. Dropping to his knees, Kane gripped Weston's clothing, rolled him into the shallow drainage ditch beside the road. The car's headlights were sweeping toward them. Still kneeling, Kane forced himself to remain motionless, facing away from the road. His heart was hammering; blood was pounding in his ears. The car was coming closer—closer. Then the engine's note dropped; the headlight glare was gone, leaving only the darkness. Kane found the pipe, picked it up. As he drove past Hampton's Pond, he would throw the pipe into the water. Then he would drive to the house on Sycamore Street. Quickly, he would shower and change. Then he would call Daniels.

But first he must bend over Weston, satisfy himself that, yes, Weston was still breathing. Gurgling and choking, yes, but still breathing.

12:20 A.M., EDT

At Tim's Place she'd learned that, yes, Jeff had been there earlier. Hours earlier. Driving the Cape Cleaners truck, someone had said. Still making deliveries, because he'd gone to Boston earlier, and his car had broken down. Not the van, but Jeff's Camaro, almost ten years old. But now the Camaro was parked beside the dry-cleaning store, and the van was gone.

At random, she turned on a blacktop road, driving away from the lights of Carter's Landing. Had she been on this road before—maybe only minutes before? In the darkness, she couldn't be sure. On the highways, the interstates, there were the lights, the billboards, the signs. Hold the steering wheel, press down on the accelerator, and the interstate did the rest. The interstate, and the motion of the car and the beat of the music. And then, once she'd gotten to Carter's Landing, one Xanax, the topper, after the two Valiums.

But all of it together, the combination, still wasn't enough to shut out the contempt in her mother's voice telling her so plainly to leave them alone with their millions. And millions. And millions.

Her mother's words, followed by his words:

"You were there."

The three words had seeped into her consciousness. The three words, the sound of Daniels's voice when he said it, the look in his eye—all of it had begun to fester, as if—

Ahead, she saw red and blue and white strobes flashing. Police lights. Ambulance lights. And now the policeman with a flashlight was waving her around the official cars and vans strung out along the road, blocking the right-hand lane.

As she braked, downshifted, turned out, she saw Constable Farnsworth eyeing her closely. Now he was waving to her. Did he want her to stop, was that why he was waving? Uncertain, she pressed the brake pedal harder, downshifted to first gear, crawling now.

And then she saw it: the Cape Cleaners van. It was parked between two rows of trees that bordered a narrow lane leading to a scattering of weekend cottages.

The van's door was standing open, as if Jeff had carelessly abandoned it.

FRIDAY,
July 27th

3:30 P.M., PDT

As Bernhardt twisted the key in his front-door lock he heard the telephone inside the flat begin to warble. On the other side of the door, Crusher, Bernhardt's newly acquired Airedale, sixty pounds of pure kinetic energy, began a steady barking. It was the first phase of Crusher's frenetic welcome-home celebration. The barking wouldn't cease until Bernhardt went inside, gave Crusher a hug.

The lock released: the door swung open. As Bernhardt put his attaché case inside the door and knelt to hug the ecstatically wriggling Airedale, he heard a woman's voice on the answering machine. As Bernhardt straightened, Crusher's next phase began: wild, random leaping on his master, a bad habit that Bernhardt blamed on Crusher's previous owner.

Using arms and legs to fend off the dog, Bernhardt went through the flat's long, turn-of-the-century hallway to the rear door. Now the dog began leaping against the back door, demanding to be let outside. As Bernhardt opened the door and Crusher bolted through, Bernhardt heard the beep signifying that the caller had left her message and disconnected. He walked back to the front door, locked it, picked up his attaché case, and stepped into the front bedroom that he'd converted into an office. Pencil and notepad ready, he switched on the answering machine.

The first four messages were routine. Two were from Terry Tricomi, the computer whiz who needed more information on a circus acrobat who'd jumped bail after a wife-beating indictment. The third call was from a wrong number who apparently hadn't listened to Bernhardt's recorded message.

The fourth message was the last one, recorded while Crusher was celebrating Bernhardt's safe return. It was a woman's voice—a young, unformed, unsure-sounding woman's voice. But nevertheless a determined voice:

"Mr. Bernhardt, my name is Carley Hanks. Caroline Hanks, that's my full name. You don't know me, but you know my mother, Emily Hanks. You directed her in two plays, and I've heard about you ever since I was about fifteen years old. I even met you once, at a party at our house. They're divorced now, my folks. My mother is remarried, and lives in Santa Barbara. My father lives in Los Angeles now. I'm eighteen, and I've been here in San Francisco almost a year. I'm studying design at the Dexter Academy, but I'm working now, for the summer." There was a pause. From the small garden in the rear of the flat, Bernhardt heard Crusher barking, demanding to be let inside. Reflexively, Bernhardt glanced at his watch. Yes, it was Crusher's dinner time.

"The reason I'm calling," Carley Hanks was saying, "is—well—it's about a friend of mine. Her name is Diane Cutler, and I think she's in trouble. My mother says that you're a very good private detective. And she also says that you're very sensitive about people, very—" She broke off, searching for the word. "Very caring. So I was wondering whether I could talk to you about Diane. I live in Noe Valley, and I see by the phone book that you're on Potrero Hill. So I could be at your place in fifteen minutes. So—" She hesitated. "So I'll hope to hear from you." She slowly recited her phone number, and hung up. Bernhardt copied down the number, double-checked his appointment calendar, then dialed the number.

"Hello?"

"This is Alan Bernhardt, Miss Hanks. I just got your message. It was playing when I came in the door."

"Oh, yes, I—I just called."

"Would you like to come over now? Four-thirty, say? Is that all right?"

"Oh, that's—yes—that's fine. Just fine. Thank you."

"You're welcome. I'll see you at four-thirty."

4:35 P.M., PDT

Bernhardt was at the sink shredding lettuce when the doorbell rang. He put the lettuce in a plastic bag, put the bag in the refrigerator, dried his hands. In the rear garden, having heard the doorbell, Crusher was loudly barking, demanding admittance. Whereupon, by way of greeting, the Airedale would jump up on Bernhardt's guest—any guest. Ignoring the dog, Bernhardt called out, "Just a minute, please." He walked to his office, where his corduroy jacket was draped over a chair. He was a tall, lean, angular man, slightly stooped. His face was unmistakably Semitic: a high-bridge, slightly beaked nose, a broad forehead, a full mouth. Like the body, the darkly pigmented face was angular, deeply lined in a pattern that suggested both reflection and sadness. The dark, perceptive eyes were also reflective, also sad. In his midforties, Bernhardt had thick, unruly hair that was flecked with grey. The rhythm of his movements was neither graceful nor without grace. But he moved purposefully, meaningfully. He wore a soft button-down tattersall shirt without a tie, slacks that needed pressing, and loafers that needed polishing. His corduroy jacket was creased for comfort, not style.

He took a sheaf of files from his visitor's chair, considered, decided to place the files atop a bookcase, precariously balanced. Then he went to the front door, drew the bolt, and greeted Carley Hanks. She was a small woman, a blue-eyed blonde with a shy smile and a soft, hesitant voice. She wore an oversize cable-knit white cotton sweater, khaki safari pants with expanding patch pockets, and scuffed running shoes. Her shoulder-length hair was loose; she wore no makeup or jewelry.

Bernhardt was the first to speak: "So how does your mother like Santa Barbara?"

"I don't think she likes it much. She grew up in San Francisco, and she misses it here." She spoke calmly, concisely. Her eyes were steady.

In person, Bernhardt was deciding, she was more decisive than her telephone manner suggested.

"Give her my very best wishes," Bernhardt said. "She's a good actress. Better than a lot of pros."

"She's doing little theater in Santa Barbara." It was a grudging admission. Could it be, Bernhardt speculated, that Emily Hanks liked Santa Barbara more than her daughter was willing to acknowledge, another sad story of divorce?

Bernhardt nodded. "Good. I'm glad to hear she's acting."

"She says you write plays—that you wrote a play that was produced off-Broadway."

Bernhardt's smile turned reflective, then wry. "That was a long time ago, I'm afraid."

"Still—Broadway."

"*Off* Broadway. There's a big difference." Now the wry smile twisted inward as he said, "Which is why I'm a part-time private detective."

"Mother says you have an interest in the Howell Theater."

"That's yet another reason I moonlight. Most little theaters are supported. Not vice versa."

"Hmm . . ." Carley frowned.

"So tell me about your friend," Bernhardt said. "What's her name again?" He drew a notepad closer, clicked a ballpoint pen.

"It's Diane Cutler. And I'm afraid that—"

"Wait." He raised a hand. "Before we get into that—her problem—give me a rundown on her."

She frowned again. "Rundown?"

"Vital statistics. Age, marital status. What kind of work she does. Her history, in other words."

"Oh." She nodded earnestly. "Okay. Well, she's my age. Eighteen. And we grew up together. Ever since we were both five years old, we lived within two blocks of each other."

"Were you best friends?"

Gravely, she nodded. "Yes. At least, we were until we were about fifteen. And then—" She drew a long, deep, heavily laden breath. "And then our parents both got divorced. It was within just a few months of each other, that they got divorced. And then—" Now her clear blue eyes went dull, clouded by regret. "Then, also just within a few months of each other, our mothers both got married again, and moved away.

My mom went to Santa Barbara, and Diane's mom went to New York. She married Preston Daniels. Have you ever heard of him?"

"Sure." Bernhardt nodded. "The real estate tycoon."

"Yeah." It was a sarcastic acknowledgment. "Right."

"You don't think much of Preston Daniels, I gather."

"That's right, I don't."

"Have you ever met him?"

"Yes. They have a place on Cape Cod. A wonderful beach house. I spent a week there, last summer."

"Does Diane live in New York?"

"She's going to college. Or, at least, she was going to college. She just finished her freshman year at Swarthmore. But her father lives here, in San Francisco. He's remarried, just like my dad. He's a lawyer— Diane's dad, I mean. His name is Cutler. Paul Cutler. So, a week or two ago, Diane came out here—drove out here, in her car. See—" Earnestly, she leaned toward Bernhardt. Carley Hanks had come to the crux of it, the reason she desperately sought help. "See, she had a terrible fight with her mother. And with her stepfather, too. Daniels. So—" She spread her hands, evoking the eternal plight of the powerless teenager. "So she came out here, to San Francisco. Except that she doesn't get along with her stepmother, either. So—" As if she were admitting to a defeat, she grimly shook her head. "So she's staying with me."

"It sounds like Diane has problems with both her stepparents." Watching her, Bernhardt spoke quietly, evenly.

"Yeah, well—" She broke off, considered, then decided to say, "Well, the truth is, the past couple of years, Diane's been pretty hard to get along with herself."

"What about her and her father?" He glanced at his notes. "Paul Cutler. Do they get along?"

"Yes, they do. But she can't live with him and his wife."

"Do you think she's talked to her father since she arrived in San Francisco, told him what was bothering her?"

"I don't think so."

"Why not?" But, even as he asked the question, he knew it was meaningless. The answer was lost in the mystery of the parent-child relationship.

"What about you?" he asked. "Will she talk to you?"

63

"She tells me a little. But not enough. That's why I called you. Sometimes strangers can help more than friends or family. You know—like psychiatrists."

"On my machine, you said Diane's in trouble. What kind of trouble?"

She looked away, shifted in her chair. The body language was definitive: she was deciding how much to tell him—and how much not to tell. Finally she admitted: "The fact is—the truth is—that the past year or two, Diane's done more—" She looked away, bit her lip.

"She's done more drugs than she should have," Bernhardt offered. "Is that what you were going to say?"

Sadly, she nodded. "Yeah, that's what I was going to say."

"What kinds of drugs does she do?" There was an edge to Bernhardt's voice, a sharpness in his eyes. If Diane Cutler was a junkie, he would stay clear. It was the second lesson he'd learned. The first lesson was to always get a retainer.

"She drinks a lot, and she smokes a lot of dope."

"That's it?"

"She also takes pills. Lots of pills. And if she does the pills with the booze, she gets really spaced out."

"How about cocaine?"

"I'm sure she's tried it. But she's not really hooked. I'd know if she was doing a lot of it."

"Heroin?"

"No, not heroin."

"So she does booze and grass and pills."

Gravely, she nodded.

"You say she gets spaced out. What's that mean?"

"She just kind of—kind of floats off."

"Would you say she's self-destructive? Does she get in car accidents, things like that?"

"No, nothing like that. She loves her car. If she drinks too much, pops too many pills, she's extra careful."

Judiciously, he nodded. "That's a good sign."

Carley nodded in return. "I thought so too. Except that she's so—so sad. So terribly sad. It's like she's got nowhere to go. Nowhere at all."

"Is she suicidal, would you say?"

Hopelessly—helplessly—she shook her head. "I don't know. I just don't know."

"This trouble she's in, has it got anything to do with drugs? A supplier that wants his money?"

"No, it's nothing like that."

Thinking now about the time he'd already put in, Bernhardt spoke crisply now, all business: "So what's the problem you called about, Carley?"

"I called you because she's scared. So scared, and so—so lost. That's the only way I can say it."

"Scared of what? Scared of who?"

"I don't know. The only way I get any information is when she's high, lets things slip out, and I piece them together. Otherwise, when she isn't high, she won't talk about it. But it's got something to do with—" She swallowed. "It's got something to do with murder. Maybe with two murders." Her voice was hushed. Her eyes were very blue, very round.

"Do you mean that she was a witness to murder? Is that what you're saying?"

"I—I don't know, Mr. Bernhardt. I honest to God don't know. All I know is that she's afraid. Deathly afraid."

"Afraid of what?"

"Afraid that she'll be killed."

He studied her for a long, thoughtful moment. Yes, she believed it, believed Diane Cutler was in mortal danger.

"So how do you think I can help?"

"Well, I—I was thinking that if you talked to her, maybe you could find out what happened. You know, the way people talk to their psychiatrists, like I said. And if you could get some information from the police, maybe, then you could advise her."

"You say she's living with you."

"Yes."

"Where do you live?" He drew the notepad closer.

"At forty-one-seventy-four Noe. That's in Noe Valley, between Clipper and Twenty-sixth Street."

"What's your schedule? Do you work?"

"Yes. Nine to five. Not today, though. The owner of the business died."

"What about Diane? What's she do during the day?"

She shrugged. "Hangs around. Reads. Drives her car."

"What kind of building do you live in?"

"It's a lot like this place—a big old Victorian that's been cut up into four apartments. They're small apartments, though. One bedroom." As she spoke, she looked wistfully around Bernhardt's office, originally the flat's master bedroom. "I wish I had a place like this—a flat with a garden and everything. This is great."

"Thanks." Bernhardt rose from behind the desk, went to the window that looked out across a small front garden to the street. He stood for a long moment with his back to Carley Hanks, a Holmesian pantomime of deep, reflective thought. It was, Bernhardt admitted to himself, a deliberate actor's turn, calculated to impress. But, after all, the best investigators were the best actors; fiction was the investigator's best tool.

Finally he turned to face his visitor as he said, "There's my fee—forty dollars an hour for most things, sometimes a little less for surveillance. And there's a two-hundred-dollar minimum, for something like this. That's—ah—in advance. I don't charge for what we're doing now, for the first consultation. But after that, I charge."

While he'd been talking, she'd looked at him steadily, undismayed. Carley Hanks could pay the freight, then. And, confirming it, she opened her big saddle-leather shoulder bag, rummaged, and came up with a checkbook, all in one single, self-assured movement of the hands. "I've decided to go up to five hundred dollars," she said. "After that, maybe we'll have to hit up Mr. Cutler." She opened the checkbook, then looked at him directly, all business now. "Is that one 'l' in Alan?"

Amused, Bernhardt smiled. "Right. And there's a 'd' in Bernhardt."

8 P.M., PDT

"What I can't decide," Bernhardt said, "is how to approach her. I can't just ring her doorbell and say 'Hi, I'm Alan Bernhardt, and I've been hired to find out what's bugging you.'"

Across the table, Paula Brett smiled. She was a small, trim woman with serious eyes and a quick laugh. Ten years younger than Bernhardt, she'd majored in drama at Pomona and then managed a firm foothold on the bottommost rung of the Hollywood acting ladder. But she'd married a sadistic second-rate screenwriter with two ex-wives and a diabolically concealed drinking problem. The marriage had lasted eight years, long enough to inflict psychic wounds that were just beginning to heal. Even though both Paula's parents were tenured professors at UCLA, she'd had to get out of Los Angeles after the divorce. San Francisco was the obvious choice—and acting in little theater was the obvious therapy. She'd met Bernhardt while he was directing her in *The Buried Child*. They'd gone out for pastrami-on-rye sandwiches and beer after the first rehearsal. A week later, he'd taken her to his favorite Italian restaurant. The next week she'd cooked dinner for him at her place. Four days later, at his place, they'd made love.

"Maybe Carley Hanks could introduce you, and then leave," Paula suggested.

Bernhardt gestured to the salad bowl. "More?"

"Is there dessert?"

"Just mangoes. And ice cream, if you want it."

Promptly, Paula reached for the salad bowl, announcing that she would skip the ice cream. They were eating in Bernhardt's small dining room that adjoined the kitchen at the rear of the long, narrow, ground-floor flat. The dining room was the flat's rearmost room, with a window overlooking the small garden. The garden was carefully tended by the building's owner, who lived on the second floor. She—Mrs. Bonfigli—was a spry, quick-witted, sharp-tongued, tight-fisted woman whose husband had earned a precarious living making harpsichords in the building's full-length basement workshop, where his carefully oiled tools still hung on wooden pegs. When one of Bernhardt's clients had left Crusher the Airedale with Bernhardt for a weekend, and the client had then jumped bail, Mrs. Bonfigli had ordered Bernhardt to get rid of Crusher. But when Bernhardt had dolefully described the details of Crusher's certain fate at the animal shelter, Mrs. Bonfigli had relented. Now, when Bernhardt left town, Crusher stayed with Mrs. Bonfigli.

"What you should do," Paula was saying between small, precise bits of French bread and salad, "is let me talk to her."

It was, Bernhardt knew, yet another variation on a theme that Paula had lately been pursuing with increasing determination. Paula, he was

beginning to realize, was stubborn. Quiet and ladylike, but stubborn.
"Listen, Paula ..." He refilled his wineglass, refilled her glass. "We've
been all through this. And I just don't think—"

"The problem, it seems to me—the first step—is to get Diane
Cutler's confidence. And it's only natural that she'd confide in a
woman."

"What's bothering her," Bernhardt said, "is murder, at least according
to Carley Hanks. Suppose Diane saw a murder committed. Suppose she
saw who did it. Suppose the murderer's after her. Then let's suppose you
win her confidence. Let's suppose she tells you everything—because
you're a woman. So then—"

"You're being facetious. I'm being serious. You've said yourself that
women make great investigators."

"Paula. Please." He reached across the table, took her hand,
squeezed. "I'm not saying you wouldn't make a great investigator. But
that's not the point. The point is that I'm in love with you. We make
wonderful, exciting, imaginative love. We have breakfast together the
next morning. While we eat, we pass sections of the newspaper to each
other across the table. All this is very important to me. And I think we'd
be very silly to mix all that with business."

"Then you shouldn't talk shop at breakfast," she said promptly.

"You're right. Absolutely right."

Both of them sipping the wine, they shared a long, silent moment.
Then, gravely, she said, "That part about the paper, at breakfast. I like
that."

"I know."

11 P.M., PDT

"So?" In the bedroom darkness, Paula's voice was soft and low. On
Bernhardt's bare chest, her fingers traced a slow, sinuous design, lazily
erotic.

"Okay. *Jeez.*" It was Bernhardt's burlesque of a grifter's heartfelt protest upon being conned at his own game. "We'll see how it goes. But I'm going to talk to her first. Fledgling private investigators don't start off doing interrogations. They start at the bottom. Which means surveillance. Which means long, cold hours parked in some car. Long, cold, *miserable* hours. So buy yourself a good thermos bottle. You'll want a transistor radio, too, with spare batteries. And an empty coffee can."

"An empty coffee can?"

"Think about it."

SATURDAY,
July 28th

9:30 A.M., EDT

"I think," Paula said, "that you should talk to her father. I think that's the way to go."

Bernhardt looked at her empty cup. "More coffee?"

"No, thanks."

"Want half of my croissant?"

She smiled: her slow, knowing smile. "You're ducking the question. Stalling."

"I'm buttering my croissant. And I don't believe in discussing business at breakfast."

"I've been in San Francisco for six months, at least. I'm bored. All I've done is act in one Alan Bernhardt production."

"You have no idea what boredom is. Not until you've done a stakeout or two."

"Maybe so. But I want to try."

He sighed, spread orange marmalade on the croissant, took a bite. "Let's think about it. Let's both think about it."

"I *have* thought about it."

"There's an art fair in Sausalito. Want to go over there, hang around for a while, then drive out to Point Reyes, have a picnic on the beach?"

"I don't see how you can think about picnicking while Diane Cutler is suffering."

He sighed again, took another bite of the croissant. "It's Saturday, after all. I figure, this week, I've put in maybe seventy hours being a private detective. I figure I'm entitled to hang around with the one person in the world that I—"

"You see? You see what I mean? You're overworked. Overextended. You need someone."

73

He groaned, finished the croissant, drained his coffee cup, returned the empty cup to its saucer. He sat silently for a moment, staring thoughtfully at Paula. When he'd first known her, it was the intensely feminine piquancy of her face that had first attracted him. Then he'd discovered the understated perfection of her body. When she entrusted her body to him, she also entrusted the vulnerabilities and self-doubts that were the bitter ashes of her divorce. Only later had he discovered how persistent she could be, how stubborn.

"When I first started working part-time for Dancer Associates," he said, "I got ten dollars an hour."

She listened equably, placidly. Paula didn't gloat. Neither did she anticipate victory prematurely.

"I'll start you at fifteen."

"Fine."

"I'll bill your time to the client at forty dollars."

"Naturally." She rose, smiled, began collecting the breakfast dishes while Bernhardt packed a picnic hamper.

11 A.M., EDT

Kane's hand went to the control console. He eased back on the power, changed the propeller pitch. They were flying through light turbulence, characteristic of this altitude, at this time of the year. Twenty miles ahead, Cape Cod began to solidify, a familiar shape emerging from the summertime mist.

Was he concentrating?

Could he concentrate?

It had been almost exactly two weeks since he'd flown this same approach, at this same altitude, at this same speed. Daniels and Carolyn Estes had been in the cabin. They'd been dressed alike, in white slacks and striped boater shirts. She'd been breathtakingly beautiful. When he'd looked at her, touched her, Daniels had come alive, randy as a teenage stud.

But the next day Carolyn Estes had disappeared.

And two days later, in the darkness just east of Carter's Landing, Jeff Weston had died, killed when his skull had cracked where the pipe had struck him. But he hadn't died then. He'd still been breathing when—

"King Air Five Zero Sierra Romeo." It was Cape Cod Approach, ready to hand him off. He pressed the yoke's "transmit" button with his thumb. "Five Zero Sierra Romeo."

"Contact the Barnstable tower on one one niner point five."

"Zero Sierra Romeo." He changed frequencies, keyed the radio again. "Barnstable tower, this is King Air Five Zero Sierra Romeo. Twelve miles southwest for landing with Delta." He released the transmit button, adjusted the radio's volume as the controller responded, "Zero Sierra Romeo, make left traffic for runway two four, report on the forty-five three miles out."

"Zero Sierra Romeo." Kane checked the altimeter, checked the airspeed, came back again on the power. As he entered the landing pattern he wanted a thousand feet on the altimeter, a hundred thirty knots airspeed. He glanced at Daniels, sitting beside him in the copilot's seat. "Harness fastened?"

Staring straight ahead, eyes slightly narrowed, mouth tight, aristocratic chin raised, Daniels grimly nodded. Daniels didn't mind the takeoffs, and he liked to fly, liked the views, maybe because he could look down on everything, not up. But he was ground-shy. In the boardroom, Daniels was king. But in the right-hand seat, with the ground coming up, Daniels was just another fearful passenger.

Fearful of what could go wrong on landing—

—terrified, probably, of what could be waiting for him on the ground.

But Daniels was right to bluff it out. There were only two choices: bluff it out, or fold the hand. And Daniels, give the bastard his due, was a gambler, a balls-out risk taker.

Eight miles out, two thousand two hundred feet, a hundred fifty knots. Once more, Kane adjusted the power. Then he tripped the intercom switch that connected him with the cabin.

"Ready to land, Mrs. Daniels?"

"All ready, Bruce."

Double-checking, he twisted, looked back into the cabin. Yes, she'd turned her seat to face the rear. And, yes, he could see the harness tight across her shoulders. Millicent Daniels was a good passenger.

Kane glanced a last time at the rigid line of Daniels's profile, then began the landing checklist: fuel on fullest tank, gear down and locked, flaps set, propeller pitch coarse. In three minutes, give or take, they would be on the ground.

Win or lose, they'd come back to the Cape. Balls out.

11:04 A.M., EDT

Watching Kane's hands on the controls, confidence incarnate, Daniels felt the airplane bank to the left, turning to make their final approach. Within inches of Daniels's hands, the dual control yoke moved to Kane's touch; within inches of Daniels's feet, kept carefully flat on the floor of the cockpit, the rudder pedals shifted. Ahead, the runway was coming closer—closer, rushing toward them at a hundred miles an hour. Now the wings rocked sharply, the airplane's nose lifted in light buffeting. The yoke moved, the wings steadied. On the radio's loudspeaker, the controller's voice said something unintelligible: their call sign, followed by a short string of numbers. In response, Kane spoke cryptically into the tiny microphone attached to his headset. Suddenly they were over the broad white stripes of the runway's threshold. The nose was coming up—and up. If anything went wrong now—if a gas truck should come out on the runway, they would surely—

A soft thud, a reassuring squeak of tires on the runway, and the main wheels were down. Slowly, gently, the nose lowered until the third wheel touched. Another perfect landing, right on the runway's white center line, a Bruce Kane specialty.

"Very nice."

Kane nodded, smiled briefly, then began flicking switches, adjusting knobs, talking to the ground controller as they rolled down the runway, slowed, turned off onto a taxiway. Over the loudspeaker, the ground controller continued to give instructions and answer questions, many of them impatient. Something, apparently, had gone wrong.

"It's going to take ten minutes, at least, to get to the goddamn terminal building," Kane said grimly, braking the airplane to a full stop on the taxiway. "Some asshole collapsed his nose gear when he landed, and they've got to—" He interrupted himself, listened briefly to the controller, then advanced the throttles slightly as the airplane moved twenty feet forward before stopping again.

"No problem."

"Cape Cod on a Saturday in July." Kane glowered at the corporate jet crossing in front of them on an intersecting taxiway. "It may as well be Coney Island."

Making no reply, Daniels touched the buckle of his harness, about to release himself. He should, after all, go back and see Millicent, explain the delay.

But instead, in these next few minutes, sitting in this aluminum and steel cocoon, his free will suspended, his minute-to-minute fate in the hands of an anonymous voice on the radio, he would gather himself, prepare himself.

For most—for the vast press of faceless humanity—ten minutes meant nothing. For the masses, these minutes would differ little from the minutes just passed, or the minutes just ahead: lives of quiet desperation, Thoreau had said.

Yet, in minutes—in seconds—a bullet fired into an emperor's brain could change history. In minutes, a stock market crash could begin.

In seconds, a skull could crash against the corner of a slate coffee table—

—A pipe could crash against the skull of a strutting, slick-haired, Saturday-night stud.

Accidents. Two accidents. Two lives, ended.

The woman—a woman whose name happened to be Carolyn Estes—had kept her date with death because, thirty years ago, she'd been born beautiful. Only that, nothing more.

The man—a man whose name happened to be Jeff Weston—had died because, the night before his death, he'd happened to be at a certain spot on the surface of the earth at a certain time.

77

But the two of them, dead, could topple an empire. The headlines, the final rap of a black-robed judge's gavel, and the Wall Street sharks would begin circling.

For two weeks, underlying every thought, shading every movement, every gesture, the images had endlessly, remorselessly rolled: Carolyn, dead on the Persian carpet; Carolyn, wrapped in the blanket, an amorphous, unmanageable burden as he struggled to lift her into the Cherokee.

Followed by the other images: the surreal midnight landscape of the landfill, where he'd labored like a sweating, grunting peasant, conscious only of the sound of the blood in his ears, raging.

Followed by that terrible night, lying sleepless, sweat-drenched, trembling from the inside out, uncontrollable, himself destroying himself.

And, for all the nights since, the image of Carolyn's decomposing hand protruding from the earth, turned up by the bulldozer's blade. The image was immutable, a constant that would remain forever just beneath the surface of his consciousness. It was there now, this instant, the terror that never ended, the wound that would never close.

And then, the next day, the letter from Jeff Weston.

Followed, later, by the conversation with Kane, in the bar at Westboro. Kane listening to the proposition, the deal. Kane, eyeing him thoughtfully, the pilot's face registering a bully-boy's pleasure at the prospect of violence.

He'd gone from the bar to the waiting car. As he settled into the familiar rear seat, with its phone and worktable and bar and tiny TV, dressed in his pinstripes, with his attaché case open beside him, he'd felt confidence return. On the phone, Jackie reassured him that, yes, the deal with Kent Williams was alive, still on track. During the ride to Manhattan, he'd gone over the details of the deal. Never had he felt more in stride, more cognizant, more creative. And, yes, the meeting with Williams had been a perfectly balanced masterpiece: something for everyone, his specialty. At five o'clock Monday, feeling buoyant, young, confident, he'd whistled as he'd left the office. During the drive home, with plenty of time to change for Millicent's museum appearance, he'd discussed the baseball standings with Chester. Solemnly, they'd agreed that, yes, New York was in desperate straits. The A's, they'd agreed, were unbeatable, even without Dave Sanchez.

And then, in the garage, there'd been Diane.

A word, a phrase, a hot-eyed, incoherent torrent of words from a spaced-out, strung-out teenage tramp, and it had all come crashing down. Instantly the image of the body in the landfill, the hand exposed, had flooded his thoughts. Had Diane seen the damage she'd done? Had she realized how wounded he was, momentarily helpless, unable to speak, to react, to defend himself? As he'd watched her drive away, his wild, untethered thoughts had somehow fixated on Hitler, after Dunkirk. If he'd pressed his advantage, crossed the channel, Hitler would have won the war, ruled the world.

Just as Diane, had she stayed to fight, could have ruined him. One word to Millicent, just one word—another word to the police, just one word—and she could have defeated him, left him helpless.

Instead, she'd run. But run to where? To her father, in San Francisco? Had she—?

"Finally," Kane grated as he released the brakes and advanced the throttles, sending the airplane forward another hundred yards before, once more, ground control ordered them to stop. Causing Kane to swear, say something cryptic to the controller.

Sending him helplessly back to the labyrinth of his thoughts: himself torturing himself as he remembered the confrontation with Diane.

But then, Monday night, there'd been the reprieve: Millicent's museum party. Millicent on stage. Radiant. Next year, she'd said as they'd driven home, she'd certainly be elected vice president of the museum's board of directors. And the vice president, she'd said, was always elected president.

Never—never—had he listened to her more indulgently. It had been six hours, altogether, from the time he'd watched Diane drive away until he and his glowing, preening wife had returned home. It had been all the time he'd needed to regain his balance, all the time he'd needed to tap into whatever unique wellspring gave him the gift of power, of dominance. When they'd made love that night, he'd never been better; never had Millicent pleased him more.

But the next morning, on his desk, he'd seen the phone message. The three words had been written in Jackie's hand, signifying that the call had come on his "private private" line:

"Call Bruce Kane."

Followed by the phone number of the house on Sycamore Street, on the Cape. Followed by a question mark, also in Jackie's hand. Why, she was wondering, was Kane calling him on the priority line?

First he'd told her to hold his calls. Then, with a hand that trembled, he'd punched out the number.

Like all fateful pronouncements, the words were succinct: *"That guy,"* Kane had said, *"he—ah—died, last night."*

He couldn't remember breaking the connection, couldn't remember returning the telephone to its cradle. He could only remember suddenly feeling as if he were apart from himself, an out-of-body experience. He and the telephone: somehow they were disembodied, cast loose together in the void, aimlessly orbiting. Until that moment, the telephone was his instrument of empire, the magic wand that transmuted his will into reality—ultimately into hard currency. A few words spoken into the telephone, and careers had been ruined, fortunes had been lost.

How ironic, that now that same telephone could be the instrument of his own destruction.

That guy—he, ah, died.

Two bodies, one lying on his Persian rug, one lying in the dark of night beside a two-lane road. Both of them compelling him to return to the Cape, the gracious lord and his enchanting lady, doing exactly what they'd done during the summer for two years, nothing changed.

Anything else would certainly arouse suspicion. Followed by investigation. Followed by certain discovery.

Followed by disaster, the end of everything.

11:25 A.M., EDT

Kane signed the fuel chit: a hundred gallons of Jet-A and four quarts of oil, plus landing fee. Behind the counter, Patty Walters smiled at him. It was a mechanical smile, a mannequin's smile, meant to reassure the airport manager, who always hovered nearby whenever Daniels arrived. The smile barely concealed the hostility. Last summer, it had been different. Patty had been different, and so was her smile. The second day after they met, Kane had taken her out to dinner. Afterward, they'd gone back to her place. They'd had a lot to drink, and he thought she was willing. But something had gone wrong. Badly wrong. The next day, she'd called in sick. The following day, when she'd come to work, her face had been bruised. A bicycle accident, she'd said. Five days later, her brother had been waiting for him when he'd landed. The brother was a football player, a fucking Ivy Leaguer. They'd gone behind a hangar. Five seconds, and it was over. A kick to the crotch, a knee crashing squarely into the pretty-boy face, and the brother had gone down, his nose streaming blood.

As the service manager turned away, Patty's smile twisted maliciously. "Have you talked to the constable? Did he find you?"

As if she'd struck him, a sucker punch, he felt himself go suddenly hollow. How long had it been since he'd felt this fear, this particular fear? Lost above the overcast over Guatemala with fuel running low, an engine fire in Nam, the aborted takeoff at Seattle, a near-miss on the approach to Tampa, that was one kind of fear. This was something else.

But the words came quickly, easily: "Constable Farnsworth, you mean?"

"Right. He wants to—" Her gaze shifted, slanted beyond him. The malicious smile widened. "Here he is now. I happened to hear you on the tower frequency. I knew he wanted to talk to you. So I called him. Have you been a bad boy, Bruce? Again?"

Turning his back on her, he forced a smile. "Hi, Chief. I hear you're looking for me."

As if he were debating whether to acknowledge Kane's easy familiarity, Farnsworth pursed his small, delicately formed mouth. In his fifties, grossly fat, his cheeks and jowls a glowing, cherubic pink, his shrewd little china-blue eyes sunk deep beneath eyebrows so pale they disappeared, Constable Joe Farnsworth had been Carter's Landing's chief constable for almost twenty years. Because he was appointed by the town's select board, and because he had a secret file on every member of the board, Farnsworth had lifetime job tenure. Because he was almost totally bald, Farnsworth wore his stiff-brimmed felt trooper's hat at all times. Therefore, he decreed that each of his five constables also wear their hats at all times. Just as Farnsworth had almost never been seen without his hat, so had he never been seen to smile, or laugh.

"You going out to the parking lot?" Farnsworth asked. "Get your car?" His voice was low and clotted, as if it were clogged deep in his throat. His manner was abrupt, perpetually ill-tempered. Just as most of Carter's Landing's indigenous population disliked him, so did Farnsworth dislike them. But Farnsworth's edge was the badge and the gun—and the secret files.

"I've got something in my car I want to show you," Farnsworth said. Without waiting for a reply, he turned and walked through the automatic doors that opened on the air terminal's parking lot. Farnsworth's white patrol car was parked at the curb. Farnsworth never walked when he could ride. He opened the car's rear door, reached inside, and produced a manila file folder. Leaving the door open, he moved to the front of the car and put the folder on the hood. He extracted a single sheet of paper, which he held out to Kane. It was a black-and-white fax copy of a woman dressed for tennis. She was posing in front of a tennis net, holding her racket across her chest. Squinting against the sun, she was laughing for the camera—a long-legged blonde who might have been a fashion model.

Carolyn Estes.

Before the sheet of paper could begin to tremble, an extension of his hand, of his secret inner self, Kane handed the picture back to Farnsworth.

"Know her?"

"Yeah, I know her," he answered. It was a straddle, limiting the downside risk by giving points on the upside, the market-player's strategy. He was telling the truth readily, a dutiful citizen. But, Daniels's dutiful servant, he was giving nothing away. The secrets of the castle must always stay within the castle walls.

"What's her name?" Farnsworth's voice was expressionless. His eyes revealed nothing. His hand, Kane noticed, was resting on the butt of his revolver, holstered at his hip. His other hand held the picture.

"Her name is Estes. Carolyn Estes."

"How do you know her?"

Without doubt, Farnsworth knew the answer to the question he asked. In Carter's Landing, no movement of the outlanders escaped the veiled notice of the year-round residents, the townies who depended so completely on tourist dollars.

And what the townies knew, Farnsworth also knew. Farnsworth knew it all—and more.

Compelling, once more, the straddle: the truth on one side, a servant's loyalty on the other.

Servant?

No, not servant. Beginning now, right now, the word no longer applied—had, in fact, never applied. When he said fly, they flew. The last word was always his.

"She's a friend of the Danielses."

"The Danielses? Or just Daniels?"

He shrugged. "Okay. Daniels."

"When was the last time you saw her?"

He allowed the smile to fade, then decided to thoughtfully frown. "I guess it was—yeah—" He nodded. "Yeah, it was two weeks ago, just about to the hour. I flew them up from New York, from Westboro."

"Both of them?"

"Right."

"Did she have a car here on the Cape, do you know?"

Deciding how to answer, Kane eyed the other man. But the smooth, round, pinkish face with its prim little mouth and small, innocent blue eyes revealed nothing. Finally he decided to say, "I'm a hired hand, Constable. I'm paid to fly. Period. I don't pay attention to who comes and goes, whether they drive or not."

"The word around town is that this lady—Carolyn Estes—has been here several weekends lately."

Kane decided to make no response.

"The word is," Farnsworth went on, "that you usually fly the two of them in on Saturday, for the weekend. They keep a very, very low profile. Which is understandable, since the lady isn't Daniels's wife. When they arrive, they go right from the airplane to the car, which you get from the parking lot and drive out on the tarmac. They go right to Daniels's beach house. They stay there for the weekend, pretty much out of sight. Maybe they go walking on the beach, but that's it. No servants, no eating at restaurants. Usually they go back to New York on Sunday. Same thing, run backwards—they drive out to the airport, right to the airplane." Farnsworth took a long moment to study the other man's face. Then, softly, Farnsworth asked, "Is that about the way it goes, would you say?"

Kane decided to nod, decided to smile, decided to answer, "That's about it, Constable. You've got spies everywhere, haven't you?"

"It's a small town."

"Indeed."

"You're probably wondering why we're having this little talk." It was a soft, silky question. They were getting to the meat of it—the red meat.

Kane decided to shrug. To Farnsworth, indifference would translate into innocence.

"The reason I'm asking," Farnsworth said, "is that a few days ago we heard from the NYPD. That's where Carolyn Estes lives. New York." A short, cat-and-mouse pause. "Or maybe it's 'lived.'"

"Lived?"

Farnsworth nodded. Meaningfully repeating: "Lived."

"I—" Suddenly his throat closed. His eyes, he knew, had fallen, a guilty man's reaction.

"I stopped her," Daniels had said. *"I clobbered her."*

"She lives in Greenwich Village," Farnsworth was saying. "She works for an advertising agency, some kind of an artist. When she didn't show up for work on Monday, and her landlady said she hadn't come back from her weekend, someone called the cops. In New York, they don't do anything about a missing person for forty-eight hours. Nothing. But her father's apparently a big-shot lawyer in Manhattan, and so at the end of the forty-eight hours, the police really got in gear. And it didn't take them long to find out that Carolyn Estes had met some very high roller who started taking her away for weekends, mostly to Cape Cod. Apparently Carolyn was pretty closemouthed about this guy. But a friend of hers said that Carolyn had talked about flying into Barnstable one time with this guy in the fog. Apparently she was pretty scared." Expectantly—watchfully—Farnsworth waited.

Kane spread his hands. "Fog in the summer, here, that's nothing new. With the King Air, though, it's no problem."

"I don't know anything about airplanes," Farnsworth said. "All I know is that there's a Detective First Grade McCarville, in New York, who's trying to find out whether, in fact, Carolyn Estes was here on the Cape two weeks ago today. And as I understand it, you're confirming that she was. Is that right?"

Should he call Daniels before he answered? Should he say he wanted a lawyer? No—God no. Only criminals called their lawyers.

Criminals—murderers.

"I stopped her. I clobbered her."

He was nodding, acting out the role of the good citizen. Saying, therefore, "That's right. She was here."

"She came in Saturday. Right?"

Kane nodded. "Right. Saturday evening."

"And did you take her back to New York on Sunday?"

"No. I flew Mr. Daniels back to New York Monday morning."

"Alone?"

He nodded. "Alone."

"And now he's come back. With his wife."

"Right."

Farnsworth drew a long, deep breath. "So it looks like the next person I have to talk to is Preston Daniels."

Once more, Kane shrugged.

11:45 A.M., EDT

"Yes?"

Instantly, Kane recognized Millicent's voice: Eastern schools, Western money.

"Yeah, ah, this is Bruce, Mrs. Daniels. Can I speak to Mr. Daniels, please? It's, ah, about the airplane."

"Anything wrong?"

"No, not really. But I thought I should—"

A click. Then Daniels's voice: "I've got it, honey." A pause, another click, as Millicent got off. Followed by silence. At the beach house, Daniels was doubtless waiting to make sure Millicent was out of earshot. Finally, carefully: "Yes. What is it?" The voice was clipped, the accustomed accents of command.

But those were the old rules, played according to the old game.

This was the new game. Beginning ten, fifteen minutes ago, this was the new game. Beginning with the fax of Carolyn. No more masters, no more slaves.

"Is it okay to talk?"

"What is it?" Short, terse words, demanding an answer. An order from the boss.

"I just talked to Constable Farnsworth." Deliberately, cryptically, he matched his speech to the other man's.

"Just a minute." A click, a long moment of silence, then another click. Finally: "Farnsworth, you say?"

Yes, it was showing through. He could hear it: the hesitation, the instinctive caution. Their little secret, now.

"He was asking about your friend. They're looking for her."

"Who's looking for her?"

"The police. The New York police."

"Ah." A wan, wounded syllable: score one more for the Daniels-haters. "Where are they looking?"

"It started in New York, as I understand it. Then, yesterday, Farnsworth got a picture. A fax. So he wants to—"

"Yesterday, you say? He got a fax yesterday?"

"Right. So now—" He let a moment of silence fall, maximizing the impact. "So now, he wants to talk to you. That's why I called."

"Ah." Another subdued monosyllable.

12:20 P.M., EDT

"So the way I get it," Farnsworth said, "she left here about ten o'clock Sunday night, two weeks ago. And that's the last you saw of her or heard of her. Is that about it?"

"That's about it." As he said it, Daniels could critique the nuances of his own response, an essential executive's knack. And he was satisfied. He wasn't patronizing Farnsworth, but neither was he deferring to him, as a guilty man might.

Standing together beside Farnsworth's white police car, both of them faced out toward the ocean. For this boon—for the vital minutes that allowed him to intercept Farnsworth in the driveway, well away from the beach house, Daniels knew he must give thanks to Kane. Had it gone the other way—if Farnsworth had reached the door and rung the bell, and if Millicent had answered, Farnsworth might have—

"Did you lend Miss Estes a car, Mr. Daniels?"

"No. We—ah—" He dropped his voice to a confidential note, man to man: "No. The—ah—fact is, Carolyn and I had an argument. So . . ." He smiled, shrugged, let the Daniels charm come through. "So she just picked up her suitcase and took off."

Skeptically, Farnsworth frowned. "Walking?"

"Walking," Daniels answered firmly.

"At ten o'clock at night?"

Indifferently, Daniels shrugged. "You asked me what happened. I'm telling you."

"Didn't you go after her? Make sure she was all right, at least?"

"No, I didn't. She had money—a lot of money—with her. That, I knew. So I assumed she hired a cab, drove to Falmouth. Whatever." He smiled again. As he kept the smile in place he calculated the variables, the options. How could he suggest to this fat, country-bumpkin policeman that, if he cooperated, he would be rewarded? To make bribery work, though, an intermediary was necessary. But, aside from Kane, none was available. And Kane already knew enough.

"Where does she—did Miss Estes live?" Farnsworth asked.

"In New York City," he answered. "The Village." Yes, his voice was calm, controlled. It was, after all, the mismatch of the century: Preston Daniels versus Constable Joe Farnsworth.

"Does she work?"

"Yes. She works in advertising."

"Did you phone her on Monday? To make sure she was okay?"

"Constable—" He allowed mild vexation to shade the single word. Then, a tactical shift, he spoke affably, one good old boy to another: "Come on. You know what we're talking about here. I'm a married man. A *happily* married man. But my wife and I—" Once more, the smile, the full, direct eye contact. "We have a deal. An arrangement. Both of us, well, we get a little on the side . . . that's the expression,

I believe. And Carolyn, well, she was my summertime playmate, let's say, while my wife was in Europe. But that's all it was. Call it recreation. Okay?" As if he considered their conversation ended, Daniels moved a step toward the house. Repeating: "Okay?"

Farnsworth lifted his beefy shoulders, shrugging. Reluctantly agreeing: "Yeah. Fine. For now, anyhow. Fine."

Encouragingly, Daniels nodded. "Good. I appreciate that." A momentary, meaningful pause. Then, significantly: "I appreciate that very much."

12:30 P.M., PDT

"I still think," Paula said, "that you should talk to her father. Tell him what Carley Hanks told you. Sooner or later, you're going to *have* to talk with him, when Carley's five hundred dollars is gone."

Bernhardt shook his head. "I'd rather talk to Diane first, get a handle on her. Working with druggies is like working with alcoholics. Hopeless, in other words. A couple of hours talking with her—eighty dollars of Carley's money—and I'll know whether I want to ditch her."

"Why would you ditch her? She needs you."

"I've already told you: alcoholics and druggies have no free will. Therefore, they lie. They lie to themselves and they lie to everyone else. All the time. You can't do business with liars. That's the first rule."

"What about Carley's two-hundred-dollar retainer?"

"It'll only be a hundred-twenty, after I talk to Diane."

"Hmmm—"

He smiled at her. It was a playful smile, teasing her. During the drive from San Francisco to the Sausalito Art Fair, then on over the low, brown, sunbaked hills of Marin County to the ocean, Paula had consistently turned the conversation to Diane Cutler—and to their collaborating. Instead of being irritated, Bernhardt had discovered that, surprise, he enjoyed the joust. Why, he wasn't sure.

"Do you want me to go with you, to talk to her?" she asked.

"No. I'll do it. Monday. I'll do it Monday."

"Promise?"

"Promise." He let his smile widen languorously. It was, after all, a Saturday afternoon, one of the few off-duty Saturdays he'd allowed himself in recent weeks. They were sitting together on an old army blanket, drinking chardonnay from plastic party cups and eating French bread, salami, and Swiss cheese. They'd bought the salami and cheese presliced, but they'd forgotten to bring a knife for the bread. They'd agreed, though, that French bread tasted best torn from the loaf. Because the sky was overcast and the wind blowing in off the Pacific was cold, they wore jeans and sweaters. The beach faced the ocean squarely, unprotected by a cove. The long line of the surf broke endlessly on the sand before them, a timeless connection of the present to the past.

"We should have brought Crusher," Paula said.

Bernhardt shook his head. "He'd just get into a fight with the first male dog he saw."

She nodded, then sat silently, her eyes on the ocean. "I don't think I could live anywhere that wasn't close to the ocean," she said. Above the constant constant crashing of the surf, Paula's voice was soft and pensive.

"As long as I lived in Manhattan," Bernhardt said, "we never went to the beach much. I never felt connected to the ocean. Not like here—California."

"Really? You never went to the seashore for summer vacations? I thought that's what New Yorkers did." It was more than a casual question. They'd only known each other for a few months, and were still filling in the blanks.

"My grandparents had a place in the Berkshires, an old farmhouse on a few acres. That's where we went for the summers."

In unison, they sipped the wine as, side by side, each sitting with arms clasped about knees, they looked out to sea. Along the surf line, Paula saw a man, a woman, two small children, and two barking, frisking dogs coming toward them. As she watched, she was conscious of a void within: an awareness of a dream still unfulfilled. It was personified by the parents and their children, laughing together, touching each other. And yes, the dogs, too. The American dream incarnate. Her dream, unfulfilled.

She was thirty-four. No husband. No children. No career, really. Except for her parents, all she had was Bernhardt. In the first case, fortune had smiled on her. Both her parents were full professors at UCLA, her mother in sociology, her father in economics. Both parents loved her, their treasured only child.

In the second case—Bernhardt—fortune had smiled again. She'd found a man to love—a man who understood her, a man who laughed when she laughed.

But she wanted more, needed more. She needed a family. She needed children.

At twenty-one, it seemed as if the world would open its arms to receive her. Just out of college, a theater arts major, she'd lived at home while she made the rounds of the studios and the talent agencies, dropping off eight-by-ten glossies.

Like Alan, she'd gotten a fast start in the acting profession. At first there'd been the walk-ons. Then, lo! she'd gotten a few lines in a few second-rate films, plus one good review for the little-theater part of Vickie in Jeff Sheppard's *Jaguar*.

But then, just a year out of college, she'd met David Bell. Her parents had warned her. Almost twice her age, twice married, with two children, David Bell was the most intriguing, most exciting man she'd ever met. A screenwriter with impressive credits, an impressive house, impressive cars, impressive big-name friends, David had asked her to marry him after they'd first made love. He'd given her a week to decide, take him or leave him—his first ultimatum. Hardly had she agreed when the misgivings began: at first the very faint tinkle of a warning bell, easily camouflaged by the excitement generated by her new life.

At the end of the first year, the tinkle was a low, persistent ringing.

Eight years later the booming of the tocsin had drowned out everything. "For God's sake," her father had pleaded, "let me get a lawyer. This guy's going to destroy you. He's a drinker and a misogynist. And you're his target."

So she'd called the lawyer and filed the papers. Then she'd had to get out of town.

And now she was thirty-four.

And she was in love with a wonderful man.

But the wonderful man had had a wonderful wife—a wonderful marriage. Her name had been Jennie. They'd met at college, both of them drama majors. They'd married only a year out of college; they'd both been twenty-two. They'd gone to Manhattan, where Alan had been born and where his mother had still lived. They'd begun making the rounds on Broadway and off Broadway. While he was still in college, Alan had written two plays. Incredibly, three years after he'd graduated one of them, *Victims*, had gotten produced off-Broadway; it had had a two-month run. And, yes, both Alan and Jennie had gotten walk-on parts in a few Broadway plays.

Then, after five golden years of marriage, three teenagers had mugged Jennie less than a block from their apartment. When she'd fallen, she'd hit the back of her head on a curb. She'd died on the way to the hospital.

It had happened almost fifteen years ago. But in Alan's thoughts, Jennie had found life eternal. Never would she age; never would she be less than perfect.

Alan had talked about it only once. Strangely, perhaps, he'd told her the story of Jennie during the first hour after they'd met. It had happened after the read-through of *The Buried Child*, which he had directed at the Howell. They'd gone out for beer and sandwiches, just the two of them. Exercising his director's prerogative, he'd wanted to know her story. Where had she acted before? How long had she lived in San Francisco? Why had she come?

She'd told him the whole story; why, she didn't quite know. She remembered the irony: how few sentences it had taken, really, to tell the story of her life.

Then it had been his turn. He'd told her how his father had been a bombardier in World War II, and had been killed over Germany the month before Alan was born. He'd told her about his mother, the Jewish intellectual whose twin passions were modern dancing and banning the bomb. They'd lived in a Greenwich Village loft, Alan and his mother. She was an only child herself, much loved. Her father was a small clothing manufacturer; her mother played the harpsichord, mostly Bach.

And then, dispassionately, Alan had told her about Jennie, about how she'd died.

And then, still dispassionately, he'd told her the rest of the story.

He'd told her that in the year following Jennie's death, his mother had died of cancer and his grandparents had been killed in a one-car accident, probably because his grandfather had suffered a heart attack.

So, like her, he'd had to get out of town. Even though he loved New York, would always love New York, he'd had to leave. He'd—

"—happened to the fruit?" he was asking, rummaging in the picnic hamper.

"Isn't it there?"

"No. It was in a separate sack. We probably left it in the car." Beside the blanket, the depleted bottle of wine had been augered into the sand. Bernhardt lifted the sand-crusted bottle, examined the level of the wine. "Just enough for two glasses." Invitingly, he lifted the bottle. As he poured the wine, he asked, "What were you frowning about, just now?"

"Was I frowning?"

He made no response. But he was searching her face, looking for the answer. Sometimes she forgot how soft his brown eyes were—and how perceptive.

Did she dare to gamble?

Did she dare to say that she wanted to be married, that she wanted to have children? Did she dare to tell him she wanted to start a family now, before the clock defeated her? Did he know how real Jennie was, to her?

The last question answered the first. No, she couldn't gamble. Instead, lightly but meaningfully, she could say, "I was thinking about you, as a matter of fact."

"And?"

"And I was wondering when you're going to start writing another play."

"Hmmm." He was still looking directly into her face, searching for something. Did he realize that her question was a cop-out, a tactical retreat?

"Originally," she said, "you were going to moonlight while you acted and directed—and also wrote plays. And then you left Dancer, and went into business for yourself. So then—"

"I *liberated* myself from Dancer. I hummed the "Marseillaise" for weeks after I—"

"The point is, though, that you don't have time to act or direct, since you're in business for yourself. That's understandable. Rehearsals have to be scheduled, and that's a problem, no question. But writing, you can make time for. You could write on stakeouts, I'd think. Things like that."

"Is this really another pitch for me to put your name on the letter-head? Is that what this is all about?"

"What this is all about," she said, "is that I care about you. I think you have a gift. I'm a fan."

He leaned close to her, rocked his body against hers, a companion-able nudge. "I'm a fan, too. Your fan."

"Hmmm." She nudged him in return. Then: "Don't forget. Monday."

"Monday?"

"That's when you talk to Diane. Monday."

"Hmmm."

2 P.M., EDT

"I think," Millicent said, "that we should hire private detectives. It's been two weeks. A private detective can get access to credit card slips, and find out where she is."

They were seated side by side on the deck, looking out across Nantucket Sound. Millicent was wearing a one-piece emerald-green bathing suit, sunglasses, and a floppy white cotton hat. With her chair tilted back, partially offsetting gravity, her breasts had never looked riper, more desirable. That night, they would make love. Nothing, he knew, disarmed a woman like sex, the more carnal the better. So when—

"—talked to Paul, just before we left New York," she was saying. "He hasn't heard a word from Diane."

"Well," he answered, "she isn't going to starve, not unless you cancel her credit cards. And she probably isn't going to kill herself on the highway. So what can happen to her?"

"Christ, Preston, she's hurting. She's my child, and she's *hurting*."

"She's Paul's child, too. Let him take the duty for a while. Whenever the two of you have a fight, she threatens to go to San Francisco. Maybe that's where she belongs. At least for a while."

"Paul's got his own family. And Diane doesn't get along with Paul's wife. You know that."

"Diane doesn't get along with me, either. In fact, she doesn't get along with a lot of people. It's time you faced it, Millie. Diane is disaffected. She's eighteen years old, and she's running wild. She should be in—" He caught himself. *In therapy*, he'd been about to say. But secrets came out in therapy.

Did therapists take VISA cards, American Express cards?

"In what?" she demanded. "What were you going to say?"

He lifted a hand from the arm of his chair, let it fall. "Never mind." He turned his gaze to the beach. An hour ago, Millicent had said she'd go swimming. When she did, he would have his first chance to go into the living room, turn back the rug and pad, look at the floor. He would—

"—private detective, when we get back to the city."

"Wh—what?" With an effort, he forced himself to concentrate. "Sorry. I was daydreaming."

"I said, I think I *will* hire a detective. I know I'd feel better if—"

"Let's not do it yet. Let's give it another week."

Above the white frames of her smoked glasses, her eyebrows came together. "But I want—"

He let his voice go flat as he said, "I want to wait, Millie."

"But why? I don't see why we can't—"

"I don't want private detectives—or anyone—poking around in our life."

She took off the sunglasses, waited until he looked at her directly. Then, coolly: "What're you afraid of, Preston?"

"Afraid of?" He drew a deep, deliberate breath. "In what sense?"

"Something's bothering you. Badly. What is it?"

"If anything's bothering me, it's the usual—too much to be done, not enough competent people to do it, take the load off. Except for Jackie, I could fire my whole staff. I swear to God, I think any M.B.A. right out of Harvard could—"

"I'm not talking about business." A carefully calculated pause. "Am I?"

"I don't know." His own pause matched hers. "Are you?"

It had been the wrong response. Millicent hated to fence, hated word games.

"Look, Millie, I—as the saying goes—I've had a hell of a week. So if you don't mind, I'd rather—"

"Did you and Diane have a fight? Is that the reason she left?"

He contrived a weary smile. "I'm always having fights with Diane. So are you."

"That's not what I mean. The day she left, did you—?"

As if he were suddenly exasperated, he quickly cut her off: "Millie. Please. We've been all over this. *You* were the one that had a fight with Diane just before she took off. Yes, I saw her in the garage after she'd left you. And, yes, she told me to fuck off before she got in her car and drove off. But that's it. Period. Another hour in the life of Diane Cutler."

As if she accepted his rebuke, his edict, she made no response. Instead, in icy control, she put the sunglasses back in place, turned her gaze away from him, once more staring out to sea. Another long moment of heavily laden silence passed. When would he be alone long enough to fold back the rug? Should he suggest that she go into town, to shop? They'd talked about buying a painting by a local artist, good community relations. Should he suggest that she—

No.

If she went into town, and Farnsworth questioned her, then—

"Why are we here, Preston?"

Aware that the question was rhetorical, a tactical opening gambit, he made no response. She was still staring out to sea. Her features were composed. Icily composed. It was, he knew, an ominous sign. Millicent didn't strike out at random.

"As I understand it," she began, "we have what's called an understanding. That's to say, if you run across someone you want to play with for a while, amuse yourself, it's all right as long as you don't rub my nose in it. I don't embarrass you, and you don't embarrass me. The JFK solution, in other words." As she said it, she moved her head slightly to the left, aligning her gaze with Hyannisport and the

Kennedy compound, less than five miles directly across Craigville Bay.

"That's to say," she continued, "that Kennedy didn't take his floozies through the front door of the White House. And he certainly didn't take them to Hyannisport." A hard, flat pause. Then: "Which is to say, Preston, that I wouldn't expect you to bring your floozy here."

On his response could depend his future. Everything. Therefore, certain words must be spoken—and certain words must never be spoken. Some marriages depended on the truth. His marriage depended on fiction—on what was known but never acknowledged. Unspoken words. Lies.

"I'm wondering," he said, "why you're telling me this."

"I happened to run into Susan Piernan at the museum. We went out for coffee. It was the first time I'd seen her since I got back from Europe. She said she'd been up here—on the Cape—for three weeks, with her kids."

Watching her profile, so exquisitely formed, so perfectly composed, he waited. If she went on, crossed the line, then everything would go. Yet, strangely, he was conscious of a composure, a distancing, as if he were someone apart, evaluating his own response:

First he must smile. But the smile must register puzzlement, not displeasure. "I've been here the last couple of weekends, and I don't remember seeing Susan."

It was the final word. If, beyond this, there were other words, they would be the first words in a legal torrent: her lawyers and his lawyers, endlessly enriching themselves.

While, at the landfill, only a few miles away, the worms were at work on the flesh of that which once had been a woman named Carolyn, last name Estes.

While, in New York, police computers were—

She was rising, stooping to pick up her beach towel and her swim cap. Saying: "I like our marriage, Preston. It's an exciting life. It suits me, and I think it suits you, too." As she spoke, she worked at the strands of her hair, tucking them inside the cap. She was waiting for him to speak, waiting for him to recite his required lines:

"I like our marriage, too, Millie." And, then, extra insurance: "I wouldn't want anything to happen to it."

"Good." She snapped the bathing cap, slung the towel over her shoulder, and smiled down at him. It was a new smile, one that, most certainly, he would often see as time passed.

If time passed, for them.

"Are you going to swim?" she asked.

"Not now. Later, maybe." As he watched her walking down toward the ocean, he was conscious of an enormous backwash of relief. Once more, they'd dodged the bullet.

He waited until he saw her begin wading out into the surf before he opened the glass doors that led to the living room—and the slate coffee table, resting on the Persian rug.

3 P.M., PDT

As the doorbell sounded she heard Carley's voice from the bathroom. "That's Dale. Let him in, will you, Diane? I'm still doing my eyes."

"Right." She went to the door, pushed the button, waited. Finally, she heard steps on the stairs, then a quiet knock.

"Dale?"

"That's me." It was a cheerful, confident-sounding male voice. She unbolted the door, opened it. He was short, muscular, sandy-haired. A second-year law student, Carley had said, at Hastings. Rich parents in Los Angeles. Big, happy family, the all-American sitcom cast. Dale even drove a vintage Mustang, cherried out. And he could fly, too. His father, Carley had said, owned two airplanes, one of them a biplane.

"I'm Diane." She stepped back, gestured him inside. She liked the way he moved: easily, smoothly. His eyes were direct; his smile was easy, friendly. His clothing was all cotton, exactly right for San Francisco in the summer.

Always, even when they were only twelve or thirteen, Carley had found the right guys—the ones you brought home for dinner.

Dale, the law student. Alive.

Jeff, the Saturday-night stud. Dead. Lying beside the road in a pool of his own blood.

"You live in New York." As he spoke, Dale went into the living room ahead of her, went to the big bay window, looked down into the street. Explaining: "I left the top down, and there's some stuff in the car."

She went to the window, stood beside him. She could feel his closeness, his masculinity. "Is that yours? That red sixty-six?"

He nodded. "It belonged to my grandfather, if you can believe that. I spend more time worrying about that car than I do hitting the books."

"Have you got a garage?"

"Definitely. That car wouldn't make it overnight, parked on the street."

"In New York, it wouldn't make it over the lunch hour."

He smiled, for the first time looked at her directly. "How long've you lived in New York?"

"Three years, give or take."

"So are you coming back to San Francisco? Is that it? Carley says you were both born here, you and her."

"To be honest, I don't know what I'm going to do. My mom lives in New York, my dad lives here. I guess I'll know more when I've talked to him."

"You drove out from New York."

She nodded.

"How long did it take you?"

"It took a week."

He nodded, looked away, calculated. "So you averaged—what—about four hundred miles a day?"

"Just about. I didn't push it. I—"

"I'm ready." Carley stood in the doorway to the hall, posing for them. She was smiling her big smile. Last night, talking girl talk, she'd said that Dale could be the guy—Mr. Right.

"We'd better go, then." Dale was moving to Carley, touching her, letting his hand linger. For a moment—one long, intimate, oblivious moment—they were smiling into each other's eyes. Were they making it together, Carley and Dale? His touch—her eyes—said that, yes, they were making it. Did Carley realize how much one person's happiness could hurt another person?

"That bridge traffic . . ." Dale was saying.

Promptly, her master's voice, a standard strategy, Carley turned, walked briskly to the door. Calling out: "There's some ravioli in the fridge, Diane. Help yourself."

"So long, Diane." In the open doorway, Dale turned back, smiled, waved. "See you soon. Welcome home."

"Thanks." She didn't smile, didn't wave in return. If it had been turned around, and Carley had come to New York, she wouldn't just walk away with a guy and leave Carley alone. Not without asking, at least, whether Carley had plans for the rest of the day—Saturday, when everyone was doing something, sharing.

Through the open window, one flight up, she heard their voices on the street below. She turned, saw them get into the fire-engine-red Mustang, a convertible, black top. Would they look up, wave to her? No.

She watched the car turn the corner, disappear. She glanced at her watch. Almost three-thirty. What were the options? In San Francisco, the town of her birth, the place where she'd lived for fifteen years, on a sunny Saturday afternoon, what were her options? Do her laundry? Buy a paper, check out the movies? Go to a sidewalk café, watch other people laugh?

Phone her father?

First take a pill, to calm down, and then call her father?

Soon—within days—she would need a connection, for the Valium and the Xanax. Carley had grass connections, and she had her own fake ID for the booze. But pills, that took a doctor, a drugstore—sometimes both. Or else a hustler with a talent for knocking off drugstores, the toughest connection of all, because of the danger, and the guns.

The laundromat, the movie listings, or bite the bullet and make the phone call to good old Dad. Saturday afternoon in her old hometown.

When she'd lived here, there'd always been something to do, somewhere to go, someone to do something with. She and Carley and Polly and Sue, they were always together—two of them, three of them, sometimes all four of them, always together. In the eighth grade Polly had been class president. In high school, bewildered freshmen, they'd clung together—and giggled through it. By the tenth grade, fifteen years old, crazy about boys, crazy about clothes, crazy about music, always on the telephone, they'd still been giggling.

Had it been only three years? All that giggling, all those hours on the phone?

How long did a lifetime last?

Polly's father had been transferred to Hawaii. Sue was working at a summer camp, teaching leather craft. Carley and Dale were going somewhere in his red Mustang.

Her tote bag and the plastic shopping bags filled with the clothes she'd bought since she left New York were in the big hall closet. For five days, sleeping on the couch, she'd been living out of the tote bag and the shopping bags.

For five days, like a small animal tethered to a cord that constantly grew shorter, she'd circled the telephone, circles that grew smaller, compelling her inevitably to make the phone call that would decide it all. Everything.

Hi, Daddy. It's me. Surprise, I'm in San Francisco.

For five days, again and again, she'd gone to the tote, taken whatever was required to make the call. But then, each time, she'd realized that she'd taken just a little too much to talk in a straight line. And so another day passed—and another.

4 P.M., EDT

As Daniels turned into the airport parking lot, he saw Kane's Buick. Parked. Empty. He stopped the Cherokee, looked down the line of tied-down airplanes, saw the King Air with the air stairs lowered. Kane was inside the airplane, waiting. Good. Better to be seen together at the airplane than in a car, talking.

He parked the Jeep, pocketed the keys, began walking toward the small terminal. Even at Barnstable, for security, all passengers and air crew were required to pass through an electronically controlled door that could only be operated by an employee behind the reception desk.

Big Brother, watching . . .

All of them, watching, waiting, calculating.

Millicent, watching from behind her white-rimmed sunglasses. Constable Farnsworth, with his colorless pig eyes, watching. Even Kane was watching: sly, calculating glances.

The faces and the images: the amorphous shape wrapped in the blanket; the shovel, slicing through the soft, yielding earth of the landfill.

And the bulldozer blade, scraping the earth over her grave.

And, finally, the most recent image of all: the oaken floor beneath the Persian rug, after two weeks bleached white.

"Hi, Mr. Daniels." Behind the reception desk, the plump post-teenager with brassy blonde hair smiled at him.

"Hi." He nodded, smiled. As he waited for her to buzz him through, he reflected that, previously, he wouldn't have bothered to acknowledge her greeting. Did democracy have its roots in fear?

Across the tarmac, in the Beechcraft, Kane was crouched in the open doorway. As Daniels climbed the air stairs, Kane stepped back into the cabin. Uninvited, Kane settled into one of the two glove-leather swivel chairs, each chair with its own communications console, its own worktable. For underlings, four smaller chairs were bolted to the floor, facing front.

Kane spoke first, another breach of protocol: "What'd Farnsworth want?" It was a brusque question, man to man, an equal seeking information. Yes, Kane was beginning to think, to calculate.

But Kane's victim was buried in a graveyard. Not in a landfill.

Two deaths, both accidents. Two ends of the same noose. Tightening.

Sinking into the other swivel chair, Daniels shook his head. "Apparently Carolyn didn't surface after she took a hike."

"Hmmm." Kane's pale, bold eyes turned thoughtful. Then, softly: "It's been two weeks."

Daniels decided to make no response.

"Did—" Kane's eyes shifted, his voice thinned as he asked, "Did Farnsworth say anything about that Weston kid?"

"No. Nothing."

Kane nodded. Then, once more speaking brusquely, boldly, he asked, "Is that what you wanted to see me about? Carolyn?"

"No. It's about Diane."

"Diane?" Surprised, puzzled, Kane frowned. "Why Diane?"

"She's—ah—disappeared. Or, rather, she's left home. She and her mother had a fight. And Diane took off, in her car. It's certain—almost certain—that she's gone to San Francisco, to see her father."

"So how do I fit in?"

"I—ah—want to make sure she's in San Francisco. I want you to find her. She's—as I said—she's certain to contact her father, maybe even stay with him. He's a lawyer, a successful lawyer. So she shouldn't be difficult to locate."

"So what'll I do when I find her? Do I bring her back? Is that what this is all about?"

"No—no." He had, he knew, said it too hastily. "No, I don't even want her to know that you're there. That's—ah—why I'm not going. That and time pressure."

"What about Millicent? Why doesn't she go?"

He glanced sharply at Kane. Two weeks ago, it would have been "Mrs. Daniels."

"Look—" Frowning, he leaned forward in his chair. "All I want is to know where Diane is. That's it. When you find out, tell me. Call me, on my private line. That's all I need from you, at least for now."

"For now, eh?" It was a slow, thoughtful question. Then, probing: "There'll be expenses."

"Of course."

As if he was satisfied on some significant point, Kane nodded. Asking, "She took off in her car, you say."

"Yes."

"When?"

"Almost two weeks ago."

"Two weeks . . ." Plainly calculating, Kane nodded. Then, as if he were the interrogator, the dominant partner, he said, "That's about when Carolyn took off."

Daniels decided to nod—once.

Kane sat silently for a moment, eyeing him. Kane was dressed in Bermuda shorts and an expensive casual cotton beachcomber shirt— dressed as a tourist, not as an employee.

"I understand," Kane said, "that Diane and the Weston kid had something going. At least that's the gossip around town. They've been seen together. At motels . . ."

"What Diane does—who she fucks—that's between her and her mother. I just try to stay out of the line of fire."

"My point, though, is that the three of them are connected. Diane, and the Weston kid, and Carolyn. There's a connection." A moment of meaningful silence. Then: "I'd like to know what's going on. If those three are connected—if Diane's disappearance has something to do with Carolyn disappearing, and then you telling me to work Weston over, then I want to know about it. I mean—" He gestured: a short, pugnacious sweep of his tanned, muscular arm. "I mean, so far it's looking like my ass is the only one hanging out, if Farnsworth starts asking questions. He might not be any genius, but he's no dummy, either."

Rather than reply, Daniels took a blank check from his wallet and wrote it to Kane for ten thousand dollars. "Here." He handed over the check. "That's for you. Any expenses—airfares, hotels—charge it to the airplane account. I want you to fly us back to New York tomorrow about noon. Then I want you to fly commercial to San Francisco. When you find her, call me." As he rose, he saw Kane looking at the check.

"Ten thousand." Kane spoke reflectively, insolently. "That's pocket money, for you."

Daniels made no reply.

Kane waved the check between them, a gesture of mild contempt. "Considering the heat I could be taking, even though it was an accident, about that kid, this really isn't much money."

"Have you forgotten about the twenty-five thousand, less than two weeks ago?"

"Oh, no—" Kane shook his head: a slow, meaningful signal of trouble to come. "Oh, no, I haven't forgotten that. But that was before Farnsworth started asking questions. Wasn't it?" His smile, too, signaled trouble.

MONDAY,
July 30th

9:30 A.M., PDT

Bernhardt touch-toned the number Carley Hanks had given him. On the third ring, a woman answered.

"Yes. Carley?"

"No. Carley's not here. Can I take a message?" She spoke abruptly. Diane Cutler's voice. Almost certainly, Diane's voice.

"No, that's all right. It's a personal call. I'll get her later, when she comes home from work. Thanks."

"Who shall I say called?"

"Tell her Tony called."

"Tony . . ."

"Thanks." He broke the connection, went to the back door, let Crusher inside, bolted the door. The Airedale had found a bedraggled tennis ball, one of dozens that had somehow disappeared in the small rear garden since Crusher had come to live with him. Bernhardt wrestled the ball away, loped to the front of the house, faked the dog out, tossed the tennis ball down the full length of the hallway. Paws slipping, churning on the waxed floor, Crusher got under way, hurtled down the hallway, caught the ball on the rebound off the kitchen door, skidded to a stop before he crashed into the door. Prancing, Crusher returned for another turn—and another. Finally, laying out two dog biscuits to ease the pain of parting, Bernhardt slipped into a corduroy jacket, took his attaché case, and left. Munching the dog biscuit, the Airedale nevertheless managed to look betrayed as Bernhardt closed the front door on him.

10:15 A.M., PDT

On the other side of the door, through the small optical peephole, Bernhardt saw reflected movement.

"Yes?"

He hadn't decided on an opening, a strategy. Improvisation, he'd learned, was his fate. Or was it his talent?

"Diane?"

"Yes . . ." Cautiously.

"My name is Alan Bernhardt. Carley asked me to come by, talk to you for a few minutes."

"Talk about what?" Suspiciously.

"I wanted to talk to you before I talk to your father. It'll just take a few minutes."

"I don't understand what you're talking about. What d'you *want?*" Petulantly now.

"I'm a private investigator." He held up the plastic laminated ID.

"So?" It was a quick, glib question.

"If you'll just let me in, Miss Cutler, I'd appreciate it. We can't settle anything with the door closed."

A moment's silence. Then: "What's Carley's last name?" Cleverly. Cautiously. Alertly.

"Hanks."

"You know my last name. Do you know my father's first name?"

"It's Paul. Paul Cutler. He's a lawyer with offices in the Embarcadero Center. And I'm not answering any more questions until you let me in."

Finally: "What the hell. I'm not doing anything else." A lock grated, a chain rattled, the door came open.

She was short and heavily built. Her hair was dark and tangled, closely crowding a thick-featured oval face. Her complexion was bad, her mouth was shapeless, her nose was too small and too flat, and her dark eyes were lusterless and opaque, muddied by chronic confusion.

Barefooted, she wore jeans and a bright-orange sweatshirt. Beneath the sweatshirt, her breasts were full; beneath the jeans, her thighs were round and thick. Her stance was defensive, her expression sullen; the tilt of her head was dogged, defiant. Diane Cutler was one of the lost ones, caught in the hopeless tangle of teenage angst, a little girl with big problems.

"So?" In the narrow hallway, standing with her bare feet spread, she folded her arms, her chin up another defiant fraction. "What's it all about?"

"Can we——" He looked over her shoulder, nodded toward the spacious, high-ceilinged living room that overlooked Noe Street. "Can we go inside, sit down?" He smiled, spread his hands. "I don't plan to hassle you. At least——" He tried to improve on the smile. "At least not if you wouldn't mind getting me a glass of water."

She studied him for a final moment before she shrugged, gracelessly stepped back, jerked her head in the direction of the living room. "Sit down. Would you like some coffee? It's already on."

"That'd be great. Black." As he strode into the living room he took the automatic inventory: an expensive sound system, an upscale TV, the traditional student's brick-and-plank bookshelves crowded with dog-eared paperbacks, threadbare hand-me-down furniture that had once been expensive; assorted posters, most of them friendly to the earth. The room itself was vintage Victorian: high coved ceilings, walls paneled beneath a plate rail, a big bay window with a curved window seat. Most of the furniture was clustered around a turn-of-the-century oak dining table that had been cut down to coffee-table height. The coffee table was stacked with magazines, newspapers, books, dirty cups and glasses. At the entrance to the living room, a large coat rack displayed a collection of hats: a safari hat, a pith helmet, a Sam Spade fedora, several baseball caps with unlikely logos, a cowboy hat, and a badly dented top hat.

As Bernhardt sat down on the couch, Diane Cutler entered the room from the hallway, a steaming mug of coffee in either hand. She placed one of the mugs in front of Bernhardt, then sat in a director's chair, facing Bernhardt across the table. As Bernhardt sipped the coffee, he noticed a lipstick stain on the rim of his mug. He shifted the mug to his left hand, sipped again.

"You said Carley asked you to come by. Does that mean she hired you?"

"She asked me to come. I don't discuss who pays me."

"It was my mother, wasn't it? She knew I'd come to San Francisco. She hired you."

"It wasn't your mother. But that's all I'll say."

"Then why should I talk to you, if you won't talk to me?"

"Because," he answered, "Carley thought it might make you feel better, take some of the pressure off."

She smiled. It was a sardonic, show-me smile. "Take the pressure off. Just like that, eh?"

"No, not just like that. I think she figured that sometimes it helps to talk to a disinterested party."

"Talk about what?"

"Carley didn't say. Except—" For emphasis, he let a beat pass. "Except that she said it might have something to do with the law. That's why she thought of me, you see. I know her mother. We're friends. So Carley thought that—"

"What d' you mean, 'the law'?"

"I don't know what I mean. Frankly."

"Great. The blind leading the blind." She drained her mug, banged it down on the cluttered coffee table.

"If you're in any trouble—anything I can help you with—why don't you tell me? What's the harm? Even if you're on the wrong side of the law—even if you're running—maybe I can help you. Or, at least, advise you. Maybe I can—"

"I'm not in any trouble with the law. None. A couple of parking tickets, and that's it."

"Fine. You don't have a cop problem. So what is it?"

"What I've got," she said defiantly, "are family problems. Just like everyone else. *Everyone* else."

"Carley thinks you're scared. She thinks you're running from something—or someone. And so do I." As he said it, Bernhardt saw her face change, saw her eyes wander speculatively away. When her gaze returned, he could see the calculation.

"Suppose I *was* having a problem with the law," she said. "What could you do about it?"

"Obviously, that'd depend on the problem."

"You said you were going to talk to my dad. What'd you mean by that?"

"I meant that if I couldn't talk to you, then I'd try to talk to him, see if I can find out what's bothering you."

"Suppose I had a problem in Massachusetts. And suppose I ran away. Let's say—" Plainly to let the words catch up with whatever angle she'd decided to play, she broke off. Then: "Let's say I was drunk, spaced out, whatever. Let's say it was a hit-and-run. But I was so spaced out, I wasn't even sure what really happened. All I knew was that I had to split, get away, before it all came out, whatever happened. I panicked. I had to run." Once more, she broke off. As if she'd been animated by her own story, true or false, her eyes had quickened.

"You want me to find out what happened on a certain day on a certain road in Massachusetts. Is that what you're saying?"

Her mouth twisted into a small, sardonic smile. "It was just a story. Remember?" But now she was watching him carefully.

Deciding to go deadpan, the stereotype of the bored P.I. who'd heard it all before, he spoke quietly: "Who was it, Diane? Who're we talking about?"

She hesitated. Then, perhaps because she'd decided to trust him, she said, "Could you find out what happened? Can private detectives get that kind of information?"

"It depends on what happened, and why. Private detectives can ask questions. And there're data bases—a lot more data bases than most people think. But don't forget, private detectives take an oath to uphold the law. Some of us take that oath seriously. Of course, there's a gray area, otherwise known as client privilege. Different private investigators interpret that privilege differently. Some don't want to know the whole truth about their clients. Sometimes it's easier that way. But I don't work like that. If I've got a client who's broken the law, I want to know about it. I want him to tell me what happened, and why. I'm not going to blow the whistle on him. The way I see it, that'd be a breach of confidence. But if the law asks me, directly, whether a certain client committed a certain crime, I'm not going to lie. So—" Having finished with the standard spiel, he leaned back, drank some of the coffee, which was going cold. "So you should keep all that in mind, if you're considering retaining me. People who ask cops questions usually get asked questions in return."

"I've already told you. It's just a story. I wasn't talking about me."

"Good. I'm glad to hear it." He decided to drain the mug, put it on the table, make the motions of departure. Either she'd tell him more, or she wouldn't. Whichever way it went, he'd already put Carley Hanks's check in the mail for deposit. He rose, took a card from his pocket, put it on the coffee table. The girl rose with him, but made no move toward the door. Her expression was unreadable, frozen by something sad and secret.

"I haven't been a private detective for very long," he said. "At least, not running my own operation. I've still got a lot to learn. One thing I've discovered, though, is that it's hard to work for one person who's trying to help someone else. Maybe that's because the whole process breaks down if the person who's being helped doesn't want to be helped. It's a little like—" He hesitated. "It's a little like alcoholism. Unless someone wants to be helped—admits he has a problem—he can't be helped. So—" He moved toward the short hallway, and the door. "So I won't be seeing you again, Diane. Not unless you want to see me." He thanked her for the coffee, turned his back on her, walked to the door. He was reaching for the doorknob when he heard her say:

"Mr. Bernhardt. Wait."

7:45 P.M., PDT

"Poor kid." Deeply sympathetic, Paula shook her head. "Poor little rich girl. God, it sounds like she's really hurting." She gestured to the salad bowl. "More?"

Bernhardt shook his head, raised his wineglass, sipped. He'd bought the bottle at his friendly corner grocery store, ostensibly a medium-priced French Bordeaux, drastically reduced. It had been a mistake. For less money, he could have gotten a good local product—complete with preservatives.

"It also sounds like she trusts you, Alan. It sounds like she needs you."

"That's the real pathos," he said. "Apparently there isn't a soul on earth she trusts enough to confide in. She can't get along with her mother, and I get the feeling her father has to choose between her and his new family. Except for Carley Hanks, she doesn't have a single friend, I don't think."

"She trusts you, confided in you, though."

He put the wineglass down, shook his head. "Not completely. All she's told me is that she wants to find out how a guy named Jeff Weston died. If he was murdered, she wants to know whether there's a suspect. But that's it. She won't tell me why she wants to know."

"So what happens now?"

"I have three choices. I can make some phone calls to Cape Cod, and hope the local authorities feel like giving out the information to a mere private investigator, which is very, very unlikely. Or I can go to Cape Cod and take a few days to poke around—which is expensive. Or else I can call in some markers at SFPD. Except that I don't have a surplus of markers. I'm just about running even."

"What kind of markers are you talking about?"

"I know the two lieutenants who run Homicide, Pete Friedman and Frank Hastings. Every once in a while they need something done that's not entirely legal. Entering places they can't get warrants to enter, for instance, looking for evidence. So they provide cover, hopefully, and I do the dirty work for them. In exchange, they check things out for me. Things like how Jeff Weston died, who the cops think killed him."

"So give them one of your markers. I'm sure your credit's good."

"Except that I don't want to use up a perfectly good marker when I'm not playing with a full deck. Especially since the money doesn't look all that good."

"Did you talk about money to Diane?"

"She's living off her VISA card. Which means Preston Daniels could pull the plug anytime."

"Why don't I talk to her? Maybe she'll tell me things she wouldn't tell you. Why don't I have business cards printed up, and interview her? I can get cards printed overnight."

"Paula. Listen. I thought we'd agreed on this. I'm not going to use you unless I pay you. Which brings us back to money. So far, the most

I can make on this case is five hundred dollars. And in an investigation like this, five hundred is nothing. Christ, the round-trip airfare to Cape Cod would be twice that. At least."

In silence, Paula finished her linguine, finished her wine, raised the empty glass for more. As Bernhardt poured, she spoke quietly, significantly:

"For a girl, eighteen can be a terrible time. Wonderful, sometimes, but terrible, too. Either the guys are trying to get in your pants, which is a problem, or they aren't trying to get in your pants, which is a lot bigger problem. It's a time when a girl like Diane needs someone like you, to—"

"I understand all that. But I don't run a consulting service. And even if I did, I'm not a philanthropist. I'm a businessman. And I—"

"She'll have to get in touch with her father." It was an authoritative statement. "He's her only hope."

"On that point," he said, "I agree with you. Here—" He held up the bottle. "Let's finish it."

8 P.M., PDT

As she touch-toned the last digit she felt herself go hollow, a sensation both numbing and searing.

"Yes?"

For as long as she could remember, her father had answered the phone like this: just the one word, both a statement and a question.

"Daddy . . ."

She hadn't meant to say it: that little girl's greeting, so dependent sounding, so sappy.

"*Diane.*" An explosion, a rush of emotion, of overflowing pleasure. "Jesus, where are you, Diane?"

"I'm here. In San Francisco."

"Your mother's been calling me every day. Sometimes twice, three times a day."

"Great." Flatly. Angrily.

"She's worried about you, Diane." It was a reproach. Already, instantly, he was criticizing her.

"Diane?"

"Yes." Another flat, show-me syllable.

"Wh—where're you staying?"

"I'm staying with friends."

"Who? Carley?"

She made no response. Would he keep at it, force her to respond, therefore to either lie or defy him?

But why should she lie? Why was it necessary? Why couldn't she talk about Carley? Why couldn't she talk about the past?

"How long've you been in San Francisco, Diane?"

"A couple of days."

A short, terse, calculating silence. Then: "I want to see you, Diane. When can you come over? Tonight?"

"No, not tonight."

"Tomorrow, then. Come for dinner."

"No, not dinner."

Another silence. She could imagine him, his forehead furrowed, the fingers of his right hand touching his mouth, a mannerism that revealed tension, uncertainty.

"Listen, what about lunch tomorrow? Come by the office, and we'll have lunch. How about it?"

"I—"

"Diane. Please. Lunch, tomorrow. Come to the office. Will you do that?"

She sighed. It was a staged sigh, loud enough for him to hear the resignation. "Okay."

"And will you call your mother? Will you call her tomorrow?"

"I—"

"Or would you rather I called her?"

"Jesus, don't keep at me about her, do you mind? She kicked me out, did she tell you that?"

"Diane, I—I can't believe that. God knows, we've had our problems, your mother and I. But she loves you. She wouldn't—I know she wouldn't kick you out. She wouldn't—"

"All right. *They* kicked me out, she and her rich, photogenic husband. How about if *they* kicked me out?"

"Oh, Jesus—" It was a ragged, shaky exclamation. Then: "We'll talk about it tomorrow, Diane. Okay? We'll—" Suddenly he interrupted himself: "Oh, Jesus, I've got to be in court tomorrow. I was thinking I could substitute Ralson. An associate. But he's got a deposition, I'm almost sure." Another silence. "Listen, call me at the office tomorrow. We'll set something up for Wednesday, Thursday at the latest. Will you do that? Will you be sure and call me?"

"I'll call you."

"Do you need anything, Diane? Money? Anything?"

"I've got money."

"I want to help you, Diane. You know that, don't you? You believe that."

"I'll call you tomorrow." Spoken in a stranger's voice. A cold, controlled stranger's voice. Perfect.

8:30 P.M., PDT

Consulting the slip of paper Daniels had given him, Kane punched out Paul Cutler's phone number. As he waited, he let his gaze wander appreciatively around the large, luxurious hotel room, billed to Daniels, Inc. Never, as a corporate pilot, could he have lived so lavishly. Never would—

"Yes?"

"Is—ah—is this Mr. Cutler?"

"That's right. Who's this?" It was an impatient question.

Trying for the shallow, tentative inflection of his younger self, Kane said, "My name is John Williams. I'm a friend of Diane's, from New York. Could I speak to her, please?"

"John Williams?" It was a cautious question. "From New York, you say?"

"Yes, sir."

"Did Diane tell you she'd be here?"

"No, she didn't. But she told me she was coming to San Francisco. She said it'd be okay to call, even though the number's unlisted." He tried for a youthful, earnest note: "I hope that's okay, Mr. Cutler."

"Of course. No problem, John. But she's not here now. I'll tell her you called, though. Where can she reach you?"

"Well, ah, I can't be reached, not really. I'm—see—I'm staying with friends. Or, anyhow, I was staying with friends. I'm not even sure how long I'm staying in town. I'm headed down south, really, to Los Angeles. But I promised Diane I'd call her, if I got to San Francisco. So that's what I'm doing."

"Are you friends from college?"

"No, sir. From New York. My dad is in business with Mr. Daniels. Real estate."

"How long has it been since you've seen Diane?"

"About two weeks, I guess it was. Something like that."

"Did she—" Cutler broke off, then continued more slowly, as if he was exploring, experimenting: "Did she—had she planned to come to San Francisco? That's to say, did she think about it for a while? Or was it a sudden decision?"

"Oh, it was sudden. Very sudden. She just called me, and said she was taking off. Driving her BMW. And then she was gone. Just like that."

"Yes . . ." Cutler said it slowly, speculatively. Then, as if he'd made a decision, he spoke crisply, decisively: "As a matter of fact, I just got off the phone with Diane. She's in San Francisco. The, ah, truth is, I'm not sure where she is, who she's staying with. Friends, that's all I know. She, ah—" A delicate pause. "She and my wife—my present wife—don't get along all that well. So . . ." Cutler's voice trailed off.

"I know, sir. Diane told me about it. She has the same problem with Mr. Daniels, I guess."

A rueful laugh. Then: "You and Diane must be good friends."

"Yes, sir, we are."

Another moment of silence. Finally Cutler said, "The fact is, John, that I'm worried about Diane. She—she makes things hard for herself. Do you know what I mean?"

117

"Yes, sir, I do. And I think you put it just right. She *does* make things hard for herself. That's just how she is."

"You understand, then. You understand why I'm concerned."

"Oh, yes, sir."

"The reason I say it, John, is because I'd like you to do me a favor."

"A favor?"

"Yes. If you do find her, I wonder whether you'd be good enough to call me. Would you do that?"

"Why—why yes, sir, I certainly will."

"Let me give you my office number. It's my private line, so you won't find it listed."

"Yes, sir." Smiling broadly, he copied down the number and repeated it. Then: "Any idea where I could find her?"

"I'd try Carley Hanks, if I were you. They're old, old friends. Try her first. I don't have her number, but she's probably in the book. If she isn't, call me. I can put you in touch with her father."

"Yes, sir. Thanks."

"Thank *you*, John. I hope to hear from you."

"Yes, sir. I hope I can find her."

"Good. Well, good-bye, John. And thanks again."

"Thank *you*, sir." Still smiling broadly, he broke the connection, went to the small wet bar and poured bourbon from a crystal decanter. Adding water and taking ice from a silver ice bucket, he turned to face his reflection in the mirror behind the bar. He raised the glass in grave self-salute. Murmuring: "Thanks, Jeff Weston. Thanks very much."

10 P.M., PDT

Slumped low behind the steering wheel, the approved stakeout posture, Kane switched on the car radio, found a station playing light rock. It was one of the Beatles tunes that had endlessly revolved in his consciousness during those long months in the hospital, the beat of the music and the throbbing of pain an amalgam of hopelessness, of bitterness, of rage.

He was twenty-one when he was shot down. It had only been his eighth artillery control mission over Vietcong territory, only his third solo mission. "Stay low," Captain Lowery had warned. "Don't climb out over enemy territory. That's when they'll get you, when you're climbing out." And Lowery had been right. Just exactly right. He'd missed a checkpoint, fucked up the coordinates, ended up thirty degrees off course, lost, too low for a radar fix. Asshole puckered, he'd fire-walled the throttles and the mixture and the propellers and climbed out while he called for a fix. He'd only gotten to five hundred feet AGL when he'd felt the Skymaster shudder, saw the holes in the forward engine's cowling, felt the vibration begin. He'd shut down the forward engine, lowered the nose, turned toward the south, switched to the Mayday channel. Then he'd—

In the building across the street, the two-story Victorian building where Carley Hanks lived, he saw lights come on in one of the two big second-story bay windows that faced on the street. According to the names on the mailboxes, there were four tenants. Minutes before, a young blonde woman wearing jeans and a bulky-knit sweater, good body, easy, fluid movements, had entered the building. And, yes, the same young woman now appeared in the bay windows. She was looking down into the street. Was this Carley Hanks? The age was about right: late teens, early twenties. Assume, then, that this was Carley Hanks. Assume, then, that he was halfway home: find Carley Hanks, thought Cutler, and he would find Diane Cutler.

Find Diane Cutler, and he was a winner.

Find Diane Cutler, find out what happened on the Cape that Sunday night, and he unlocked the door to the treasure house. When he was a child, he'd dreamed that he could pick up gold and jewels on the sidewalk, endless riches. Even in Vietnam, feverish, the same dream had come back.

And now, more than twenty years later, the dream could come true.

11:15 P.M., PDT

"When you find Diane," Daniels had said, "when you find out where she's living, what she's doing, then call me. Don't contact Diane. Repeat: don't contact her. Just call me, on the private line. Anytime."

How many knew Preston Daniels's private phone number? How many at the White House had the number? How many oil barons, how many real estate tycoons?

How many women?

Carolyn Estes, and how many others?

Carolyn Estes, missing.

Carolyn Estes, missing and presumed dead.

Kane switched off the car radio, yawned against the jet lag left over from yesterday, stretched, glanced at his wristwatch. Fifteen minutes more, and he would return to the hotel, have a drink at his own private wet bar. Tomorrow, he would buy some stone-washed jeans, running shoes, and a sweater, the uniform of the with-it San Franciscan, all of it charged to Daniels.

Carolyn Estes, presumed dead . . .

Using a calendar, he'd gone over it again, plotted the sequences: On Saturday, July fourteenth, as he'd done on two previous Saturdays, he'd flown Daniels and Carolyn from Westboro to Barnstable, arriving about six in the evening. He'd parked the airplane south of the terminal building, away from the arrival-departure action. While Daniels and Carolyn waited in the airplane, he'd gone to the parking lot, gotten the Cherokee, driven it onto the ramp, parked it beside the King Air. Keeping a low profile, Daniels and Carolyn had carried their own luggage down the air stairs to the Cherokee and driven away. He'd stayed at the airport for more than an hour, supervising the fueling and checking out the response circuit of the transponder. Then he'd driven his own car to the house on Sycamore Street that Daniels maintained in Carter's Landing for the hired help. That night, July fourteenth, lying in bed, he'd imagined Daniels and Carolyn, making love in the beach house. They'd hardly get inside the door before they'd begin undressing each other. There would be champagne and caviar in the refrigerator, left by Bessie, the housekeeper. All night, Daniels and Carolyn would gorge themselves on champagne and sex, feasting on each other's bodies. All night, and most of Sunday, too. *Saturday Night and Sunday Morning*—it was the title of an old movie.

But instead of flying them back to New York Sunday evening, he'd been ordered to fly alone to Westboro. He was to leave a hand-carried letter for Jackie Miller, the only person Daniels trusted fully. Then, that same night, he'd been ordered to return to the Cape. He'd been told to leave a telephone message for Daniels, confirming that he'd landed.

During that time, during the night of Sunday, July fifteenth, Carolyn had disappeared.

Except for the weekends he spent with Carolyn on the Cape, Daniels was in the habit of leaving for New York early Monday morning. With luck, Daniels could be in Manhattan by ten a.m., having already done an hour's work on the plane and another hour's work in the limo during the drive from Westboro to Manhattan. It was in the airplane and the limo, Daniels often said, that he got the most work accomplished, made his best decisions.

But on Monday, July sixteenth, the day after Carolyn disappeared, Daniels hadn't left Barnstable until almost noon. And after he'd read the letter from Jeff Weston, Daniels had done nothing but stare out the window.

And then, when they'd landed, there'd been the proposition: work Jeff Weston over, the rougher the better.

In Manhattan, the whole Daniels empire awaited the arrival of the king—while the king was finalizing the details of a common, ordinary, everyday mugging.

A mugging that had become murder.

At the thought, the image of Jeff Weston's head lying in the pool of blood suddenly surfaced, like some obscene creature emerging from the depths of a stagnant, poisonous pool.

The same pool that might someday give up the body of Carolyn Estes.

Because, yes, Carolyn had died on Sunday night, the fifteenth of July.

There'd been a fight, and Daniels had killed her. Jeff Weston had seen it happen, and he'd told Diane Cutler what he'd seen. They'd decided on blackmail, Diane the mastermind, Weston the front man, the muscle. But when Weston had died, Diane had run, all the way to California.

Diane, the time bomb. Ticking.

Someday, somewhere, Diane would talk. If the police listened—if Constable Joe Farnsworth found Carolyn's body, the law would come for Preston Daniels.

On the first day, they'd come for Daniels.

On the second day, they'd come for him.

Meaning that they must help each other, must protect each other, he and Daniels. Partners in crime: it was an ancient expression, probably as old as history. And now he knew its true meaning. Now he knew that—

A car was coming slowly, hesitantly, toward him, as if the driver were looking for a parking place. Was the car—? Yes, it was the BMW. Diane's car. Without a doubt, Diane's car.

Diagonally across the street there was a parking place large enough for the BMW. Yes, she was slowing, coming to a stop, putting the car in reverse. The parking place was small, but she handled the car skillfully, as she always had. Only minutes, and she switched off the headlights, killed the engine. Cautiously, Kane slid low in the seat as he watched Diane get out of the BMW, lock the door, and begin walking toward Carley Hanks's apartment building. On the second floor, Carley Hanks's apartment was lighted. And, yes, soon after Diane entered the building, light patterns moved within the apartment.

Kane started the rental car's engine and pulled into Noe Street. At the Clipper Street intersection he switched on the headlights. Heading for Market Street, where he'd turn right, toward downtown, he drove cautiously through the unfamiliar streets.

Tomorrow he would call Daniels, on the private line. What would Daniels instruct him to do, what orders would the great man give him?

What orders would Daniels give . . .

What orders would he obey?

What orders, soon, would *he* give?

TUESDAY,
July 31st

6:30 A.M., PDT

A thousand feet below, the jungle was rich, endless green, blossoming with blooms of billowing orange napalm streaked with black smoke, some of the bursts shaped like atom-bomb mushrooms. Then there was the explosion. He was engulfed by an oily, impenetrable black cloud. Flying with one hand, he opened his safety harness, tripped the door latch, kicked open the door. Smoke was choking him, blinding him, about to claim him. The Skymaster, with one of its engines in the rear, was a killer airplane to leave in the air. Alarms were warbling, shrieking over the engine's roar.

Alarms?

Did the Skymaster have alarms for—

The telephone, on the nightstand beside the bed. Groping, blearily blinking, Kane reached for his wristwatch. Six-thirty.

Daniels. It had to be Daniels. In New York, the time was nine-thirty. Already, Daniels would have increased his net worth, made the standard multimillion-dollar deal, warming up for the day ahead.

"Hello."

"Yes. Bruce. Have you found out anything?"

"Yes. Just last night. Late. I didn't want to call you then."

"Well?" Daniels demanded.

But they were talking through the hotel switchboard. Was it a risk?

"I—ah—did what I came to do. She's—"

Quickly, the other man broke in: "Has there been any contact? Any conversation?"

"No. I didn't think you wanted me to—"

"There's been a—a new development. Just now. Just a half hour ago. That's why I'm calling."

125

Sitting on the edge of the bed now, Kane felt the sudden dryness of fear begin, deep in his throat. And, yes, he felt his bladder constricting—tighter, almost unbearably tighter. All night, he hadn't urinated. And now this: the fear he could hear in Daniels's voice. The fear that might match his own fear.

He realized that he was pressing hard on his genitals, something his mother had hated: *"Don't do that, Bruce. Puleeze."*

"It's—" Daniels hesitated, an uncharacteristic uncertainty. "It concerns our fat friend. The one who—who was asking you questions. He just called."

Farnsworth. Constable Joe Farnsworth. Shrewd Joe Farnsworth.

"Where'd he call you? At the office?"

"Yes . . ." The single word was heavily laden.

"Jesus. What's he want?"

"He was asking about"—now, furtively, Daniels's voice thinned—"about that, ah, accident. Two weeks ago. The man."

Jeff Weston. The death of Jeff Weston.

Now the urge to urinate was too much to bear. Had Preston Daniels ever been told to wait, while—

"Listen. I've got to take a piss."

"But—"

"Sorry. It can't be helped." Without waiting for a reply he put the phone on the pillow, walked carefully to the bathroom, emptied his bladder. Never had he felt this much relief, afterward. He raised his shorts, quickly returned to the bed, picked up the phone. "Sorry. It just couldn't wait."

"It—it's got to do with the—ah—Buick."

On the Cape, Daniels kept four cars. Stalking Jeff Weston, he'd used the Buick, the least distinctive of the three cars. But someone had seen the car, recognized it.

Recognized the car—recognized him?

"Jesus. I don't like that."

There was no reply. But the silence was more meaningful than words.

"Has—" Kane hesitated, searching for the phrase. "Has our friend made any—any connections?"

"If he has, he didn't say so. But I don't think he'd say anything

126

specific, not yet. Not even if he thought—" Stifled by the enormity of whatever Farnsworth might suspect, the rest of it was choked off, lost.

"Shall I come back there? Is that why you're calling?"

"No. I mean, that's not why I'm calling. I—I just wanted to update you. Warn you."

"So what now? What about this San Francisco thing, the reason I'm here? Are you going to—"

"No. I was going out there. But now I—I don't think it'd be wise. I wanted you to find her, and then I'd intended to come out there, to talk to her. Find out—" Once more, the words died. Then: "Find out how she fit into all this."

Jeff Weston and Diane . . . Daniels had to learn how much they suspected, how much they knew. For the first time, Kane could hear the thin note of desperation in Daniels's voice. Desperation, and—yes— guilt. Murderer's guilt.

"You've got to know about Diane. I can see that."

"But I can't contact her. Not now."

"I know . . ."

"That leaves you, Bruce."

"Me . . ."

"You're the only one who can do it. There's no one else."

"You've got to trust me, then. You don't have any choice. You understand that, don't you?"

No reply.

"*Don't you?*"

"I—" For a moment, one final moment, Daniels plainly couldn't bear to say it, pronounce the words that meant capitulation. Meaning that Kane must force the silence to continue. Until finally, in a low, resigned voice, Daniels said: "Yes, I understand that."

"Good." Another beat, another turn of the screw, one final twist. Then: "I'll be in touch." Without permission, he broke the connection.

9:10 A.M., PDT

The mists were thickening, swirling; concealing, then revealing. Was the figure ahead a man or a monster? Overhead, dark clouds crossed a pale crescent moon. The surf was the only sound, a distant muttering. Face turned away, arms slack, the monster was motionless. The sand surrounding him had turned to eddying slime, putrefied by decaying flesh. Why was he coming closer, even though he still stood motionless? Why was the distance between them closing? The monster's shoulders were scaled, his hands were talons. Now his face was visible: amorphous and scabrous, pulsating, the flesh itself as alive as a Gorgon's cluster of writhing worms, the eyes two red coals, the nostrils two pits, the mouth a shapeless, blood-dripping maw.

What did he intend for her? What was she meant to do? And what was the sound that suddenly suffused them, that high-pitched keening—

—the doorbell buzzer.

Someone at the door.

Carley, locked out?

The room was bright with morning light. Turning, she looked at her watch, on the table beside the couch. Almost nine-fifteen. Propped on one elbow, she felt her head begin to throb, felt the dull ache of recollection beginning. Yes, it was coming back: the cheap red wine and the Xanax. Today, she'd promised Carley, she would buy some good red wine, ten, fifteen dollars a bottle, a cupboard full. And groceries, too. And—

Again, the buzzer sounded.

Barefoot, wearing only panties, she stood up, waited, felt the room begin to steady. Slowly, carefully, she walked to the hallway door. With Carley gone, the door was unbolted. Latched and locked, but unbolted, a security no-no.

She put one eye to the peephole, saw a man's head, full-face, as, with a sudden jangling shock, the buzzer sounded again.

Kane. Bruce Kane.

Bruce Kane?

In San Francisco?

Now he was looking directly at the peephole: directly into her eye. Had he seen the movement? Yes, backlit, he could see her: see motion, see light and dark, shifting.

"Diane? Is that you?"

Bruce Kane . . . She'd never liked him, never trusted him. Bruce Kane, a schoolyard bully grown up.

"What d' you want?" It was all she could think of to say, a dumb question. One more dumb question; one long, bad joke. God, but her head ached.

"I want to talk to you. It won't take long."

Bruce Kane, with his flat, hard eyes and his scarred, street-fighter's mouth and his bulging weightlifter's biceps—and his hard, trim buns. The packaging was good, but the price would come high.

"Is my—is Daniels with you?"

"No. He's in New York."

Could she refuse to open the door? No. Somehow she couldn't refuse.

"Just a minute. I was still sleeping. I've got to put something on."

She saw him smile. His particular smile, without humor, without warmth. "Take your time."

"I will."

9:25 A.M., PDT

"D'you want some coffee?" she asked.

Kane shook his head. "No, I've already had three cups. Your—Daniels, he called at six-thirty, for God's sake." As he spoke, he sank into one of two director's chairs. About to prop his feet on the battered, littered coffee table, a gesture of equality, of easy goodwill, he decided instead to cross his legs. Across the table, Diane was sitting in the nest of her sleeping bag, spread on the couch. Her running shoes and socks were on the floor in front of the couch. The socks looked dirty.

"Did he tell you to find me?" she was asking. "Is that what this is all about?"

"I had to come to San Francisco anyhow. As long as I was here, he wanted me to try and locate you."

He saw her eyes sharpen skeptically, then harden. He'd forgotten how tough she could be—how smart, how shrewd. Instead of responding, she was simply waiting for him to go on, to explain. Advantage Diane.

"He wanted me to find you," he said, "because he wants to know what you're doing."

Her mouth twisted, mocking a smile. "It's summer. Vacation time. I'm taking a vacation."

"Maybe you should've told your folks."

"I *did* tell them. I guess they didn't tell you."

"What is it that they didn't tell me?"

She shook her head, waved the question away. "Never mind."

"Listen, Diane, you've got a lot of people worried. Do you know that?"

"Yeah, well, a lot of people have got me worried, too. Do *you* know *that?*"

"I know that something's bothering you. Maybe I can help."

"I don't think you came to help me, Bruce. I think my stepfather paid you to find me. Just like he pays you to fly him around the country. There's no difference. He says jump, and you say how high."

Letting silence work for him, the policeman's trick, he stared at her until she began to shift uncomfortably. Yes, a teenager's uncertainty was there, buried deep. Finally he said, "You've got it wrong, Diane. You've got it all wrong. That's the way it used to be."

Contemptuously, she made no response. Instead, sullenly, she stared past him, toward the big bay window that fronted on the street below.

"Now," he said, "when he says jump, I ask where—and why. Then

I make up my own mind." He spoke softly, one confidant to another.

She snorted. "When did all this happen?"

He drew a long, slow breath. It was decision time, pick-up-the-chips time. He spoke very deliberately, very precisely: "It happened just about two weeks ago."

She flinched. As the words registered, struck home, her teenager's cool deserted her, leaving her staring at him warily. "You say—" She broke off. Then, cautiously: "You say two weeks?"

He nodded. "Two weeks, maybe a little more. Just about—" A final pause before he must commit himself, push it all the way. Everything: "Just about the time Jeff Weston was killed."

As if he'd gone for her, threatened her, she drew away, her back pressed hard against the couch. Her eyes widened; her voice was a ragged whisper. "What d' you know about Jeff?"

"I know that he died. And I know that he and you were—friends."

"Friends—" It was a brief, bitter echo.

"I know that you left home, left New York, the same day Weston died. And I know you've been running ever since." As the words fell, he saw fear come into her eyes, saw her hands tighten on the sleeping bag that surrounded her, a runaway teenager's nest.

"Wh—what else do you know?"

"I know about Daniels's girlfriend. I know when she disappeared."

"His—" Clutching the sleeping bag, her fingers suddenly tightened, the giveaway. "His girlfriend?"

"She disappeared the night before you took off. And now the police are looking for her."

"Oh, Jesus." Suddenly she sprang to her feet, went to the far corner of the room, faced away from him: a child standing in the corner, arms rigidly at her sides, fists clenched, head low, braced against punishment. "The police. Sweet Jesus."

Also on his feet, he moved to stand behind her. He spoke softly: "I know all about her, Diane. I know her name, and I know where she lived. And you know what happened to her that Sunday night. Don't you?"

Suddenly she began to sob: deep, wracking sobs. Without hope, she began to shake her head. Repeating: "Sweet Jesus."

"I want you to think about it," he said. "I want you to think about what you know, and what I know."

11 A.M., PDT

How long had it been since he'd left her? An hour? Less than an hour? Yes, almost certainly less than an hour. Yet, already, she'd caused Kane's visit to pass into the shadows, a memory, no substance, therefore no menace. No menace, therefore no fear. No fear, no terror. One small round capsule on an empty stomach, and she'd caused Kane to cross over, dissolve, shrink into the shades beyond.

But memory remained. She'd left the warm, secure cocoon of her sleeping bag to find him at the door. Instantly, she'd sensed danger. Yet she'd let him in. It was, she knew, Daniels, his power. Svengali. Extend his arms, fingers spread, eyes wild, compelling, Daniels's will be done. *Thy will be done,* the minister's scam. Dress up, drop a dollar in the collection plate, and *Daniels's will be done.*

Yet she'd let him in. Kane, with those flat, watchful eyes. Snake's eyes, portrait of Kane. Pilots were heroes—pilots were killers. A burst of machine-gun fire, black smoke trailing the enemy airplane across the sky, curving down, score one more dead.

One more dead—and Jeff dead, too.

If Kane hadn't done it, then Kane could have done it. Crash and burn, the hot-rodder's creed.

She'd been with Jeff, that Sunday night on the dunes. Kane had known it, known they'd been together. And Jeff had died.

And Kane had tracked her down, rung her doorbell, waited politely for her to dress.

I want you to think about it. The con man now, not the hit man.

Hit man?

It had been her first thought when she'd seen him on her doorstep. Yet she'd let him in.

132

I want you to think about it.

Translation: Together, they could ruin Daniels. Forever.

Dressed in a dark skirt and blouse, funeral clothes, she would watch the judge pronounce sentence. She would watch, and she would smile. Daniels, guilty of murder. Preston Daniels, in convict's denims, locked in a cell.

But suddenly she saw it again: Jeff, and all the blood. Jeff, no longer human, as meaningless as a bundle of clothing discarded beside the road.

Jeff, so curiously flattened on the bottom. When she'd stood there beside his body a wayward fragment of memory had flickered: a big blow-up water toy, a sea horse she'd once had that had lost most of its air.

Before Daniels let her testify against him, before he allowed her to send him to prison, he would have her killed. First Jeff. Then her.

She was sitting on the couch. Because the morning fog hadn't yet cleared, San Francisco's arctic summertime, she'd pulled the sleeping bag around her, as much for protection as for warmth. In front of the couch, on the floor, lay the leather tote bag. When she went to sleep at night, everything went into the tote bag: wallet, keys, contacts, whatever paperback she was reading, money, address book—and the pills, and the grass. Her stash. Herself. Whatever she had, whatever she was, it was all there, in the tote bag.

So that now, without moving from the couch, she had a choice: she could find Alan Bernhardt's card, probably in her wallet. Or she could call her father, tell him she had to see him. She could tell him what happened—what could happen.

But why did it seem so shameful, to tell her father? Why did it feel so wrong?

Just as wrong as it would feel to tell her mother. Just as wrong. Just as lost.

One choice—two choices—

Leaving the third choice, the last choice: the tote bag again, and the pills. Rest in peace.

11:20 A.M., PDT

"Wait," Bernhardt said into the phone. "Hold it, Charlie, until I get the goddamn file. Or, better yet, let me call you back. How long'll you—" The telephone warbled: call forwarding. "Listen, Charlie, there goes my other line. I'll get back to you before noon. Okay?"

With Charlie Foster's grudging approval, Bernhardt broke the first connection, took the second call. Reacting to Bernhardt's irritation, Crusher, lying beside the desk, raised his head, flopped his tail twice, sighed, yawned, let his head fall back between his paws.

"This is—ah—this is Diane Cutler, Mr. Bernhardt."

"*Diane.*" Squaring himself before the telephone, Bernhardt concentrated, focused on the voice in his ear. It was a softer, more tentative voice than he associated with Diane Cutler. "How's it going?"

"Well—ah—I thought I'd like to talk to you. Someone—something. I mean—" She broke off, began again: "Something's happened that I—I'd like to talk to you about. I mean, it—it's like you said, maybe if I talk to you about it—a stranger—I can make more sense out of it, out of what's happening."

"We can sure give it a shot. When would you like to talk?"

"Could—would—I mean, this afternoon. Have you got time, this afternoon?"

"Can you come over here? Have you got wheels?"

"Sure."

"It's on Potrero Hill. Do you—?"

"Sure. I grew up here."

"Right. I'd forgotten. How about two-thirty? Is that all right?"

"It's fine, Mr. Bernhardt. Just fine. Thanks."

"How about 'Alan'?"

"Yes—Alan. Thanks."

"See you at two-thirty."

1 P.M., PDT

From New York, he could hear the intermittent buzzing: Preston Daniels's private line, ringing. At the third ring, Jackie Miller came on the line. She recited the number, nothing more.

Should he identify himself? Would she recognize his voice? If she did recognize his voice, and he didn't identify himself, would she be suspicious?

"Jackie—is Mr. Daniels available?"

"Bruce?"

"Yes."

"He's in a meeting. I don't think—"

"Just tell him I'm calling. Let him decide. Okay?"

"Just a moment." It was her Ivy League accent. Vassar, of course.

A long silence. Then Daniels came on the line: "Yes. What is it?" A short, terse question.

"I—ah—think I should come back to New York. Now."

"Are you finished there?"

Unaccountably, he laughed, a momentary eruption. It was nervousness, he knew. Tension. Momentary loss of control. And control was essential now. Who would take control? Daniels, with his billions?

Or him, with what he knew, what he'd found out?

"I don't know whether I'm finished or not. But we should talk." In the background, he could hear voices. Yes, Daniels was in a meeting. In a meeting, yet taking this call. Leverage. Winner take all.

"I'm leaving for Atlanta at noon tomorrow," Daniels said. "You fly to Atlanta. Stay at the Hilton. I'll contact you there."

"The Atlanta Hilton. Right."

Abruptly, the line went dead.

2:30 P.M., PDT

"Cup of coffee? Seven-Up?" Bernhardt smiled, an attempt to put her at ease. "A glass of white wine?"

"No, thanks."

"Are you sure? Because I'm going to have some coffee." He gestured to an automatic coffee maker that shared bookshelf space with rows of well-thumbed books, most of them paperbacks.

"Okay. Black."

"I'll just be a minute."

"Fine." She watched him as he rose, went to the machine, poured the coffee. He was a tall, lean, loose-limbed man, slightly stooped. He was dressed casually: rumpled corduroy sports jacket, tattersall shirt open at the neck, slacks that needed pressing, loafers that needed shining. His face went with the clothes: a dark, Semitic face, reassuringly creased. The nose was slightly hooked, the mouth was wide and expressive: a mouth meant to smile. His eyes were soft and dark. His thick salt-and-pepper hair curled just over his collar, and needed trimming. Only the glasses evoked the actor, the intellectual: expensive-looking gold-framed aviator's glasses. The glasses suggested that Bernhardt understood the game; the clothes suggested that he chose not to play.

Carrying the two steaming mugs of coffee, Bernhardt carefully handed one mug to her, then sat facing her across the small, cluttered office.

"I haven't done anything about finding out about Jeff Weston's death," he said. "I may as well tell you that, right out."

She sipped her own coffee, which tasted Colombian: good, strong Colombian, another touch of class. Covertly, she eyed Bernhardt, imaging the body beneath the clothing. What would it be like, making love to a man like this? Pillow talk—what would the pillow talk be like, after the sex? What would make a man like this laugh?

She put the mug on the table beside her chair. "I didn't think you'd done anything."

"Oh?" He looked at her. Partly, she decided, it was a shrink's look: eyes not quite friendly, mouth not quite smiling. Setting the limits. Asking the questions. Always, asking the questions: sly, deft little questions: "Why's that?"

"Because," she said, "I didn't think you figured I was being straight with you. Or at least telling you everything, the whole story."

The small smile widened appreciatively. "That's very perceptive, Diane. I'm impressed."

She nodded acknowledgment, but made no reply. Instead, lowering her eyes, she drank from the mug. But could she use the caffeine jolt? An hour ago, to steady herself, get control, she'd taken a pill. So if she drank too much coffee, it could—

"Why don't we start," Bernhardt was saying, "by me telling you everything I know about you—everything I know, and everything I surmise. How's that?" As he spoke, he took a sheet of paper from a file folder that lay on his desk. Scanning the paper, he tilted his head up. Bernhardt wore bifocals.

She shrugged. "Fine."

"I know," he began, "that you grew up in San Francisco. Millicent and Paul Cutler were—are—your parents. They divorced when you were about fourteen. Your mother married Preston Daniels, real estate tycoon. You moved to New York when you were just starting high school. Which has got to be the worst time to move, especially so far away, and especially since your father remarried, I gather, just about that time. Right?"

She knew she must respond, knew she must nod. Soon, she knew, the probing would begin. First the probing, then the pain.

Always, the pain.

"So now," he was saying, "we come to the present." He tossed the sheet of paper on the desk, an actor's flourish, and spread his hands to include the two of them, sitting here in the office that once had been a bedroom, eyeing each other, deciding about each other.

"So—" Once more the professional smile, his eyes crinkling behind the trendy glasses. "So what's happened, since yesterday?"

"What's happened," she answered, "is that a man named Bruce Kane came to see me this morning. He's my stepfather's pilot, his personal pilot."

"And he scared you."

Cautiously, she scanned his face. "Why do you say that?"

"Because you were already scared of something yesterday. But you weren't willing to talk to me about it. Now, though, you've come to tell me what's bothering you." Expressively, he spread his hands. "So I figure that Kane has something to do with your change of heart. Maybe a lot to do. Maybe everything."

"I—I'm not sure. I'm just not sure."

"Tell me about it, Diane." He spoke quietly, seriously—as friends speak. "Start at the beginning. Tell me the whole story. It's the only way."

Slowly, resigned, she nodded. Then she began.

3:15 P.M., PDT

When she'd finished telling the story, Bernhardt sat silently for a moment, his expression thoughtful. Finally: "That's some story, Diane. If it happened the way you think it happened—if Daniels killed his girlfriend, and buried her, and then had Jeff Weston killed to shut him up—" Incredulously, Bernhardt shook his head. "That's a big deal. That's a *very* big deal."

She made no response.

"On the other hand," Bernhardt said, "there's also the possibility that Daniels's girlfriend OD'd, and he panicked. It'd make sense. A scandal like that—girl found dead in tycoon's love nest—it could ruin him."

"What about Jeff, though? What if he tried blackmail, and got murdered?"

"What if he got in a fight, and lost? Or he could've gotten mugged for the money he'd collected."

"Yes, but—"

"It could've all been coincidence. Pure coincidence."

"But it could also—"

"How long was it between the time Daniels's girlfriend disappeared and the time Weston was killed?"

"A day. Almost to the hour."

"Yeah. Well—" Dubiously, he shook his head. "See, that's where, frankly, I think it could all fall apart. I mean, you don't hire a murderer in twenty-four hours, not unless you happen to have one on the payroll. And even if you *do* have one on the payroll, it still takes time to plan a murder."

"It only takes a few seconds to kill someone."

"True. But how could the murderer have known Weston's delivery schedule? That's the kind of question the police are going to ask."

"Are you saying you don't believe me?"

"Not at all. I believe you absolutely. You and Weston saw Daniels load a body—or something suspiciously like a body—in his Cherokee. Then he drove to the landfill. However, you—"

"Wait a minute. What'd you mean, 'like a body'?"

"I mean," he answered, carefully measuring the words, "that you don't really know—not a hundred percent—that it was a body. You—"

"It *was* a body. Just the way he was acting, it couldn't've been anything else. And there was the arm, the hand—I saw it fall out."

"Diane—" Reluctantly, he drew a deep breath. "Imagine yourself on the witness stand. The defense attorney, who probably makes half a million a year, asks you whether, *in fact*, you're certain it was a body. You tell him exactly what you've told me. 'A hand?' he asks, jumping right on it, not backing away. And then he starts: 'How far away were you? Was there a moon? Had you been drinking?' You know how it goes, you've seen the movies. Then he'll ask you whether, *in fact*, you actually saw Daniels burying the body, actually eyeballed him. And then he'll—"

"But what about Jeff? You're saying it was coincidence that he was killed? But I'm telling you that—" Angrily, she broke off, began shaking her head. Suddenly she reached for the coffee mug. If it couldn't be booze, at least she'd be swallowing something, anything. But the mug was empty, the story of her life.

"More coffee?" Bernhardt asked.

Sharply, she shook her head.

"The odds are," Bernhardt said, "that it'll take a trip to Cape Cod to find out how Jeff died. And that's expensive, Diane. That's thousands of dollars."

"So I'm wasting my time talking to you. Unless I can come up with money, I'm wasting my time. Is that it?"

"No," he answered, his voice measured, his eyes steady. "No, that's not it. But airline tickets cost money. Rental cars, too. Then there's me. I've got rent to pay. And—" He smiled, an overture. "And I've got an Airedale to support."

Unsmiling, she shifted sharply in her chair, looked at her watch. It was time to go. Time for a drink, for a pill—for relief from the pain that was beginning. Anger could only carry her so far.

As if he hadn't noticed her restlessness, Bernhardt asked, "What about Bruce Kane? How's he figure in all this?"

She shrugged, shook her head, gestured impatiently. "I'm not sure. I think originally he was hired to find me, which wasn't too hard. I mean, it was pretty plain that I was coming to San Francisco. And then it was easy to figure I'd stay with Carley. But now—" She frowned. "Now, from the things Kane said this morning, I have the feeling that he might be out to blackmail Daniels."

Bernhardt sat up straighter. "Why do you say that?"

"He hinted that he and I are the only two people besides Daniels who know what happened. He didn't say it in so many words, right out. He's too shrewd for that. But I think he flew Daniels and his girlfriend into the Cape, maybe on Saturday. Everyone in Carter's Landing knew Daniels was shacking up on weekends. So when Daniels left for New York, alone, on Monday, I think Kane started to suspect something was wrong. So between the two of us, with what he knows and what I know, we could ruin Daniels. And I think Kane knows that."

"But if that's true," Bernhardt mused, "then why would Daniels hire Kane to find you? I'd think he'd want to keep you and Kane apart."

She shrugged, shook her head. She couldn't answer the question.

"Do you believe Kane's capable of blackmail?"

"I believe he's capable of anything."

"Murder?"

"Probably."

"Could he have murdered Jeff Weston?"

"Why would he do that? What would he gain?"

"If Weston was thinking about blackmail, too, then he might've been competition."

Impatiently, she shook her head. "That's crazy. It was only the day after the girlfriend disappeared that Jeff died. It'd be too early for Kane and Jeff to be at each other's throats. Besides, there's enough for everyone, if you're talking about blackmailing Daniels. Plenty to go around."

Genially, Bernhardt nodded. "You're pretty good at this, Diane. You've got a gift for imagining why people do what they do. Otherwise known as a devious mind."

"Mmmm." Her smile was tentative; her eyes were speculative.

"That was meant as a compliment. I could've just plain said you're a very smart lady."

Her smile widened almost imperceptibly. Plainly, Diane Cutler distrusted compliments.

Picking up on the cue, Bernhardt shifted ground: "So why're you here, Diane? Why'd you come to San Francisco? Why're you running? Yesterday you said it was family trouble. Then you talked about Jeff, about how he might've died. Then—now—you tell me that seeing Daniels and the body freaked you out. So what is it? All three?"

As if the effort cost her pain, she grimaced, then nodded. "It's all three. It's—Christ—it's everything. I hate New York. I hate Preston Daniels. What I had with Jeff—" Sadly, she shook her head. "That was nothing. Worse than nothing, really. So then—" Struggling to frame the thought, put it into words, she broke off, sat silently for a moment, staring down at the floor. Finally saying: "So then, when I saw that— that scene, on Sunday—the great Preston Daniels, humping to load a dead body in the same car I'd ridden in, and then the next night, when I saw Jeff lying in the gravel beside the road with his eyes wide open and blood everywhere—well, I just had to split, that's all. I—I just couldn't handle it."

"You'd already split from your mother, though, earlier on Monday. Isn't that right?"

"Yeah, well—" She shifted in the chair, a sharp, restless protest, a teenager's mute admission of the pain within. "Well, that's happened before. I mean, that wasn't the first time I slammed out of the apartment. But then, Christ, then I drove up to the Cape, and—"

"You saw Daniels, though, after you slammed out of the apartment. You said you saw him in the parking garage of your building. Isn't that so?"

"Oh, yeah—" Her voice was bitter. "Oh, yeah, I saw him."

"And from what he said to you in the garage, you were convinced that he'd been doing away with a body, the night before."

She nodded.

"And you think he realized that you knew what'd happened."

"Right."

"And you think that if Jeff was murdered to shut him up, then you could be next."

Once more, she nodded.

"Okay, so if that's true—" Bernhardt leaned intently forward, locking his eyes with hers. "So if that's true, and if you hate Daniels so much, then why didn't you go to the police, blow the whistle? You've got Daniels right where you want him. One word to the police, and he's ruined."

She grimaced, looked away. "One word to the police from me, and I'd die. Just like Jeff died. Witnesses die all the time, you know, before trials begin."

"Hasn't it occurred to you that you could go to your mother, tell her everything you know about this—everything you suspect? Don't you think that'd be your best insurance?"

Once more, her mouth twisted into a bitter smile. "Do you think my mother would believe me if it meant blowing the whistle on Daniels? Christ, a scandal like that, and she might not be president of the museum board."

Thoughtfully, Bernhardt studied her face, now drawn so painfully tight, eyes cast down, defeated. Finally, speaking softly, he decided to say, "If you went to the police, blew this whole thing open, then you could ruin both Daniels and your mother. Two for one."

Her response was a quick, involuntary shudder, as if he'd caused her pain.

Still speaking softly, he said, "You don't want to blow the whistle because you don't want to hurt your mother. Isn't that right, Diane?"

"I—Christ—" Desperately, she shook her head. "I—I don't know. I just don't know anymore."

Plainly, the admission had left her spent. It was, Bernhardt knew, time to close out the scene, begin the exit lines:

"Do you know where Kane is staying? What hotel?"

"No."

"Any idea how I could reach him?"

Exhausted, she shook her head.

"Does he have Daniels's airplane, do you know?"

Once more, she shook her head.

"What kind of an airplane is it?"

"I don't know the name of it. But it's got two motors, and it can go three hundred miles an hour, I know that."

"Is it a jet? A Lear jet, like that?"

"No. It's got propellers."

"Okay." With an air of finality, he moved forward in his chair as he said, "I'll see what I can do. Stay close to Carley's phone. Okay?"

"Yes. Okay."

WEDNESDAY,
August 1st

11 P.M., EDT

"When she heard that Carolyn was missing," Kane said, "and I said the police were looking for her, she freaked out. I mean, she *really* freaked out."

Dressed in dinner clothes, seated in Kane's hotel room, legs crossed, willing his hands to relax as they rested on the arms of the chair, Daniels allowed himself a single carefully calculated nod. It was, after all, what he'd expected, and therefore prepared himself to confront.

"What is it," he asked, "that Diane thinks she knows? Did she tell you, in so many words?"

"She didn't *have* to tell me. It was all there in her face. She was with Weston the night Carolyn disappeared. What Weston saw, she saw."

"Ah." Daniels nodded. "Yes. I thought that must've been it." As if he were a medical clinician assessing the nature of his own responses, he took the critical inventory again: hands steady, face expressing gravity but not fear, body satisfactorily aligned, voice under control.

"You did, eh?" It was a toneless, expressionless question, a question without an answer, signifying nothing.

Nothing but suspicion that had turned to certainty.

Nothing but disaster, the end of everything.

Silence. A terrible, empty silence, each of them avoiding the gaze of the other. Finally, with great effort, he looked directly at Kane. The moment held, tightened; finally drew unbearably taut, forcing him to say:

"It was an accident. She came at me. I had to hit her. She fell, hit her head."

"Like Weston. That was an accident, too."

147

"Yes . . ." Gravely, he nodded.

"But then—" Kane hesitated. "Then you—you did something with her. With her—" He cleared his throat, blinked. Finally saying: "With her body."

"I didn't have a choice. It was either that, or see everything blow up."

"You'd beat it, though. Tell the truth, and you'd beat it. You'd never go to jail."

"I'd be ruined, long before I went to trial. Millicent would have to get a divorce. She wouldn't have a choice. So she'd take hers. So then the credit would go. And that'd be it. The whole thing, gone."

"That's hard to believe."

"In real estate, finance—credit—is what it's all about. No credit, and it's all over."

"Didn't you have a prenuptial contract?"

Wearily, he raised a hand, let it fall. "I don't want to talk about it."

"So you wouldn't be a billionaire anymore. But you'd never go broke. I *know* you'd never go broke."

Mirthlessly, Daniels allowed himself to smile. "There're different definitions of disaster."

"If Farnsworth starts putting all this together," Kane said, "that's one definition. Right?"

"Right." It was a heavily laden monosyllable. This, he knew, was the preamble to the ceremony of surrender. The minions were taking over.

"By the way," Kane said, "speaking of money . . ." Delicately, he let it go unfinished.

Daniels withdrew an envelope from an inside pocket of his dinner jacket; negligently, tossed the bulky envelope onto a nearby table.

Kane looked at the envelope. A week ago, he would have thanked Daniels. Now he only nodded. Saying: "I guess that's a down payment. Another down payment."

Daniels nodded in return. "Exactly."

"Diane."

"Yes. Diane. There's nothing else to do."

THURSDAY,
August 2nd

8 P.M., PDT

"How long'll you be staying in San Francisco, Mr. Carter?" As he asked, the night clerk offered a registration form and a ballpoint pen.

"Two days," Kane answered, writing "William Carter" on the form, followed by a Los Angeles address.

"And what credit card'll you be using?"

"That'll be cash." Kane took out his wallet and began counting the bills out on the counter. The plate-glass countertop was cracked. The night clerk's knuckles were bruised, as if he'd been in a fight. The lobby smelled of disinfectant.

8:30 P.M., PDT

"What d' you think? Should we order another one?" Bernhardt held up the empty bottle of cabernet sauvignon.

Paula shook her head. "Not for me."

He nodded, then caught the waiter's eye, at the same time pointing to their basket containing only one piece of French bread. Carrying three steaming plates of Italian food, harassed, the waiter nodded as he edged between two nearby tables.

"You take the last piece," Paula insisted. "Sop up your white clam sauce. That's the best part."

"You sure? I doubt that he'll be right back."

"Sure I'm sure. I've got lasagna. There's nothing to sop up." As she spoke she took the piece of bread, placed it decisively on his plate. Then, equally decisive, she said, "I'd like to meet her, Alan. I—" Expressing a puzzlement at her own determination, she frowned, then shook her head. "I don't know what it is, but I've got a *feeling* about her."

Considering how best to respond, Bernhardt wound linguine on his fork, successfully conveyed it intact to his mouth.

"Maybe you should talk to her father," she urged. "Cutler. Maybe if he knew the whole story he'd come up with enough money for you to go to Cape Cod." She smiled. "Maybe we could both go. Business and pleasure."

He grimaced. "Cape Cod in the summertime. Unless you've got a ton of money, it's a zoo."

"Still, I think you should talk to her father."

"As far as I know," he said, "Diane hasn't even seen him yet, much less told him what's happening. And if she hasn't told him, then I'm not going to tell him. That'd be just plain dumb."

"But where else'll we get the money?"

He put his fork aside, sipped his wine, drew a long, elaborately patient breath. "Paula—listen—you've got to cut me some slack on this thing. You might not realize it, but I've got three open cases right now. All of them, as it happens, working for law firms that pay very, very well. They also pay promptly, and often. Bread-and-butter accounts, in other words. Now, you keep saying you want me to arrange my life so I can have time to write plays. And that's fine, I'm all for it. But I can tell you that taking on someone like Diane Cutler and her problems is no way to operate a profitable P.I. business. In fact, it's—"

"But that's why I'm saying that you should contact Cutler. You should—"

"Please. Paula. Give it a rest." He pointed. "Eat your lasagna."

"Like a good girl, eh? Is that what you're saying?"

"That's what I'm saying."

9 P.M., PDT

If the phone went to four rings, she'd decided, and the answering machine came on, she would—

"Yes? Hello?"

The voice cut like a knife. Phoebe Randolph Cutler, wife number two. The lady account executive, six-figure income. High style, hard as nails. Nine years younger than her husband. Both of them earning six figures each.

Did Phoebe ever sweat, when they were screwing? Did—?

"Hel-*lo.*" Audibly irritated. Strike one.

"Th—this is Diane. Is my—"

"Just a second, Diane. Your father is anxious to talk to you." The plainly audible message: *You're bothering your father. You're bothering all of us. You're an inconvenience.*

"*Diane.*" Breaking in, her father's voice. Warm. Welcoming. "How're you *doing?*" Her father, trying to sound like her father. Trying too hard, Ozzie and Harriet.

"I'm okay."

"So how about lunch? Tomorrow. One o'clock. Okay?"

"Yes. Fine."

"I don't suppose you packed a skirt." Still warm. Still imitating the All-American Dad.

She sighed. "No skirt. You're right."

"Just kidding, Diane. See you tomorrow. I can't wait."

"Yeah."

FRIDAY,
August 3rd

10:30 A.M., PDT

"I'd like a short length of three-quarter-inch galvanized pipe," Kane said. "About eighteen inches long."

"Do you want it threaded or plain?" the clerk asked.

"It doesn't matter."

"We've got it both ways."

"Then I'll take it plain."

1:15 P.M., PDT

Across the small, elegantly set table, Diane watched her father as he handed their menus to the waitress. He was smiling politely. It was, she realized, yet another difference between the two men, her father and her stepfather. Daniels looked through servants. Straight through.

Now, she knew, it would come. They'd done the small talk, done the father-daughter smiles, gotten through the first small silences. Now came the hard part:

"I guess you know," Cutler said, "that as soon as you called, Monday, I called your mother." Ruefully—yet another good-guy try, Ozzie and Harriet—he smiled. "It was almost midnight, New York time, when I called. She wasn't too pleased. At least, not until I told her why I was calling."

Leaving her to say what? Do what? Pretend what?

She lowered her eyes, sipped her coffee. When she raised her eyes she saw that, yes, his smile was gone. As, yes, she saw his mouth tighten, saw the shadow of pain behind his eyes. Could he see the same shadow in her eyes, sense the same pain?

"Diane, I—I don't pretend to know what's happening. I mean, I know you and your mother are having problems. And Daniels, too—I know you and he are having problems. And I know that, according to your mother, you don't want to go back to college next year." As he spoke, he searched her face. Then, a shift, a lawyer's change of pace, keep them guessing, he experimentally sampled the salad. Saying: "This is good, a great dressing. Have you tried it?" Followed, yes, by the smile. But was this a lawyer's smile, no longer a father's smile?

In silence, she picked up a fork, ate some of the salad, put the fork in the salad plate.

"So what'd you think?" Now it was the father-of-the-year smile, his specialty. Yes, he fit perfectly into the sitcom frame: a summer-weight pinstriped suit, an expensive white Oxford button-down shirt, rep tie, all very casual, all very with-it. And the face went with the clothes: an Ivy League face, slightly modified for the laid-back San Francisco scene.

"It's fine. Good salad." She nodded.

Erasing the smile. God, it was so easy to erase his smile. His smile, and all the others. All except for Daniels's smile—the smile that never was.

"Listen, Diane—" He laid his own fork aside, a solemn, measured signal. "If you'll just tell me what it's all about, I'd like to help you. Do you want to come here to live? With—" A moment's hesitation. Then, dutifully: "With me?"

"You mean 'us,' don't you? Phoebe and you."

He raised his hand to his mouth, pressed his lips with is fingertips, looked at her with stricken eyes. Then, in a voice gone ragged, he said, "I—I know the two of you don't get along, Diane. But that's got nothing to do with us—with you and me. You know I've always—"

"Are you happier now? Do you think your life's better now, with Phoebe?"

"It—" In denial, he sharply shook his head. "It's got nothing to do with Phoebe, Diane. Surely you understand that. It's—your mother and I—it just wasn't working out. You know that. We've explained to you that—"

"You explained nothing to me, Daddy. You gave me a lot of bullshit, that's what you gave me. 'We no longer love each other,' you said, something like that. How about if you said something like, 'Your mother's got a chance to land a genuine tycoon, and I can't stop her from doing it.' How about if you'd said something like that, Daddy? How about the truth, for a change?"

"The truth . . ." He spoke softly, bitterly. "What the hell is the truth? Who knows what the truth is?"

"The truth is what really happens. The truth is what people think about, but don't talk about."

"Diane, you were fourteen when we got divorced. You couldn't expect us to—to—"

"To tell me the truth? Is that what you were going to say? Well, I'm eighteen now, and you're still not telling me the truth." As she spoke, she snatched up her coffee cup, drained it, slammed the cup back in its saucer. Almost instantly, a busboy was there, refilling the cup from a silver pot. He was a slim, smooth-moving Latino with dark, dusky eyes.

"How about you, Diane?" her father was saying, challenging her now. "Do you tell the truth?"

Defiantly: "Sure."

"How about drugs? Do you do any drugs?"

"Is that what Mom told you?"

"Never mind what your mother told me. You say you tell the truth. So I'm asking you, do you do drugs?"

A deep breath. Then, nothing to lose, let go and drop, finally fall free: "Sure I do. I smoke pot, and I drink booze and I pop pills once in a while. I've tried cocaine, too. But I don't do anything else. I'm not into needles, if that's what you're getting at. I don't like to have holes in my skin." She watched him for a moment, saw the words strike, one after the other, neatly timed, neatly spaced. Slow-motion machine-gun bullets from old war movies, kicking up the dust. Power.

Then, following up, hit them when they blink: "What about you, Daddy? Booze, and what else, you and Phoebe and your button-down friends? A little coke, on Saturday nights?"

"I've tried cocaine." His eyes were steady, his voice was firm. "But I didn't like it much. I don't like being that much out of control."

As he said it, the waitress arrived with their entrees. Truce declared.

A truce, or a draw? Finally, a draw?

For a few moments they talked about the food, about San Francisco, about the earthquakes: the last one, and the Big One yet to come. Finally, down to business again, her father said, "We've talked many times the last couple of weeks, your mother and I. As I said, she's very worried about you, very concerned for your welfare. I'd like you to believe that, Diane."

She made no reply, gave no sign.

"I didn't tell her that Carley was living here. I didn't think Carley would appreciate getting involved."

In reluctant acknowledgment, she nodded.

"And I didn't call Carley, either, if you noticed, looking for you." He smiled: a small, tentative smile, almost a shy smile. "I was pretty proud of myself for that."

Another grudging nod. Another silence. Then, another try, the lawyer, probing, boring in, he said, "From what your mother said, from the way she talked, I had the impression that the reason you left had something to do with them—with her and Preston Daniels, with some problems they're having."

She laughed: a short, bitter eruption. "Did she say that?"

He studied her face for a moment. Then, putting aside his knife and fork, putting his hands flat on the table, pleading now, he said, "Diane, are you in trouble? Is that what this is all about? Are you running from some kind of trouble, back in New York? Because if you are, we can work it out. Has it got anything to do with the law? Is that it?"

As they sat silently, each searching the other's face for some special sign, some assurance, something hopeful, something worth saving, she realized that, yes, she should tell him.

But, just as clearly, she knew she wouldn't tell him.

Why?

She could tell Bernhardt, a stranger. But she couldn't tell her father.

Why?

2:20 P.M., PDT

"Is that yours?" Cutler pointed to the BMW. It was a politely interested question, small talk.

"Yes."

"How do you like it?"

"It's great. I'd rather have a Porsche. But it's great." Within a few feet of the car now, she began rummaging in her shoulder bag for her keys. Somehow she needed to have the keys in her hand before she turned to him, offered her cheek for a kiss.

"Oh," he said, "I forgot to ask. Did you connect with John Williams?"

At the car now, no escape, she frowned as she turned to face him. "John who?"

"Williams. Your friend from New York. He called just after you called. Monday night."

"I don't know any John Williams."

"Well, he definitely knows you. Or at least I assumed he knew you, since he seemed to know all about your plans." He smiled. "He sounded like an admirer. Does that help?"

"But—"

"Listen—" He lifted his arm, looked at his watch. "Listen, I'm sorry, pumpkin, but I've got to go. There's a deposition in twenty minutes."

"This John Williams. What'd he say?"

"He said he was on his way to Los Angeles, and hoped to see you here. He sounded pretty casual, just passing through. Listen—" He took her shoulders, held her, then quickly hugged her, hard. He spoke into the hollow of her shoulder: "I really do have to go. I—" His voice caught, but just for a moment. "I love you, pumpkin. I hope you know that."

2:30 P.M., PDT

"Room six-twenty, checking out."

"It's after checkout," the clerk said. "I can't give you a refund."

"No problem." Kane dropped the key on the desk.

"Was everything all right?" It was a disinterested question.

"Sure. It's just that something came up." He picked up his suitcase, picked up the canvas satchel containing the pipe and some dirty clothing, and walked outside. On Powell Street, on the cable-car line, the tourists were thick, a constant stream, clogging the sidewalks, tangling traffic, jostling, laughing, calling to each other.

The nondescript hotel he'd chosen was midway between the affluence of Union Square, up the street to his left, and the T-shirt shops and schlock camera shops and dirty-movie arcades to his right, down the hill toward the cable-car turntable. Powell Street was the eastern border of San Francisco's Tenderloin. Just a block to the west, downhill, everything was for sale: girls, boys, drugs, guns.

He turned to his right, walked two blocks, turned right again. He passed a dirty-book stall and a girlie bar with a top-hatted barker out front. The next storefront was a peep show parlor, open full width on the sidewalk. Leaving the suitcase just inside, then taking out his wallet, he went to the counter and changed a ten-dollar bill: a five, three ones and eight quarters. Carrying the canvas satchel, he went to the rear wall. With his back to the street he decided on a machine featuring "Fighting Girls." As he put a quarter in the slot, he glanced over his shoulder. Yes, the suitcase was gone.

162

2:50 P.M., PDT

She turned her shoulder bag upside down on the couch, emptied it, sorted through the contents. If the card wasn't in her wallet, then it must be—yes: ALAN BERNHARDT. INVESTIGATIONS. She took the card to the phone, punched out the number. Her fingers were unsteady. Her mouth was dry. When she heard Bernhardt's voice on the answering machine she felt herself go hollow. It was, she knew, associative, a word she'd just learned. With Bernhardt's voice, she associated the terror remembered: Bodies wrapped in blankets. Jeff, lying beside the road, staring sightlessly at the sky.

Should she hang up, steady herself, try again? She should have taken a pill before she called. She should have—

The beep. She was on.

"Mr. Bernhardt. Alan. This is Diane Cutler. It's about three o'clock Friday afternoon. And I wanted to tell you that—"

"Diane." Yes, it was his voice. And, in the background, a dog barking. Loudly. "Wait just a second, Diane. I just walked in, and this Airedale's going crazy. Can you hold on?"

"Yes . . ."

"Just a second, then. The plan is to get a dog biscuit, throw it out in the garden, and hope for the best."

And, moments later, he was back on the line. "Sorry. Airedales are great dogs. But they're—ah—taxing."

"I can tell."

"So what can I do for you?"

"Well, I—I just had lunch with my dad. I just got home from having lunch. And he said that, Monday night, someone called him asking about me—someone who gave him a false name."

"When you say 'asking about you,' what d'you mean? Did he sound like a bill collector, someone official?"

"He said he was a friend of mine, that his name was John Williams,

I think that was it. And my dad said he sounded like he knew all about my plans, where I'd be, what I'm doing. But the thing is, I didn't tell anyone I was coming here. Nobody."

"And you're worried about it."

"Someone killed Jeff. And now someone's tracking me."

She heard him draw a deep breath. "You're assuming that Jeff's death is connected to the disappearance of your stepfather's girlfriend. And if that's true, maybe it's logical that this guy—John Williams—is tracking you for some dark purpose. But there's another scenario. It could be that the two events are unrelated. It could be—"

"What I'd like is some protection."

Once more, she heard him draw a deep, reluctant breath. "And I'd like to offer you some protection, if only to ease your mind. But I've got to be honest with you, Diane. And the truth is, I run a one-man operation. There's me and an answering machine and that's it. And—"

"But, Christ, I'm trying to tell you that—"

"Wait. Let me finish." It was a crisp, stern command. "If I provided protection for you—a bodyguard—I'd have to hire someone by the hour. I'd have to pay someone—a free-lancer—twenty-five or thirty dollars an hour. Then I'd have to add ten dollars to that, for overhead."

"So we're back to money, you and me."

"I *need* money."

"I thought Carley gave you some money."

"She gave me a two-hundred-dollar retainer, and said she'd go to five hundred, total. If I hire someone to guard you, one shift at forty dollars an hour, that's the end of the five hundred."

"What about Kane? Have you tried to find him?"

"I've tried the airports, looking for your stepfather's airplane. No luck."

"Kane might've been the one who called my father."

"Anything's possible. But, offhand, I can't think why he'd use a fake name. After all, you know he's here. He knocked on your door."

"He's a shifty bastard. I've already told you that."

"I know. And I'd like to talk to him. It just hasn't worked out."

"Yeah . . ." As she said it, she looked at her watch. How long had they been talking? Fifteen minutes? Billable? Lawyers, she knew, charged two hundred dollars just to talk on the phone, give advice.

How much did her father charge?

How much would her father pay, for someone to protect her?

Why couldn't she tell her father what happened? Why couldn't she—?

"Diane?"

"Yes?" She tried to put it all in a single word: all the questions, all the anger.

"I've just had a thought."

"A thought?"

"I've got a friend—a good friend—who wants to learn the business. This might be a good place for her to start."

" 'Her'?"

"You might not realize it, but more than a third of the private detectives are women. And they make damn good investigators, too. In lots of situations, women can get more information than men can get."

"So what'll she do if someone goes for me? Scream? Christ, I can do that."

"You're going to laugh at this, but I'm going to tell you what she'd do. She'd blow her whistle. You'd be amazed what the bad guys do, when they hear a police whistle."

"Jesus."

"Then there're car phones."

"Hmmm."

"Shall I talk to her?"

"I'm going out tonight. Carley and her boyfriend and I are going to the movies."

"Will you be home for the next couple of hours?"

"Yes."

"Okay. Stay put. My—ah—assistant will call you, make the arrangements."

"A woman . . ."

"Believe me, she'll deliver. And I'll be backstopping her."

"You will?"

"Guaranteed."

"What's her name?"

"It's Paula. Paula Brett."

165

"What is she, some kind of lady jock? Is that it?"

"No," Bernhardt answered, "that's definitely not it."

4 P.M., EDT

"The problem with Houston," Daniels said, speaking into the speakerphone, "is the oil situation. I just don't think we should commit to—" On his console, the blue light blinked: Jackie, with a call on his private line. "Just a second, Herb. There's my other line. Hold on." He pressed the button. "Yes?"

"It's your wife, Mr. Daniels."

"Tell her she can hold for two minutes, or I'll call her back in five."

"One moment." Jackie left the line, then quickly came back. "She'll hold."

"Talk to her about clothes, Jackie."

"Hmmm."

He went back to the first call. "Sorry, Herb. My wife."

"No problem."

"I've got her on hold, talking to Jackie. So this is the nub: If Ernie's realistic about this, if he realizes that he made a mistake, and he's willing to take sixty, sixty-five cents on the dollar to get out clean, take the loss, write it off, then I think we'd be interested. But I want Ernie to feel right about this. I don't want him to feel like he's being fucked. He's only thirty-five, and he's smart. There'll be other deals."

"I agree."

"I don't think you should do this on the phone. I think you should go down to Houston Monday. Even tomorrow, if you can work it out with Ernie. Play a little golf, have a couple of drinks. The point being, I want Ernie's goodwill. The deal itself, even at fifty, fifty-five cents, I think we can take that or leave it. But Ernie's someone we can work with, down the line."

"I absolutely agree."

"Okay. Keep me posted."

"Right."

"How *is* your golf game, by the way?"

"It seems to vary with my waistline, a direct relationship."

Daniels decided on an appreciative chuckle. "Okay. Gotta go." He switched to his private line. Yes, Millicent and Jackie were talking about clothes.

"Okay, Jackie. Back to work."

"Yes, sir." A humorous, relaxed response.

"Preston." Millicent's voice was low, stricken.

Stricken?

Instantly the images came back, the images that only the moment-to-moment pressures of work had erased: Diane, dead on some San Francisco street. Diane, no longer a mortal threat. Replaced now by the police, the reporters. Replaced by the eyes, watching.

Were other calls waiting, on other lines down the chain of command? Would there be headlines in tomorrow's tabloids?

"What is it?" he asked. "You sound worried."

"It's Justin. He had a heart attack this morning."

Justin Faye, their host for tomorrow's dinner party. The invitation was a bright star in Millicent's firmament, a prize. And for him, too. Senators and CEOs and, yes, a cabinet member, they were all on the guest list. Society columnists would be holding the presses for this one, the crown jewel of the summer social season.

Poor Millicent, with the Aubergé gown in the closet, and the hairdresser reserved.

"So the party's off."

"Of course," she answered peevishly. Then, letting it all hang out, yet another grievance, she said, "Did you know that Freddy's having people in tonight after the performance?"

Freddy King, the choreographer, unsurprisingly gay, currently anointed New York's favorite media darling. Hold the presses again.

His response must be low-keyed, pitch-perfect: "No, I didn't know." Then: "Are you sure?"

"Of course I'm sure. After all I've done for him, that son of a bitch."

"Maybe he's just having a few people. Maybe it's all guys. I don't think you should—"

"He's having Inez and Jimmy." It was the ultimate indictment. Assuming, as one must, that Freddy knew of the Millicent-Inez rivalry.

"Hmmm." He allowed her to hear a deep, sympathetic sigh. Then: "Listen, it's after four, and I've got to—"

"I want to go to the Cape. Tomorrow. Early tomorrow. Or tonight, even." It was a command, not a request.

He felt his stomach contract, felt his whole body take the shock, felt substance fall away, leaving only the emptiness.

Yet, certainly, she suspected nothing. She simply had to get out of town. Regroup. Plan vengeance. Have two martinis before dinner, not just one.

If he objected, said he couldn't make it, she would certainly go by herself, fair game for Constable Joe Farnsworth.

So he must go with her. He must tell Millicent to tell Jackie to arrange it: a charter flight, up to the Cape tomorrow, return Sunday night. Either a charter flight, or get someone else to fly the King Air.

While, in San Francisco, Kane was otherwise occupied.

6 P.M., PDT

She pressed the button beside "Hanks," leaned closer to the grille of the small speaker while she positioned herself to grasp the doorknob if the electric door opener buzzed.

"Hello?"

"I'm Paula Brett. I'm working with Alan Bernhardt. Is this Diane?"

"No, this is Carley. But Diane's expecting you. I'll buzz you in—"

—As, yes, the door's buzzer sounded. Paula pushed open the vintage oak door and climbed one flight of stairs to the second floor. The building was turn-of-the-century Edwardian: high, coved ceilings, elaborate woodwork and trim, wide hallways. The rooms, certainly, were spacious and airy, with generous windows. There were two apartments to each floor, front and back. Carley Hanks's apartment, Alan had told her, was the second floor front. On her knock, the door immediately swung open.

"Diane Cutler?"

The young woman nodded. She was short and thickly built. Her shoulder-length hair was dark and full and tangled; her jeans and blouse weren't suited to her figure. Because her hair was too full, her face seemed too small. Her eyes were dark and hard-focused, smudged by teenage disaffection. Her lipstick was too vivid, a touch of defiance gone wrong. The skin of her face was coarse.

"I'm Paula Brett."

Nodding, Diane Cutler was stepping back, gesturing without enthusiasm to the interior hallway. Paula closed the hallway door, followed the young woman into a large, sunny living room. They sat facing each other across a big, low coffee table.

"Alan's filled me in." Paula ventured a smile. "We've spent a lot of time talking about you."

No response.

"He wanted me to tell you that I've got a walkie-talkie, plus the whistle." She patted her shoulder bag, tried another smile. "I've also got a cellular phone in the car. So you'll be getting Alan, too, as backup."

"Good." No inflection. No warmth. No answering smile. Poor Diane Cutler, with her eyes gone muddy, with her closed, embittered face and her stocky, awkwardly articulated body. Poor little rich girl.

"Is there—" Paula hesitated. Bernhardt had warned her: this wouldn't be easy. Nothing, she suspected, would be easy with Diane Cutler. "Is there anything you'd like to ask? I mean, we'll want to make plans, for tonight."

"I already told Alan. I'm going out with my roommate and her boyfriend. We're going to have something to eat, and then go to the movies."

"Is her boyfriend coming by here?"

Diane Cutler nodded, glanced at her watch. "He's coming in about twenty minutes."

"Where's your roommate?"

"She's in the bathroom."

Considering, Paula nodded, let her eyes wander to the front window that overlooked the street below. Like most San Francisco residences, the majority built on lots only twenty-five feet wide, Carley Hanks's apartment building was attached to its neighbor on either side, with garages beneath. Assuming that the rear entry was secure, one person parked in front of the building could cover the whole surveillance area. Just as, she suspected, Alan had already concluded.

"So the three of you are leaving here about six-thirty or seven. Right?"

Diane nodded.

"Will you go in one car?"

"I guess so."

"The three of you will eat, and then go to the movies."

"Right."

"Then what?"

"Then I guess maybe we'll have a drink someplace. Or we might just go home."

"All three of you'll come here?"

"Either that, or maybe they'll drop me off, and the two of them'll go to Dale's place for the night. That's up to them."

"If that's the way it goes," Paula said, "then the only time you need me would be when they drop you off—the time between when they drop you off and the time you're back here, safe." She gestured to the room, the apartment.

Diane shrugged.

"Will Carley's boyfriend be coming here in his car?"

"I suppose so." She considered, then nodded. "Sure. He wouldn't take a bus."

"It'd be easier if you all went from here in one car," Paula said. "That way, you wouldn't have to worry, not if you're with your friends. Then, when you get back here, I'll be parked outside."

Expressionlessly, the other woman looked at her for a long, silent moment. Then, in a flat, resentful voice, she said, "I don't see what good it'll do, if you're parked with your—" A short, contemptuous pause. "With your whistle."

For this objection, she was ready, rehearsed: "If someone's out to harm you, Diane, they don't want a witness. Especially a witness who's making noise."

The other woman looked away.

"Very few private investigators carry guns, Diane. A lot of them are licensed—Alan, for instance. But he almost never carries a gun. Because guns can create problems—a lot of problems, sometimes."

"They can also come in very goddamn handy, I'd think."

"A gun's no good unless you're willing to pull the trigger. And if I saw someone making a move on you, I'm not going to shoot him. I'd be in jail if I pulled the trigger first. And if *he* pulled the trigger first, you'd be the victim. So I'm going to yell. And, yes, blow the whistle. And he's going to split."

"Okay." Sullenly, the other woman shrugged, looked pointedly at her watch. Saying in the same flat, hostile voice: "Whatever."

7 P.M., PDT

"Let's take the BMW," Carley said as she locked the apartment door and tested the latch. "Okay, Diane?"

"Sure." Then, remembering Paula Brett's instructions, she said, "We'll go to the movies in my car, and then all three come back here. If you guys go to Dale's afterward, you can go in his car from here. Okay?"

Carley and Dale looked at each other and nodded. "Fine."

7:02 P.M., PDT

Sitting on the passenger's side of the rental car, Kane shifted on the seat, moved his legs to a more comfortable position, switched on the radio, found a light-rock station. It had been two hours since Diane had returned to the apartment after a trip to the corner grocery store. In that time, four others had entered the building. One of them, a dark-haired, attractive woman in her thirties, had arrived about an hour ago, and had left a half hour later. Her clothing and her manner had suggested that she'd come on business. Of the three others, one had been a young blonde woman, one had been a dark-haired, casually dressed young man in his twenties. The fourth visitor had been a refrigerator repair man, just departed. Minutes after entering the building, the dark-haired young man had briefly appeared in the window of the second-floor front apartment. Then the blonde had appeared in the same window, standing close to the man. Meaning that, certainly, the blonde was Carley Hanks. Meaning that the dark-haired man must be visiting Diane and Carley. Meaning that—

Across the street, the door to the apartment building was opening. The three of them—Diane, Carley, and the dark-haired man—were coming out. Carley and the man were touching each other, laughing into each other's eyes. Diane, unsmiling, was looking straight ahead.

As Kane slid to his left, under the steering wheel, the two women and the man turned left, walking toward Clipper Street. Kane started the Buick's engine, backed up, moved forward. Once more back, once more forward, until the car cleared the bumper of a pickup truck ahead. At the corner of Noe and Clipper, the trio turned left, disappeared behind a small apartment building.

It was around that corner, Kane knew, that Diane's BMW was parked, faced east on Clipper. Slowly, cautiously, he was driving north on Noe, toward the four-way stop at the intersection. Glancing in the mirror, he saw two cars behind him. He was too close to the intersection to double-park, gesture for them to go around. But if he stopped too long at the intersection, waiting for Diane to start the BMW, the drivers behind him would surely begin sounding their horns. Meaning, certainly, that Diane would look toward the sound, see him, recognize him.

Two choices, then: turn right, on Clipper, or drive straight ahead. Fifty-fifty.

Inching the car forward as, yes, a horn blared behind him, he saw the three getting into the BMW, closing the door. Behind the wheel, Diane was settling herself, ready to drive off. Through the intersection now, out of her sight, he pulled to the right, stopped, gestured for the irate drivers behind to go around.

As, in the mirror, he saw the green BMW turning left, coming toward him. Giving him time enough to turn his head away, put his hand up beside his face. The BMW passed him with only a few feet of clearance. He waited for the BMW to get a half block ahead, then put the Buick in gear and drove slowly forward.

10 P.M., PDT

"I've got to admit," Paula said, "that you were right. The life of a private detective is pretty dull. So far, at least." She spoke into a cellular phone mounted between the front seats of Bernhardt's aging Honda Accord. Across the street, lights went on in the apartment beneath Carley Hank's big bay window. Accounting, therefore, for the downstairs front tenants, a man and a woman who'd just entered the building.

On the telephone, Bernhardt chuckled. "How about if I come over there? We could schmooze."

"No, thanks. I want to be treated just like any other employee. No perks."

"Hmmm."

"I could come over later, though. Make my report."

Lasciviously: "Hmmm."

"How long should I give it, after she comes home?"

"I guess that'll depend on what happens. If Carley's boyfriend stays all night, I'd leave as soon as they're all inside, locked in. If Diane's alone—if they drop her off—I'd intercept her on the sidewalk. I'd go inside with her, make sure the rear entrance to her building is secure. Then I'd go into her apartment with her, check that out, mostly to reassure her, get her settled. I'd make sure she has our phone numbers. Then, after I'd checked the lock on the front door of the apartment house, which I'm sure is in good shape, I'd go back to the car. I'd wait for her lights to go out, then I'd give it another hour. And then—" His voice changed to a playfully erotic note. "Then I'd come back here. I'd say hello to Crusher, maybe give him a dog biscuit. Then I'd get into bed, and make my report."

"Hmmm."

11:10 P.M., PDT

Parked three cars behind the BMW, Kane saw two uniformed policemen coming toward him, walking their beat. One of the policemen was eyeing two women walking on the same side of the street. One of the women, a garishly bleached blonde, wore skintight black leathers studded with bright steel. Defiantly, the blonde was returning the cop's stare. The blonde's companion, miniskirted, her spiked hair dyed a bright orange, leaned close to her friend. They said something to each other, looked at the policemen, then laughed. As the policemen and the women passed shoulder to shoulder, one of the policemen tapped the blonde's buttocks with his nightstick. The reaction was a professional-looking shimmy, then loud, good-natured laughter.

On Friday night, on Polk Street, the natives were looking for action.

Kane yawned, blinked, tried to find a comfortable position behind the steering wheel. Moving from one parking place to another for more than two hours, he'd been watching the BMW—while the cops had begun to eye him as they passed. Soon, he knew, one of them would say something to him. While one of them was questioning him, the other cop might run his license plate through the police computers, playing the percentages. Paying cash, he'd flown from Atlanta using a fake name. He'd used the same name at the cheap, no-questions-asked hotel, also paying cash. But when he'd rented the Buick, he'd had to show his driver's license and credit card.

Did professional hit men use fake ID? Did the professional establish a complete identity, a trail that led nowhere?

Fifty thousand dollars Daniels would give him, when the job was done . . .

Once it would have seemed like a fortune. Now it seemed no more than a down payment on a life of power, a life of privilege. One skull accidentally crushed on Cape Cod, and he'd joined the firm, Daniels and Kane. Another skull crushed in San Francisco, a street killing, and he became a full partner. First hit her with the pipe, to put her down. Hit her again, for insurance—and again. Five, ten seconds, no more. Take her purse, get back in the car, get away. One more mugging that went wrong. In New York, it happened every night, hundreds of times a night. In San Francisco—

Diane and Carley Hanks and the man were coming toward him, part of a crowd leaving the theater, just around the corner. They went to the BMW and Diane opened the passenger door. Kane started the Buick's engine, put the car in gear, backed up beside a fireplug, ready to follow. As he waited, Kane reached beneath his seat to touch the iron pipe. Then he opened the glove compartment, found the surgical gloves, slipped them on.

11:40 P.M., PDT

"We're going to Dale's," Carley said from the back seat. "You can have the apartment to yourself."

"For the whole weekend," Dale added.

"Almost the whole weekend," Carley corrected. "I'll be back late Sunday. We're going up to the Sea Ranch tomorrow."

"Whatever." Diane downshifted, stopped the car for a traffic light at Castro and Twenty-fourth Street. A few blocks more and they'd be at Noe near Clipper, home.

Carley's home. Not her home.

"Would you let me drive this car someday?" Dale asked.

"Sure. We can go over to Marin County sometime."

"Great. We can go up the coast to Bolinas. This car'd be great on that road."

"We can have a picnic," Carley said. "How about next Sunday?"

As they all agreed, Dale pointed ahead. "My car's parked in the next block, to the right. You want my parking place, Diane?"

Considering, she braked, downshifted again, turned the corner, slowed the BMW to a crawl. Yes, Dale's red Mustang was parked on the right side of the street.

"You'd better take it, Diane," Carley advised. "You won't get any closer to the apartment, believe me. Not on Friday night."

They were on Clipper Street, almost two blocks from the apartment, around the corner. Should she ask them to wait for her, give her a ride to the apartment after she'd parked her car? She could imagine their conversation, after they dropped her off. Poor Diane. Spooked. So easily spooked.

She braked to a stop just behind the Mustang, and waited for them to get out of the car. Politely, they both were saying good night. But, plainly, they were thinking about each other—about their Friday night of love.

11:46 P.M., PDT

Ahead, the BMW was stopping. With a half-block separating them, Kane braked the Buick to a stop. Now the BMW's passenger door was swinging open. The man was getting out, holding the door for the woman, Carley Hanks. The couple was smiling and waving at Diane Cutler, still inside the BMW. Now, as the man turned to a vintage red Mustang parked nearby and opened the passenger door, the BMW was backing up and then stopping, its front bumper aligned with the rear bumper of the Mustang. When the Mustang pulled out, Diane would take the parking place, a block and a half from the apartment.

Kane put the Buick in gear, checked the mirrors, then drove forward, past the BMW and the Mustang. At the corner, he turned right onto Noe. Her apartment building was midway in the block. He passed the building, made a U-turn at the next intersection, came back on the opposite side of the street. He pulled into a double driveway, to face her as she came walking toward him. He switched off the Buick's headlights, set the handbrake. Already, he calculated, she would be parked, would be walking toward the corner.

In minutes, it would be settled. Finished. Daniels's empire, secured.

And for him a fortune. Daniels with his checkbook open, he with his hand at Daniels's throat.

Should he restart the engine?

Yes, start the engine, let it idle. Play the percentages.

Twisting the key, his fingers were trembling. His fingers, his legs, the pit of his stomach, everything. On Cape Cod, there had been no trembling. On Cape Cod, he'd—

Ahead, a figure was turning the corner, coming toward him. A woman. Diane. Surely Diane. Looking to his left, he verified that, yes, the window of her apartment was dark. No one was expecting her, watching for her.

Was the engine running? Yes, slowly ticking over. Soon the engine would be his single salvation. The engine that propelled the car, the arm that swung the pipe: there was nothing else. Nothing more. Nothing less.

Seconds, now, as she came steadily closer.

With his left hand, carefully, he tripped the door latch, began pushing the door open. On the other side of the street, she was coming closer—closer. The pipe was in his right hand, grasped so tightly that it was part of himself.

Closer—closer—

When she was directly across the street, he would—

The light.

The car's interior light, exposing him.

Should he draw the door shut again, switch off the light, making himself once more invisible in the darkness? Or should he get out of the car, commit himself?

The minutes were gone; only seconds remained.

11:46:20 P.M., PDT

Watching the dark-colored sedan approaching on the opposite side of the street, Paula saw it pass the apartment building, saw it continue to the next intersection, where it made a U-turn. Still traveling at hardly more than a crawl, the car was returning on her side of the street. Inside the car there was only the driver: a man, his shadowed face turned straight ahead as he passed. His manner, the speed of his car, everything suggested that he was searching for a parking place, a ritual she'd seen repeated many times during the hours she'd been parked across the street from Carley's apartment building.

The man was driving a new American car, a Buick, she thought, or an Oldsmobile. Three cars ahead of her, he was pulling into a double driveway, switching off his headlights. With the three cars between them, it was impossible for her to see the driver. But he was parked beneath the sodium-bright cone of a streetlight; if he left the car, she would see him clearly. Could it be John Williams, the mysterious voice on the phone? Could it be Bruce Kane, Preston Daniels's pilot? Kane, she knew, was a man of medium build, muscular, with short cropped hair and a barroom bouncer's face. He—

At the corner of Noe and Clipper, a solitary figure appeared, turned right, passed beneath another streetlight.

Diane. Almost certainly, Diane. Alone.

Had her friends simply dumped her out of the car, instead of bringing her to her door? Hadn't Diane told them of her fears?

The answer, she knew, was no. It was part of Diane's self-imposed teenage isolation that she wouldn't tell her friends she was afraid. Neither would she—could she—tell her parents, the antagonists who, together and apart, had burdened Diane Cutler so cruelly.

As her solitary figure came steadily closer, Paula saw a plume of exhaust gas rising from the car parked in the double driveway ahead.

But the car wasn't moving.

As, ahead and across the street, Diane had covered almost half the distance from the corner to Carley Hanks's apartment building. The building was in the middle of the block, almost directly across the street from Paula's position. Diane was—

In the car ahead, the interior light came on.

11:48 P.M., PDT

She looked over her shoulder, back the way she'd come. The sidewalk was deserted. Where was Paula Brett—in which car, on which side of the street?

Paula Brett, lady private eye. A soft-talking socialite, a dabbler.

Alan Bernhardt, the actor turned detective. Jokes, both of them. Carley's little joke. Could protection be bought for a few hundred dollars? Security at bargain-basement prices, amateur night?

If she'd known the restaurant would be so crowded, and the movie so dull, she would have let Carley and Dale go alone. Politely, they'd asked her to go along. Carley, the do-gooder, Rebecca of Sunnybrook Farm. Shirley Temple, with her hair in ringlets. Dale, the fraternity man, Mr. Clean. Show him a line of coke, and he would be out the door, gone.

And Carley, too—gone.

Jokes.

A few more buildings and she would be home. When she was in the apartment, Paula had said, she must—

On the other side of the street, in a car parked across two driveways, an interior light came on. The driver's door was swinging open; a man was getting out of the car: a familiar figure, under the streetlight.

Kane.

11:49 P.M., PDT

Without realizing that she'd done it, Paula had opened the driver's door, stepped out into the street.

Just as, ahead, the door of the stranger's car was swinging open. The driver was stepping out of the car, carefully closing his door. He was a man of medium build. Dark hair, close-cropped. Muscular build, muscular stance, muscular movements.

Kane's description.

Kane, moving across the street toward Diane.

Paula was moving toward the invisible line that connected Diane and the man, the three of them a triangle.

Kane. Surely it was Kane.

Kane, walking unnaturally. Concealing something along his right side.

A gun?

Paula felt herself faltering. *The whistle.* She'd left the whistle in the car, on the key ring.

Diane, momentarily frozen, helplessly turning to face the man.

Paula, advancing, closing one side of the triangle. A dozen more steps, and it would be a straight line, with her in the middle.

Kane, his eyes fixed on Diane, advancing. As, behind her, Paula heard the sound of a car, turning the corner into Noe. Headlight beams, sweeping the three of them.

Should she—?

Suddenly Diane made a high, desperate sound, then broke to her right, toward Carley's building—diagonally toward Paula. Running wildly now. Instantly, Kane lunged forward. His right hand came up. It was a weapon—a club.

"*Kane,*" Paula screamed. "*Don't. Drop it, you bastard.*"

As if he'd been struck, Kane broke stride, turned toward her. The car's horn blared; headlights glared. Diane had almost reached Carley's building; Paula, shouting abuses, obscenities, was running toward the girl, to protect her. Horn still blaring, the car was past the three of them. A man's voice, shouting. Another foul-mouthed driver, gone now. Almost to Diane, Paula turned to face Kane. His back was to her. He was running. He reached his car, pulled the door open, slid in behind the steering wheel. Defeated. Miraculously, defeated. Running.

12:10 A.M., PDT

Propped on one elbow, in bed, Bernhardt blinked, pressed the phone closer to his ear, listened intently. Then: "It was Kane? And he—what—ran away? Is that it?"

"That's it," Paula answered.

"On foot? Is that what you mean?"

"He ran to his car, and drove away. Fast. Well, medium fast."

"Did you get the license number?"

"No, Alan, I didn't." She spoke contritely. "I—Diane was so upset—I went to her, to help her. And there was a car coming. It—it all happened so quickly. I'm sorry. I'm terribly sorry."

"This car. Do you know what kind of car it was? American? Foreign?"

"American, definitely. An Oldsmobile, or maybe a Buick. Anyhow, General Motors. I think."

"And Diane's all right?"

"She's upset. Scared silly, in fact. Me, too."

Bernhardt blinked again. "You ran him off, eh?"

"I told you that, Alan. Jesus." Her voice was ragged.

"My God, you're tougher than you look."

"It was mostly reflexes, I'm afraid." Her voice was still ragged.

"And you're sure the door to the apartment is secure."

"It's bolted, if that's what you mean."

"And you're inside with Diane. You're calling from her phone. Is that it?"

"Yes."

"All right. I'll be there in fifteen minutes. Where're the keys to your car?"

"On the mantel."

"Okay. Sit tight." About to put the phone aside, he heard her say, "Your car's across the street from Carley's. It isn't locked, and the keys are in the ignition. The keys, and the whistle, too."

12:45 A.M., PDT

With Diane sitting hunched on the sofa, Bernhardt gestured for Paula to join him as he went to the bay window and looked down into the street below.

"He was parked in that double driveway across the street." Speaking in a low voice, Paula pointed. "Diane's car is around the corner, on Clipper." She pointed again. "She was almost directly across from him, when he opened the door and went for her."

"And you're sure that's what was happening. You're sure he had a weapon."

"He ran away. Instantly. If he weren't guilty, he wouldn't've run."

He smiled, touched her hand. "It's like I said on the phone, you're tougher than you look." In admiration, he incredulously shook his head. "You ran the bastard off."

"Still, I'm glad you're here." She returned the smile and touched the revolver holstered on his belt, concealed by a poplin jacket. "You and your friend."

He nodded, yawned, glanced over his shoulder at the girl. Still sitting on the couch, she was staring into the half-filled tumbler of whiskey she held in both hands before her, as if it were an offering. Then, gravely, she began drinking.

"That's her fourth," Paula whispered. "Double shots. At least."

Bernhardt nodded, walked across the room to the girl, took a chair facing her. "You'd better go easy on that, Diane. You're probably in delayed shock."

She made no reply, gave no sign that she'd heard.

To encourage a response, rouse her, he said, "You've called Carley. And she and her boyfriend are on their way. Right?"

She nodded.

"When they get here, Paula and I will keep watch outside, in front. It'd take a tank to get into the rear of this building, and the building's attached on both sides. So you'll be safe."

"Safe . . ." Bitterly, she nodded. "Sure. Safe for now."

Bernhardt made no response. Sitting beside him now, Paula moved as if to say something. Surreptitiously, Bernhardt shook his head. The tactic was rewarded when Diane began speaking without prodding:

"I guess that maybe you believe me now. Daniels killed his girlfriend and then hired Kane to kill Jeff, to keep the secret. And now Kane's come to kill me." She spoke in a dull, dead monotone. Then she finished the glass of whiskey.

"It's not that I didn't believe you, Diane. But proving it, that's something else."

"I'm not interested in proving anything. I'm interested in staying alive."

"You're alive. And by now Kane's fifty miles from here. Believe it."

"Are you going to the police?" she asked. "Tell them what happened?"

"I'm going to talk to them tomorrow. I know a couple of lieutenants. I'll talk to one of them. We do favors for each other. Are you prepared to say that it was Kane?"

"Definitely."

"And you're both sure"—he included Paula as he spoke—"you're sure he was going to attack you?"

Silently, both women nodded.

"How close did he get to you?" Once more, he included both of them in the question.

"About ten feet," Paula answered. "Maybe fifteen feet. Why?"

"There's probably a legal difference between threatening an attack and actually making an attack."

Contemptuously, Diane snorted. "Legal difference. Shit. How about—"

At the hallway door there was a click, metal-to-metal. Instantly Bernhardt was on his feet, instinctively flicking open the poplin jacket.

With his hand on the butt of the revolver holstered at his belt, Bernhardt was in the short entry hallway as the door rattled against the security bolt.

"Diane?" A woman's voice.

"That's Carley," Diane called.

Bernhardt drew the jacket together and opened the door.

1:45 A.M., PDT

With his arm around Paula, with her head resting on his shoulder, Bernhardt said, "You should go home. I've had some sleep. You haven't. And you've had a shock."

"How long've her lights been out?"

"A half hour. Maybe more."

"I'll give it another half hour."

"Why?" he asked. "I'm just curious."

"I guess I want to make sure she's sleeping. It'll help her, if she sleeps."

"Okay . . ."

"I'm so goddamn mad at myself for not getting his license number."

"Jesus, forget about it, Paula. You probably saved her life tonight." He smiled down at her. "And without the police whistle, too."

"It would've been interesting to see what the whistle would've done."

"Next time."

"So when do I get to carry a gun, like the boss?"

"No comment."

A car turned into Noe from Twenty-sixth Street. Paula raised her head, looked. It was a small car, not the one Kane had used. Letting her head sink on his shoulder, a wonderfully secure sensation, she said, "Do you really think Kane's fifty miles away?"

"I do."

"Then what're we doing here?"

"We're cuddling."

"Hmmm."

A companionable silence passed before Bernhardt asked, "Do you think Kane knows Diane recognized him?"

"I have no idea."

"But what d'you think?"

"Alan—" Exasperated, she sharply shook her head. "I don't *know.*"

"Okay . . ." Soothingly, he caressed her cheek, kissed the top of her head. "Relax."

Another silence. Then, conciliatory, she asked, "What happens to-morrow, in the light of day?"

"First," Bernhardt said, "I want to talk to my buddies at the police department. Then I want to talk to Diane's father. Paul Cutler. If this thing—"

Across the street, lights suddenly blazed in Carley Hanks's apart-ment. A figure stood at the big bay window. It was a woman's figure. A terrified woman. Carley Hanks, desperate, shouting something unin-telligible.

"*Jesus*—" Bernhardt threw his weight against the Honda's driver-side door, swung it sharply open. At the other door, Paula was doing the same.

"*No.*" Bernhardt turned toward her, leveling a top-sergeant's forefin-ger. "You stay here. On the phone."

"But—"

"*Do it, Paula.*" Momentarily he locked eyes with her. Then he turned, sprinted across the street.

2:05 A.M., PDT

"Did you call nine-one-one?" Bernhardt asked. It was an automatic question, a required question.

A useless question.

Too late.

A lifetime too late.

She lay on the floor in front of the couch. Her open eyes were sightless; her mouth was agape. Already, her skin at the neck was cool to the touch. And, yes, the room reeked with the smell of her body's wastes. As if it were a scene conceived by a director of B movies, her leather tote bag, open, spilling bottles of pills, lay on the couch beside her. One of the bottles was open; some of the pills from it had spilled out on the carpet beside Diane's claw-crooked hand. Her fingernails, Bernhardt noticed, were bitten to the quick.

Poor little rich girl.

"Dale called. nine-one-one," Carley Hanks's voice was hardly more than a whisper.

"What happened?" As he asked the question, he focused his gaze on Carley: the living, not the dead. Across the room, pale and ill, Carley's boyfriend—Dale—sat slumped on a straight-backed chair. His eyes were glazed. He looked like a badly beaten fighter, between rounds.

"As soon as you guys left," Carley answered, "she got that goddamn tote bag from the closet, and started popping pills. Three, four pills, maybe more." Numbed, she shook her head. "Then she started on the whiskey. A lot of whiskey."

A lot of whiskey, before the couple arrived. And a lot of whiskey afterward. And pills. Quaaludes, probably. Or worse. Pills and alcohol, the killer combination.

"How'd you know—" Bernhardt broke off. But she understood the question:

"I don't know what woke me up. Maybe nothing. I had a dream, I think that was it. And then—" Helplessly, her eyes returned to her dead friend, lying at her feet. At that moment, outside, the sound of a siren began.

2:30 A.M., PDT

The ambulance steward looked at Bernhardt's license, looked at Bernhardt's face. Then he shrugged. "The pills were Xanax. At least, that's the bottle that was open. Mix a few of those with five or six ounces of whiskey, and everything stops working." As he spoke, two police patrol cars turned into the block, one from either direction.

"Excuse me," the steward said. "I've got to talk to these guys, then I'll take her downtown. Any questions, ask at the coroner's office."

"Yes," Bernhardt answered. "Yes, I know."

SATURDAY,
August 4th

10:30 A.M., PDT

"My God . . ." Lieutenant Frank Hastings rose from his desk, turned away from Bernhardt, went to his office window. In his middle forties, Hastings was a big, muscular man. Born in San Francisco, Hastings had gone to Stanford on a football scholarship, then gone to Detroit to play second-string fullback for the Lions. He'd married an heiress whose father was part owner of the Lions. For a time their life was gilded with privilege and publicity. But an illegal block ended his playing days and Hastings took a make-work PR job at his father-in-law's factory. The job and the marriage had both been mistakes, and after three years a divorce was the only way out. The father-in-law used his checkbook and his clout to run Hastings out of Detroit. Drinking too much, lost without his two children, Hastings had come back to San Francisco and begun putting his life back together, a long, painful struggle. Hastings was a calm, deliberate man who thought before he acted and backed up what he said. His opposite number was Lieutenant Peter Friedman; together the two men cocommanded Homicide. Each man had been offered full command, and a captaincy. Both had declined. Hastings had seen enough interdepartmental politics working for his father-in-law. Friedman, who had a gift for playing the stock market, decided the extra money wasn't worth the grief.

"My God," Hastings repeated, "I wonder whether she had it right? I wonder whether Kane came to kill her?"

Bernhardt made no response. He'd been talking for almost an hour, and he'd only had two hours' sleep.

"Have you tried to locate this guy?" Hastings asked.

"Not really. I called the airports, looking for the airplane. But that's

191

about it. I mean—" Resigned, he spread his hands, shook his head. "I mean, I've got other clients. And they've got bigger checkbooks, if you want the truth. Mostly, what I was doing with Diane Cutler was holding her hand."

Hastings turned away from the window, returned to his desk, sat down. Outside the window the city's chronic summer fog still clouded the sky, blotting out Hastings's slivered view of the Bay Bridge and a wedge of the Berkeley hills beyond.

"Hand-holding can be important. Maybe very important in this case. She was obviously a very unhappy kid."

Wordlessly, Bernhardt nodded, dropped his eyes. Hastings watched the other man for a moment, considering. Then: "Come on, Alan. Give yourself a break. You did what you could. My God, you got paid two hundred dollars. What more could you do?"

As if to protest, Bernhardt sharply shook his head. "They're just kids, Frank. Eighteen years old. For Carley, two hundred has to be a lot of money."

Studying Bernhardt, Hastings made no response. Then, quietly, he said, "Did you come for some help—or to bleed all over my office?"

It was the right remark, expertly timed. Result: Bernhardt's expressive face began to clear, a smile began twitching at the corners of his mouth. He drew a long, resigned breath, then said, "Shit happens. Is that what you're saying?"

"That's exactly what I'm saying."

Another deep breath. Finally: "I guess I came for advice, most of all."

"Fine."

"I figure," Bernhardt said, "that I have a responsibility to find out what happened on Cape Cod."

Hastings nodded. "I agree. But to do it, you'll almost certainly have to go to Cape Cod. That'll take time. And money, too. Are you ready to swallow that?"

"I'm sure as hell willing to go to her father, and ask for the money."

"Good luck."

"He's rich. Her mother's rich, too."

"Her mother's also married to Preston Daniels. The villain."

Ruefully, Bernhardt smiled. Then, speculating: "My God, Frank—just imagine, if it's all true. Preston Daniels kills his girlfriend. Preston Daniels hires his personal pilot to kill his stepdaughter's boyfriend, because he

192

saw Daniels burying his victim. Then Preston Daniels tells the villainous pilot to track down Daniels's stepdaughter and kill her. Jesus—" Awed, Bernhardt shook his head. "This is a goddamn soap opera."

Indulgently, Hastings smiled. "That's one scenario. But how about if—" He glanced at the notes he'd taken while Bernhardt had told his story. "How about if it's all a string of coincidences? It happens, you know. It happens all the time. Or what if Diane Cutler was conning you? What if she dreamed everything up—opium dreams? That happens, too. What if Kane came out here to persuade her to go back to her mom, no hard feelings? What if Daniels's girlfriend just disappeared for reasons unknown? And the kid—Jeff Weston—he could've got killed the way a lot of people get killed, for the money in his pockets."

Bernhardt nodded. "I've thought about all that."

"Do you have the name of the missing girlfriend? Do you have an address?"

"No. Maybe Diane knew her name. But she didn't tell me."

"Pity. A name would help."

"Could you . . . ?" Bernhardt let it go unfinished.

"I can try. I'll call this place"—another glance at his notes—"Carter's Landing. I'll see what I can find out. But that's all I can do, Alan. You understand."

"Sure . . ." Resigned, Bernhardt nodded.

"For God's sake, don't take it so hard."

"She died while I was parked outside, on guard, Frank. I gave her one of the drinks that killed her. I owe somebody for that."

"She died because she was a very unhappy kid. She was on drugs. She freaked out because she thought Kane came to kill her. But she could've been wrong. It's as simple as that. Like I said, Kane could have—"

"He had a club. Both of them saw it. Diane and Paula, they both saw the club."

"Listen, Alan." Earnestly, Hastings leaned across his desk. "These things happen in seconds. And it was dark. Diane already had it fixed in her mind that someone, maybe Kane, was going to kill her. There's a name for that. It's called paranoia. And when she saw what she was afraid she'd see, she went over the edge, and OD'd. It happens, Alan. God knows, it happens. And this girl seems to fit the profile. Completely. If she hadn't OD'd last night, then it'd just be another time, another place. And soon, probably. Very soon."

"If I find that Kane was in San Francisco last night, though . . ."

"It might not prove a thing. If he denies that he was here, and if you can prove he *was* here, that's something else. Otherwise, if he says he was here on an errand of mercy—trying to help Diane with her demons—who's to contradict him? Now—" Hastings dropped his voice, deepening the emphasis. "Now, if you find the girlfriend's body in that landfill, and if you find her blood type in Daniels's car, or his house, that's something else. A tire tread matching Kane's car at the scene of the Jeff Weston killing, that wouldn't hurt, either."

Morosely, Bernhardt made no response.

"You knew I was going to say all this, Alan."

"Sure I did. But, Jesus—" He shook his head. "But it was just a few hours ago that—"

Hastings rose, put his hands flat on the desk, sympathetically shook his head. "It's no fun, seeing them dead. Some cops say they get used to it. I suppose some do. But I'd rather work with the ones who don't."

"Yeah . . ." Bernhardt, too, rose to his feet. "Well, thanks, Frank. Thanks a lot."

Ruefully, Hastings smiled. "What you really mean is 'thanks for nothing.' But the truth is, there isn't a damn thing I can do about this. Absolutely nothing, officially. There's been no crime committed in my jurisdiction, not even a reasonable suspicion. I'll make a phone call to Carter's Landing, but it could do more harm than good. Rural cops, as you may discover, can get pretty territorial. And if they decide to stick it to a big-city cop—well—they can do it."

"I'm not a cop, though."

"Even worse."

11:10 A.M., PDT

"There you are, Mr. Foster." The airline clerk handed over the ticket envelope with a practiced flourish and a mechanical smile. "That flight will be boarding in exactly an hour, gate thirty-three."

"Thank you." Kane pocketed the envelope, turned away from the sales counter, glanced up at the overhead display of gate numbers. Yes, gate thirty-three, concourse C. There would be a snack bar on the concourse. He would have doughnuts and coffee. On the airplane, they would certainly serve lunch.

At a souvenir shop he'd bought a flimsy nylon flight bag, for carry-on luggage. "Protective coloration" was the phrase. A man traveling without luggage from San Francisco to New York would surely be remembered. Then he'd bought two newspapers and two paperback books, to give the flight bag bulk. Now he walked to the security scanner, put the flight bag on the conveyor belt and stepped through the scanner, no buzzers, no alarms.

No alarms . . .

"Kane," the woman had shouted.

Over and over, the words had reverberated: *"Kane,"* followed by *"Drop it, you bastard."*

And he'd run. He'd turned his back, run to the car, driven away. His hands on the steering wheel had been shaking. He'd hardly turned the corner before the images had begun to flash: the woman, standing in the middle of the street, watching him drive away. The woman, surely a policewoman, surely copying down the rental car's license number. Then the green-on-black computer screen, displaying the name of the car-rental agency.

Followed by his name, his address, his New York driver's license number.

Ahead, he saw the snack bar sign. There was no line. He placed the nylon flight bag beside a small table facing out across the airport. He bought a cup of overpriced coffee and an overpriced butterhorn. Carrying the coffee cup, almost full, his hands were steady. Seated at the table, biting into the butterhorn without tasting it, he turned his attention to the runway far beyond the snack bar's window, where a DC-10 was about to touch down.

But the images persisted: Diane and the policewoman, at police headquarters. Constable Joe Farnsworth, his pig eyes studying a printout: Bruce Kane, current address. Occupation.

Current employer: Preston Daniels.

Preston Daniels, questioned by the police. Preston Daniels, consulting with his lawyers. Pompous, bloated lawyers, the rich protecting the rich. Making the deals. Paying off the politicians who paid off the police who took the money and smiled.

Take the money and smile.

Take the money and run.

Buy an airplane. A Beechcraft single, or a Mooney. Fly up to Canada, and disappear.

Fly down to Texas, then into Mexico. Fly low, turn off the transponder, get down below the radar. Southbound, no one cared. A vacationing Americano with an inoperative transponder, flying his own airplane into Mexico.

Olé.

12:30 P.M., PDT

"Mr. Bernhardt?" The man's voice on the phone was ragged, close to breaking.

"Yes, sir."

"This is Paul Cutler, Mr. Bernhardt."

The father of the dead girl—the girl who had killed herself while Bernhardt stood guard in the street below her window.

"Ah . . ." It was an inarticulate response, a mere monosyllable that bore an impossible burden: sympathy, remorse—

—and, yes, guilt.

"I—Carley Hanks—she told me, of course, about Diane. Carley phoned me right—right after it happened, last night. And then they— they took me to the—the—" Helplessly, Cutler broke off.

The morgue, Bernhardt knew, would have been the next words.

How long had it been since the police had knocked on Bernhardt's door, told him that Jennie had been killed when her head struck a curb during a random mugging?

A final cough. Then, painfully self-controlled: "I identified her, after the police came to tell me. And then I—of course—I called Diane's mother, in New York." Another pause, this one longer, more painful.

"If there's anything I can do . . ."

"Well, of course, that's why I'm calling. I mean, just a little while ago—an hour, maybe—Carley called again. And she—she said that she hired you, because she was so very worried about Diane."

"Yes, sir, that's true."

"Carley says she thought Diane trusted you—that Diane told you things. She—Carley—she thought that, whatever was bothering her, Diane talked to you about it."

"Yes, sir, she did."

"I see . . ." Two words that said it all: father and daughter, always at arm's length.

"I wonder, Mr. Bernhardt . . ." The words were hesitant. "I wonder whether you'd mind coming over here, to my home? Can you do that?"

"Yes, of course."

"In an hour or two, would that be convenient?"

"An hour or two . . ." Speculatively, Bernhardt broke off, to consider. It was no time to mention consulting fees, hourly rates, not with Diane's body in the morgue, awaiting the coroner's scalpel. But when would there be a better time? Now, or when—

"I'm a lawyer, Mr. Bernhardt."

"Yes, sir. Diane told me."

"And we hire private investigators. All the time. So I know about fees—about your time. It's the same with me. All I've got to sell is my expertise, and my time."

"Yes, sir. Thank you. I—ah—I charge fifty dollars an hour."

"That'll be fine. Can we say two o'clock?"

"Two o'clock."

2:30 P.M., PDT

"My God." Stunned, incredulous, Paul Cutler shook his head. "It's—it's unbelievable. Preston Daniels—all that money, all that power."

"It happens," Bernhardt said. "These people make mistakes, too. Usually, though, there's a cover-up."

"Yes . . ." Apparently dazed, Cutler nodded, then rose to his feet, paced the small, book-lined study to the far wall, where he stood for a moment motionless, staring out through French doors on a meticulously maintained garden. Finally: "That bastard. She'd be alive now, except for Daniels."

But the real damage was done years ago, Bernhardt responded in his thoughts. *A girl doesn't OD because someone scares her. She ODs because she's too unhappy to go on living.*

"Will the San Francisco police do anything?" As Cutler asked the question he turned from the window and sat behind a small leather-topped writing desk. His movements were wooden. His face was naked, a mask of stark, hollow-eyed grief.

"They'll make inquiries back on Cape Cod, but that's about it."

"No crime was committed here, after all." Staring down at the desk, Cutler spoke slowly, tonelessly. Bernhardt decided not to respond, and the silence lengthened until Cutler spoke again:

"Today's Saturday. The funeral's going to be here. In San Francisco, that is. Millicent—Diane's mother—will be here. I don't know whether Daniels will come. Considering the circumstances, I doubt that he will." Cutler let a long, thoughtful moment pass. Then: "I think it'd be useful for you to be here, for the funeral. Then, the next day, I want you to leave for Cape Cod." Cutler opened the center drawer of his desk and took out a checkbook. He put it on the leather top of the desk and pulled the drawer open farther, searching inside. Now he shook his head with sudden vexation.

"Damn. No pen."

"Here . . ." Bernhardt unclipped a pen from an inside pocket. "Use mine."

5:30 P.M., EDT

Yes, it was elemental: waves, an eternity of waves, crashing down on the seaside sand. Receding, gathering strength, rolling in again. Once there had been rocks on this beach. Now there was sand.

How many millions of years did it take, to pound boulders into pebbles, and pebbles into sand? At Palm Beach, the sand was white and fine; on the Riviera, the sand was dark and coarse: pebbles still being ground down.

Once more, the breakers came in, crashed down, ebbed, gathered force, came in again. When she'd been born, these waves were coming in.

And when Diane had been born, too.

Eighteen years ago. Only eighteen. Divide eighteen years into eons, and the time sliver was smaller than a grain of sand.

When she was in college, geology had been one of the few subjects that had held her interest. Geology and archaeology and anthropology, studies of the past. When she was a sophomore, she'd dreamed of going on archaeological digs. Wearing shorts and a halter and heavy high-topped hiking shoes and a khaki expedition hat, she saw herself on a sunbaked desert working with camel's-hair brushes to unearth fragments of bone, or pottery, or a fossilized dinosaur skeleton. Always there was a man: a European graduate student, wonderfully handsome, incredibly serious.

She'd been nineteen years old when she'd finished her sophomore year.

The next year, playing tennis on one of the campus courts, she'd seen Paul. He'd been playing on the next court with Don Kanter.

They'd been married almost exactly a year later. And, a year after that, Diane had been born.

It had been a mistake. One single mistake.

It had been a beach party, in Monterey. They'd been going to drive back to San Francisco, after the party. But they'd both drunk too much to drive, so they'd stayed with friends, slept on mattresses on the living room floor. And, God, they'd wanted each other that night. No diaphragm, try it once, take the gamble.

And Diane had been born.

They'd still been in love, then. God, they'd been in love.

The following year they'd decided that Paul should go to Stanford Law. His father had offered to pay, an offer too good to decline. Of course, Paul's father would only pay for essentials, no luxuries. Was that understood?

The problem, Paul had said later, was definitional. The word "luxury," for instance. How did they define luxury?

"How about drapes?" she'd once demanded. "Are they luxuries?" Paul's father, himself a lawyer, had come right back at her. "Drapes, no. Johnnie Walker, yes." And he'd pointed to the bottle of Johnnie Walker on a shelf.

Just then, she remembered, in the bedroom, Diane had started to cry. Situation saved. Temporarily saved.

For eighteen years, temporarily saved. Until now. Until last night, when Diane had finally saved herself from more pain than she could bear.

Last night . . .

It had been a bad night for both of them, last night. She'd been so upset because Freddy King hadn't invited her for dinner that she'd had to get out of town.

While, last night, her daughter had chosen to die.

She'd walked so far along the water's edge that she'd reached the saltwater bog that limited the beach to the north. A half mile away, the beach house seemed very small, matchbox size. When she'd left the house, Preston had come out on the lower deck, to watch her. He'd had a glass of wine in his hand. His picture-perfect profile, his white ducks and striped crew shirt, the glass held so gracefully in his hand, the million-dollar house, the soft-focused background—all of it had been perfection, a *Town and Country* picture spread.

As she'd walked down to the beach, away from him, she could feel him looking at her. When she'd reached the water's edge she'd turned to look back at him. Gravely, he'd raised his glass to her. He'd meant the gesture to express his regret, his compassion.

So that as she turned her back on him and walked away, he would understand that she blamed him as much as she blamed herself.

11:45 P.M., EDT

Damage, Daniels knew, had been done. It was measurable. The poets spoke of heartache, heartbreak. Scientists would speak of the central nervous system, of a mental state so traumatic that the blood rushed to the solar plexus, starving the brain for blood.

But it was a contradiction. Because, for almost twelve hours, ever since Cutler had called, he'd felt hollow at his center, the site of the solar plexus.

The essential fluidity of his gestures, he knew, the movements of his body, the cadence of his speech, even word control, smile control—all had been compromised, as if some essential synapses in the brain were malfunctioning. In computerese, it was as if the central memory chip were failing. Not failed, but failing. But there the analogy ended. Because the brain could repair itself; a microchip couldn't.

A drug overdose, Cutler had said.

And the images had begun: Kane, forcing himself into her apartment. Kane, subduing her. Choking her until she fainted. Kane, jabbing the needle into her arm, her thigh.

Kane, somewhere between San Francisco and Cape Cod.

Kane's face as he held out his hand for another envelope stuffed with cash.

Kane, smiling. Kane, gloating.

And the other faces. Millicent, staring at him with stone-cold eyes.

Constable Joe Farnsworth's eyes, probing.

Kane—Millicent—Farnsworth. Together, they held him hostage.

SUNDAY,
August 5th

9:30 A.M., EDT

"Where're you going?" Millicent asked.

"I'm going out for a drive," Daniels answered, searching his pockets for keys. "I'll be back in about an hour. Is there anything you want in the village?"

Ignoring the question, she asked, "When are we leaving? I want to be in New York by five o'clock, at the latest." It was a command, not a request: Millicent, dictating terms.

"I think the airplane's in New York. If it is, I'll arrange for a charter." Then, finessing: "I'll drive out to the airport and talk to them, check on Bruce, make arrangements. I—" He attempted a smile. "I've got to get out, get some air."

She made no reply.

9:45 A.M., EDT

"She's dead?" Kane's voice was almost a falsetto. His eyes were incredulous, his mouth hung slightly open. *"Dead?"*

Behind the wheel of the Cherokee, Daniels turned left to Route 28 and the airport. How long had it been since he'd done the driving with one of his employees a passenger? Democracy. The common touch. What could be more disarming?

He glanced again at Kane's face, then looked back at the traffic ahead. Saying: "I don't understand. Why're you surprised?"

"Because she wasn't dead when I split. She was alive."

On the steering wheel, his grip locked; the Jeep slewed, then straightened. But his voice, strangely, was steady as he heard himself say, "Alive?"

"I tried to do it. I was within ten feet of her. But there was a woman. And she knew me. She called me by name."

"Then . . ." The images shifted, splintered, re-formed. *A drug overdose,* Cutler had said. The images shifted again: Diane, naked on a stainless-steel table, with the top of her head removed, sawed off. Of all the day's images, that one had persisted: an electrical saw, taking off the shaven top of the skull to get at the brain.

"Then you didn't kill her."

"Hell, no. It could've been a policewoman, guarding her. I got out of there. All I had was a lead pipe. The woman could've had a gun. So I split. I got a hotel room, then I flew out of San Francisco yesterday. I decided not to phone you until I got to the Cape—a local call that couldn't be traced. By the time I got to Westboro last night it was ten o'clock. I didn't get here until one o'clock this morning, by the time I got the airplane serviced."

"So the airplane's here."

"That's what I just said," Kane answered brusquely. Then, demanding: "What happened, anyhow?"

"All I know is that her roommate called Paul Cutler about three o'clock yesterday morning, California time. She said Diane had OD'd, and her body was on its way to the morgue."

"Jesus . . ." Shaking his head, bemused, Kane stared straight ahead. Then, shrugging, smiling, he raised his hands, palms up. "So we're home free."

Daniels flipped the turn indicator, slowed for the airport turnoff, just ahead. "Except that you were recognized."

Kane's smile faded.

"Did the policewoman see the pipe? Were you that close?"

"I think—yeah—she probably saw the pipe."

"And she knew who you were."

"She called me by name. Like I said."

"So she knew you were coming . . ."

"Yeah . . ." Heavily, Kane nodded.

Daniels turned the Cherokee into a parking place, switched off the engine. He sat motionless for a moment, staring straight ahead. The images were re-forming again: the policewoman, reporting to her superior office. The officer, deciding to check on Kane. Joe Farnsworth, receiving an inquiry from the San Francisco police department. Farnsworth's desktop: the inquiry placed beside the report on Jeff Weston's murder.

Farnsworth's pudgy fingers, searching his files for the folder marked "Carolyn Estes."

As the images revolved, he spoke mechanically, as if he were reciting by rote: "The funeral's on Tuesday, in San Francisco. Millicent's going. And I'm going too. We'll fly commercial, tomorrow. I want you to fly us to New York this afternoon."

"And then what? What'll I do then?"

"You'll wait for me in New York. We'll leave San Francisco Wednesday morning. I'll be at the office until Friday afternoon. Then I'll come back here. I'll stay for the weekend. Millicent, too, I hope."

"Do you think that's smart, being where Farnsworth can get at you? I was thinking about disappearing for a couple of months."

Slowly, deliberately, Daniels shook his head. "That's exactly what we don't want to do. Everything's got to look normal. Completely normal. We're going to act like nothing unusual has happened."

"But what about Farnsworth?"

"If he's going to ask questions, I want him asking them here, not in New York. That's the last thing I want."

"Okay, that's you. I can understand how you've got to keep up appearances. But what about me? I think I should go to Mexico for a couple of months. At least."

"Six months from now, you can go."

"I don't know . . ." Eyes narrowed, mouth hardening, Kane shook his head. "I'll have to think about it. You can't split, can't disappear. But I can. And if I do split, this is the time to do it. As far as Farnsworth's concerned, it'll be a vacation."

"You've got a job here. You're on the payroll."

"Yeah—well—I can find you a pilot. I can find you fifty pilots. And as far as the payroll goes—well—I figure I'll be on the payroll permanently, whether I fly or not. Isn't that right?" As he said it, Kane turned a long, cold stare on the other man.

With their eyes locked, Daniels spoke softly, with boardroom precision: "You're talking about an income for life. Is that it?"

"That's exactly what I'm saying. The way I see it, you and me are joined at the hip. One goes down, so does the other." A short, truculent pause. Then: "Am I right?"

"You're exactly right. Which is why I want you to act like an innocent man. And an innocent man wouldn't leave town."

"If I decide to change jobs, I'll leave. And pilots change jobs all the time. It's built in."

"In six months," Daniels said, "we'll talk about it. Not now." As he said it, he withdrew a checkbook and pen from the pocket of his jacket. As he began writing, the final image materialized: Carolyn's body, decomposing. In six months, dust to dust, almost nothing would be left.

Except for the bones.

4 P.M., EDT

As Farnsworth parked the patrol car in front of the storefront police station his radio came to life: "Chief, are you coming inside?" It was Nancy Shelby, the department's full-time secretary, receptionist, and dispatcher.

"I am."

"Because there's a call from San Francisco. It's someone named Alan Bernhardt. He says he's a private detective."

"What's on his mind?"

"He's asking about Jeff Weston."

"Be right in." He returned the microphone to its bracket, flipped the communications master switch, took the keys from the ignition and began levering the mound of his stomach from under the steering wheel.

4:05 P.M., EDT

"The reason I'm calling," the voice on the phone said, "is that Diane Cutler died late Friday night."

Farnsworth scowled at the speakerphone.

"Who's Diane Cutler? I thought you were calling about Jeff Weston."

"Diane Cutler is—was—Preston Daniels's stepdaughter. Her mother is—was—Millicent Daniels."

"Daniels. Sure . . ." Unconsciously, Farnsworth sat up straighter in his oversize swivel chair and addressed the speaker phone squarely. "She died, you say? His stepdaughter?"

"She died in San Francisco. That's where I am. Her father is a lawyer here. And the police think—they're sure, really—that it was a drug overdose."

"A kind of stocky girl, lots of dark hair, not very good looking, bad complexion, big tits. Is that the one?"

"That's the one."

"Used to go out with the Weston kid, once in a while—" Farnsworth nodded at the speaker. "Yeah, I got her now." Then: "A drug overdose, eh?"

"Yessir."

"So what're you saying? That she OD'd because of the Weston kid, because he was killed? Is that what you're saying?"

"I think the two deaths are connected. I also think Preston Daniels could be involved."

"And where're you getting your information, Mr. Bernhardt?"

"I talked with Diane Cutler. Twice. I—ah—don't think this is something we should get into on the phone. I'm going to be out there in a few days. And I—"

"Then why're we having this conversation? Why'd you call?"

"I called," Bernhardt said, measuring the words, "because I wondered whether you're investigating Jeff Weston's death as a homicide. Because if you are, then I have good reason to suspect that the same person who killed Jeff Weston made an attempt on Diane Cutler's life last Friday night. Which could be why she OD'd."

"That sounds like quite a stretch."

"Maybe."

Now Farnsworth was frowning at the speakerphone, deciding on a response. "Bernhardt," the caller had said. A Jew. A smooth-talking Jewish private detective from San Francisco. A snooper. He'd dealt with them before: con artists with telephoto lenses. Hacks, bought and paid for by big-city divorce lawyers, mostly.

"Did you say you planned to be on the Cape in a few days?"

"Yes, sir. Wednesday, probably. Thursday, at the latest."

"Well, then, I'll tell you what you do. When you get here, you give us a call, and make an appointment. And we'll see what we've got. Okay?"

"Yes . . ." Reluctantly. "Okay."

"Good." Smiling at the speakerphone, Farnsworth delicately broke the connection. Score one for the home team.

5:15 P.M., PDT

"Alan."

On the phone, Bernhardt recognized the voice: Frank Hastings.

"Frank. Thanks for getting back so quick."

"You won't thank me when you hear what I got from your friend Constable Joe Farnsworth."

Your friend . . . meaning that Hastings had talked to Farnsworth after Bernhardt called the Cape.

"No luck, eh?"

"I tried to get the name of the missing girl. Nothing. Zip. I told you about some of these rural cops. But this guy Farnsworth is something else. I told him I was investigating an attempted homicide, which wasn't precisely true. He still wouldn't cooperate. All he said was that he got a fistful of missing-persons reports every week, and he didn't remember anything concerning a girlfriend of Daniels."

"Shit."

"Yeah." Hastings sighed heavily. It was a harried exhalation, signifying that, as always, Hastings was short on time. But then, speculatively, Hastings said, "There's one thing, though—he said he didn't *remember*. He was careful not to close the door completely. Covering his ass, maybe."

"So what'd you think that means?"

"I'm not sure—except that he might have his own game going."

"You mean he might be getting paid off?"

"It's happened before. When there's so much money involved, strange things happen."

"Hmmm."

"Gotta go, Alan. Keep me posted." The line went dead.

TUESDAY,
August 7th

11 A.M., PDT

"I thought funerals always started on time," Paula whispered.

Bernhardt nodded to the man and woman sitting in the first pew. "That's Cutler and his wife. They're waiting for Diane's mother."

"Is Daniels coming?"

"I don't know."

"There aren't many people, not as many as I'd've thought."

"Cutler kept it out of the papers, I think. Because it was an overdose. And she hadn't lived in San Francisco for three or four years, so I don't think she had many friends here."

"Poor kid."

He sighed, mutely nodded.

"I wish you'd let me come with you tomorrow."

"You can help more by staying here and catching phone calls, stalling clients. Believe me, Paula, if you want to help out, that's how."

"How long'll you be gone?"

"I figure four or five days. That's all the time I can afford, even though Cutler's paying well for this."

"Will Cutler—" She broke off as a palpable ripple of anticipation swept the congregation. Bernhardt turned in time to see the couple framed in the tall, backlit doorway of the church. Preston and Millicent Daniels, without doubt. Behind them, a handful of photographers were held at bay by determined men dressed in morning clothes, their arms spread wide.

"It'll be in the papers now," Paula whispered.

Not responding, Bernhardt turned as Preston and Millicent Daniels came slowly up the aisle. Behind her black veil, Millicent Daniels's

215

profile was finely drawn, a classic American beauty. Her figure was almost perfect; her bearing was almost regal: a queen advancing toward the nave of some lofty medieval cathedral. And, beside her, with her hand in the crook of his arm, Preston Daniels was a complementary figure of perfection: the prototypical captain of commerce, a prince of the realm. His profile was decisively chiseled, his expression grave. His clothing draped beautifully.

As Daniels and Millicent approached the empty left front pew, Bernhardt saw Cutler turn to look at Millicent. Responding, Millicent moved to her right, where Cutler and his wife were seated. It was a spontaneous movement, signifying a grief more profound than the bitter memories of a failed marriage. But now Daniels shifted his hand to grasp his wife's arm, propelling her to the left. Sitting on the aisle, Millicent exchanged a last look with Cutler before both mother and father, in unison, turned their eyes to the casket as, on cue, a clergyman in Episcopalian robes came through a small door to the right of the altar. As the minister approached the casket, Bernhardt's gaze traversed the assembled mourners. Most of the faces, most of the suits and dresses, were upper-middle-class or better, an assembly of the privileged. Except for Carley Hanks and a few others, there were no young faces. Yet, when she'd lived in San Francisco, Diane had been happy. And happiness equaled friendships; it was the first law of adolescence. Diane had never been pretty. Therefore, she'd probably been less popular than others; that was the second law of adolescence. But there had been Carley and a few others—enough of the others. Diane had been contented, therefore willing to see what life offered.

And then her parents had divorced.

And the downward spiral had begun. Leaving Diane a wanderer in the concrete canyons and gilded brambles of Manhattan, entangled. Adolescence without friends, privilege without love; both had destroyed Diane's dreams. Then, with all the dreams gone, she'd destroyed herself. It was simple logic.

If he'd believed Diane Cutler—really believed her—might she be alive now?

It was, Paula had sternly lectured him, a wrongheaded exercise in self-abnegation, the classic Jewish angst.

The minister was calling for a hymn. Dutifully, Paula was reaching for the hymnal, rising, turning to the hymn, beginning to sing. Eyes straight ahead, Bernhardt stood silently beside her.

"Sing," she whispered, digging her elbow into his ribs.

"I'm Jewish," he whispered.

"I'm agnostic." She dug him again. "So sing."

5 P.M., PDT

"Hello?" A woman answered the telephone on the third ring.

"May I speak to Mr. Cutler? It's Alan Bernhardt. I just have a quick question." Only hours after Diane Cutler's funeral, he spoke softly, deferring to the dominion of death.

"Just a moment." The woman spoke shortly, coldly. Was it Cutler's wife, the woman who had kept Diane at a distance? Remembering her high-styled face, her aloof manner at the funeral, he decided that the guess was a good one.

"Yes?" It was Cutler's voice. Expressionless. Exhausted.

"It's Alan Bernhardt, Mr. Cutler."

"I know."

"I'm sorry to intrude, but I'll be leaving for Cape Cod early tomorrow morning, and there's something I want to ask you."

"What is it?"

"It concerns Mrs. Daniels—Diane's mother."

"Just a moment." Bernhardt heard a door close. Then Cutler spoke in a low, cautious voice: "Yes?"

"Are you—" Bernhardt hesitated. "Are you in touch with Mrs. Daniels?"

"I don't understand what you mean."

"I want to talk to her. I know it'll be hard getting through to her. I thought you could help."

"Help in what way?"

"Their schedules for the next day or two. Private phone numbers. Maybe an introduction, over the phone. Anything."

"As far as I know, she and Daniels are going to Cape Cod, probably tomorrow. I have their number there. And their home number in New York, too. Private numbers. Just a minute." As Bernhardt waited with pen poised, he heard a drawer close. Cutler read off the telephone numbers.

"Do you have a private number for Daniels at his office?"

"No, I don't. But it's Daniels, Incorporated, in Manhattan."

"Well, these numbers are fine. Thanks."

"Why d'you want to talk to Millicent?"

"From what Diane said, I have the feeling that Millicent and Daniels are having problems. Marital problems. If that's true, and if Millicent knows Daniels plays around, it could give me leverage. Maybe a lot of leverage."

"You're thinking of the missing girl."

"That's where it all starts, Mr. Cutler. If there really was a girl staying overnight Saturday with Daniels, and if he killed her on Sunday and buried the body in a landfill, then everything Diane said makes sense. It's been three weeks now. That lady's been missed. Somewhere, there's a printout on her, a missing-persons bulletin, if nothing else."

"But you don't have a name . . ." Cutler mused. "And without a name, you're stuck."

"That's why I'm going to Cape Cod. To get a name."

"You'll keep me posted."

"Definitely."

THURSDAY,
August 9th

10 A.M., EDT

"Very nice." Farnsworth's plump face registered a small, mock-cherubic smile. With a fat forefinger he pushed Bernhardt's plastic identification plaque across the desk. Next he allowed himself the pleasure of staring at the visitor until, finally, the man from San Francisco frowned, looked briefly away, began to shift uncomfortably in the office's only visitors' chair. Yes, he'd been right about Bernhardt. A Jew, unmistakably. The face was dark and lean and hollowed out, a Semitic face, beyond all doubt. Dark, thick, half-long hair, flecked with gray. And, yes, the aviator glasses, the intellectual's trademark, a dead giveaway.

"So what can I do for you, Mr. Bernhardt?" Farnsworth pushed his swivel chair back from his oversize desk, braced one foot on an open desk drawer, tilted the chair back, clasped his pudgy hands comfortably across the mound of his stomach. "I've been thinking about what you said on the phone. When was that? Monday?"

"Yes. Monday."

"And you were asking about Jeff Weston, about how we're handling the case. Is that right?"

"Yes. You see, I wanted to know whether—"

"Wait." Farnsworth held up a peremptory hand. "I'll ask the questions." Once more, coldly, he stared at the other man until, yes, control was achieved. "Okay?"

Gracelessly, Bernhardt was nodding. "Fine." It was a hard, clipped monosyllable. Behind the aviator glasses, brown eyes snapped. Would Bernhardt be more troublesome than he'd first appeared?

"You said on the phone that Daniels was involved. What'd you mean by that?"

"Before I answer, I'd like to know—"

"Ah-ah." Farnsworth raised a forefinger, naughty, naughty. "You're forgetting again."

Jaw tightly clenched, eyes still snapping angrily, the other man drew a long, grim breath. "Sorry."

"Daniels," Farnsworth prodded gently. "Start with Daniels." Complacently, he watched the other man as he struggled so obviously to get a grip on his temper. Finally, tight-jawed, Bernhardt began to speak:

"On Sunday, July fifteenth, Diane Cutler drove up to Cape Cod from New York. She got here about ten at night. She connected with Jeff Weston at a bar called"—Bernhardt drew a folded sheet of paper from an inside pocket, glanced at it—"called Tim's Place. Then they took a drive in Diane's dark-green BMW."

"Ah." Farnsworth nodded. "The girl with the BMW. Right."

"They apparently ended up at the Danielses beach house," Bernhardt said. "As I understand it, they'd been drinking, and they'd smoked some grass. They'd probably popped a few pills, too. So they were high, and they decided to spy on Daniels. That was probably about midnight. And they saw Daniels carry something out to his car"—he glanced again at the notes—"a Jeep Cherokee. They thought it was a body, wrapped in a rug, or a blanket."

"They *thought*, you say. They weren't sure."

"When I talked to Diane, she was sure."

Farnsworth snorted. "It sounds like she could've been hallucinating."

"She could've been imagining the body, I suppose. But it's hard to imagine Preston Daniels deciding at midnight to move a rug. Besides, he took a shovel with him, in the back of the Jeep. And, furthermore, Diane saw a hand and an arm, that worked free."

"Or so she imagined." Farnsworth's voice was flat, his eyes expressionless.

"We'll never know whether it was imagination or not. There were only two witnesses. Diane and Jeff. Jeff's dead. And now Diane's dead."

"Meaning," Farnsworth said, "that all I've got is a secondhand story, which you probably know is worth about as much as a pitcher of warm spit, in a court of law."

"I'm telling you exactly what Diane told me."

"Did she ever tell her story to a policeman?"

"Not that I know of."

Signifying that the answer was a foregone conclusion, Farnsworth grunted. Saying: "Let's get back to Daniels. What happened after Daniels put the, ah, bundle into his car?"

"And the shovel," Bernhardt insisted. "Don't forget the shovel."

"The shovel." Broadly, Farnsworth nodded. "So noted."

"After he'd done that," Bernhardt said, "then he drove out to the landfill, east of town. The one with the cyclone fence around it."

"The landfill . . ." As Farnsworth said it, images began to materialize: Preston Daniels, digging a shallow grave, bent to his task beneath the night sky like some common laborer. Preston Daniels, tumbling the body into the grave.

Carolyn Estes, beyond all doubt.

Carolyn Estes, dead and buried on the night of Sunday, July fifteenth. Dump trucks, coming and going the next day, and the next, and the next, each truck creating its own mound of dirt and construction debris, mound after mound after mound. Followed by the bulldozers, leveling it all out so the process could begin again. And again. And again.

Carolyn Estes, one of Preston Daniels's blondes.

Carolyn Estes . . .

As if the name had taken control, Farnsworth found himself staring fixedly at the bottom drawer of a nearby file cabinet. In that drawer, he knew, in the missing-persons file folder, was the bulletin on Carolyn Estes.

As if someone else were talking—as if someone else had made the decision—he heard himself saying, "And then what?" Conscious of the effort required, he turned his gaze from the file cabinet to the face of Alan Bernhardt, the skinny, sad-eyed Jew who talked like a professor—and who was forcing choices that could change a whole life.

"Then," Bernhardt was saying, "the next night, Jeff Weston was killed. And Diane thinks—"

"Wait. *Wait.*" Farnsworth raised both hands, exasperated. "Let's go back to the goddamn landfill. What happened next, at the landfill?"

"Apparently there's only one way in, and Diane didn't want to get trapped inside. Anyhow, they—"

"Or maybe they were still spaced out."

Impatiently, Bernhardt nodded. "That, too."

"Okay. Go ahead. What happened next?"

"They went to a motel, Sunday night."

"A local motel?"

"Yes."

"About what time?"

"That would've been about one o'clock in the morning, I'd guess. Maybe one-thirty."

"Monday morning."

Bernhardt nodded. "Right. Monday. Later that day, Diane drove back to New York. Whereupon she apparently had a fight with her parents—her mother and Daniels. That was about five o'clock Monday evening. So she got back in her car, and drove up here."

"To Carter's Landing?"

Bernhardt nodded. "Right. She got here at about eleven o'clock Monday night. And that's when she discovered that Jeff Weston had been killed. She was sure—absolutely sure—that Daniels had Weston killed to prevent him from talking about the murder of the girl. Maybe he'd tried to blackmail Daniels. It'd make sense."

"Did she have any idea who killed Weston?"

"No, not then. Later, though, she thought it could've been Bruce Kane. Daniels's pilot." Plainly watching for a reaction, Bernhardt was eyeing him closely. As if to carefully consider the private detective's statement, Farnsworth nodded judiciously, then frowned as he allowed his gaze to wander away. "Did she have any proof?" he asked. "Or was she just guessing?"

"Kane followed Diane to San Francisco. He talked to her, made some kind of an oblique offer that could've been the first move in a blackmail try. At least, that's how Diane interpreted it. Then, the night she died, Kane tried to attack her. That's why she OD'd, that was the trigger."

"Will I find that in the San Francisco police computer? Is there a police report describing the attack on Diane?"

"No, there isn't. But I had an—an associate, guarding Diane, staking out her apartment. And she saw Kane trying to—"

"Wait a minute." Farnsworth frowned. "This associate of yours. Was that a woman?"

Obviously irritated by the question, Bernhardt nodded. "Right. A woman." His stare was defiant, belligerent.

"A woman. Hmm." Farnsworth lowered his feet to the floor, returned his swivel chair to its upright position. "Okay. Go ahead."

"Before I do," Bernhardt said, "I'd like to ask you how Jeff Weston was killed."

"Why're you asking?"

"Because," Bernhardt said, "Kane had a club in his hand when he went after Diane. Diane saw the club, and so did my associate."

"Your lady associate."

"Listen—" It was a tight, grim-faced challenge, a warning of worse to come. "Forget about whether it was a man or a woman. We've got three people dead, for God's sake. What difference does it make whether I hire men or women? The fact is—the *truth* is—that if my associate hadn't yelled when she did, Diane Cutler would probably have been killed. Just like Jeff Weston was killed."

Farnsworth decided to smile: a resigned, world-weary smile. "You say 'probably.' And that's the problem with this. It all comes down to whether we believe what a drugged-out girl told you. Isn't that about it?" He let the smile fade as he consulted his watch.

Bernhardt sat motionless for a moment, his face registering a slowly gathering contempt. Finally: "I suppose it's useless for me to ask whether you have any information suggesting that, in fact, a girl's body was buried the night of July fifteenth in the landfill site about five miles northeast of Carter's Landing."

As Farnsworth listened to the precisely worded statement, an uneasy suspicion intruded. Was it possible that Bernhardt was wearing a wire? Was it possible—even likely—that Bernhardt was a shill, a stalking horse, perhaps for the state attorney?

At the thought, Farnsworth began levering himself to a standing position, looking down on the man from San Francisco.

"You're right, Bernhardt. It's absolutely useless."

11:20 A.M., EDT

It was on Route 28 near the outskirts of Carter's Landing that Bernhardt found it: a coffee shop that catered to the townspeople, not the affluent outlanders. The sign spelling out "Kenny's" was red neon, not white-scrolled imitation Colonial. The exterior of Kenny's was stucco, not artificially weathered gray shingles. The plate-glass windows were large and set in aluminum, not multipaned and wood-framed. The booths were red Naugahyde, the counter was red Formica. The lighting, of course, would be fluorescent. And, yes, there were pickups in the parking lot, not Mercedes.

The patrons at the counter fitted the down-home stereotype. The conversation was easygoing; the topics were baseball, TV, and an accident last night involving a big rig and four drunken teenagers. All the teenagers were dead. The truck driver was in traction.

A few of the patrons looked briefly at Bernhardt, then looked indifferently away. Bernhardt sat at the far end of the counter, ordered coffee, and swiveled on his stool to face the row of customers, all of them in profile. The waitress wore a green uniform streaked with food stains. When she returned with the coffee, Bernhardt was ready with his laminated plastic identification plaque. Smiling at the waitress and pitching his voice loud enough to be heard by whoever cared to listen, he said, "Excuse me, but I wonder whether you could help me."

Having already turned away from him, she reluctantly turned back. She was an angular, middle-aged woman with a long, unsmiling face and dark, unfriendly eyes. She wore harlequin glasses decorated with rhinestones.

"My name is Alan Bernhardt, and I'm a private investigator." He held the plaque so that everyone seated at the counter could see it. As, yes, several pairs of eyes surreptitiously shifted toward the plaque, then to him. So far, so good. Curiosity, he'd discovered, could be the investigator's best friend.

"I'm looking for the Preston Daniels place."

Frowning, she studied the plaque for a moment, then reflectively scratched her neck just below the ear as she studied him. She shrugged. "Can't help you, mister. Sorry."

"You know who I'm talking about. Preston Daniels. The real estate tycoon."

"I've heard of him. But I've never seen him. And I don't know where his place is. Sorry." She turned her back again, walked to the serving window, spun a metal drum with checks clipped to it.

"Thanks anyhow." As he placed the plaque prominently on the counter and then sipped his coffee, he flicked a glance down the row of faces. Two of them, at least, had turned obliquely toward him, then turned away. Signifying, doubtlessly, that they knew the location of the Daniels beach house. He let his gaze wander to the restaurant's plate-glass windows and the tourist traffic clogging Route 28. He'd been a child the first time he'd come to the Cape. He and his mother had been living in a Manhattan loft, where she gave modern dance lessons and conducted meetings. Always, there were the meetings, the fate of the Jewish intellectual. Meetings to protest civil rights violations. Meetings to protest the Vietnam war. Meetings in support of women's rights. Meetings to plan meetings.

Every summer, his grandparents had sent him to summer camp in the Berkshires, always for the month of July. The routine never varied. All those kids, most of them Jews from New York, meeting at Grand Central Station, clustering around a Camp Chippewa sign. The train ride to the Berkshires had taken most of the day. When they reached their destinations most of the campers were hoarse—and most of the counselors were frazzled.

At the end of July, his mother and his grandparents always picked him up in his grandfather's car, always a big Buick. The four of them would take two or three days to return to New York, stopping overnight at vacation spots along the way. Once, he remembered, they'd stayed in Hyannis, at a small hotel that faced the ocean. Early in the morning, he and his mother had walked along the water's edge, where they'd found three starfish.

He hadn't known how much his mother and grandparents meant to him until they'd died. His mother had died only months after her cancer was discovered. Less than a year later, his grandparents had died when his grandfather suffered a heart attack. He'd been driving their Buick, and the car had gone across the center divider of a New Jersey expressway.

And then Jennie had died. Jennie, who'd just agreed that, yes, they must have children—two children, no more, no less. She'd been mugged only a block from their apartment in the Village. Her head had hit a curb, and she'd never regained consciousness.

The coffee cup was empty. He took out his wallet, found a dollar bill, and slipped it under the saucer. He picked up his identification plaque and slid it into the pocket of his short-sleeved sports shirt, carefully buttoning the pocket. Down the counter, two men were also dropping money on the counter. Both men were young and muscular. Both wore T-shirts; both wore the mandatory baseball caps, one cap emblazoned with a Caterpillar logo, the other with the Corvette legend. Had either of the men registered interest in Bernhardt's dialogue with the waitress? Bernhardt wasn't sure.

The two men left the coffee shop and walked toward—yes—a battered pickup truck. Bernhardt's rented Escort was parked three slots beyond the truck, perfectly positioned. The windows of the pickup were rolled down; therefore the doors weren't locked. Bernhardt lengthened his stride, bringing him abreast of the pickup just as one of the men opened the passenger's door. Catching the stranger's eye, Bernhardt smiled, nodded, expectantly broke stride. Returning the nod but not the smile, the man hesitated. Then, straightening, he turned to face Bernhardt.

"The Daniels place . . ." the man said. "Is that what you're looking for?"

"I sure am." In the three words, Bernhardt tried to convey a fraternal affability, a feel for the flavor of the local patois.

The stranger pointed a workman's hand at Route 28 and began a long, amiable series of directions. Having already gotten instructions from Chief Farnsworth's dispatcher, Bernhardt nodded, pretended to commit everything to memory. During the recitation, the pickup's driver got out of the truck and looked at Bernhardt across the truck's bed, which was filled with tools. Pushing back his baseball cap, the driver smiled: a wide, boyish, freckle-faced grin.

"You said you were a private eye, back there." He jerked his chin toward the restaurant. "What're you investigating, anyhow?"

Bernhardt looked at the driver, looked at the passenger. Their faces were remarkably similar: all-American faces, Jack Armstrong faces. Get out of high school, get a job, marry the girl next door. Drive-in movies, beer in the refrigerator, kids in the back bedroom.

How much should he tell them? How much did he want Joe Farnsworth to know—or not know?

While Bernhardt was considering the question, the passenger spoke to his friend: "I bet old Daniels got caught with his hand up the wrong skirt, sure as hell."

Bernhardt decided to guffaw, a good old boy's laugh. He nodded cheerfully, then shook his head, as if to marvel at the passenger's perception. "Hey, how'd you know?"

The driver snorted, a flatulent sound that summed up the state of guerrilla warfare between townsfolk and resort dwellers. "Everyone around here knows about Daniels. I bet, since last year at this time, he's had a half-dozen different women out to that beach house, weekends. And they're all blondes. Every single one of them." Marveling, he shook his head. "You got that much money, you get your nooky packaged any way you want, I guess."

"His wife, of course," the passenger said, "she's a brunette. And beautiful, too. Better looking than most of Daniels's bimbos."

The driver nodded judiciously. "That's true."

Projecting elaborate caution, Bernhardt looked over his shoulder, stepped closer, spoke softly, confidentially: "I'm not going to say anything that'll get me into trouble with my client. But the truth is, I'm trying to put a name to one of those bimbos. The last one. Or, anyhow, the one that was here on the weekend of July fourteenth."

The two men looked at each other, considered, then looked back at Bernhardt. "That's—when—a month ago?"

"Almost."

"Well, I can't help you with a name, friend," the driver answered. "All I can tell you, she was blonde and beautiful, just like the rest of them. But there weren't any names. Just faces."

"And bodies, too." The passenger smirked lasciviously. "Don't forget the bodies, Clinton."

"They come in Friday or Saturday, usually," Clinton said, "and they leave Sunday, mostly."

"How do they come? By car?"

Clinton shook his head. "Mostly they come in his airplane. Up from New York, or so I heard."

"Does Daniels usually come with them?"

"Usually. He doesn't always leave with them, though." For affirmation, Clinton looked at his friend, who nodded.

"That reminds me," Bernhardt said. "I'm trying to locate Bruce Kane."

"He's Daniels's pilot. Right?"

Bernhardt nodded.

"That's easy. Find Daniels's airplane, you find Kane."

"He's a real asshole," the passenger offered. "And mean, too. Give him a couple of drinks, and watch out." As he spoke, he looked at his wristwatch. "Jesus, Clinton, we gotta go." He smiled affably at Bernhardt. "Get Clinton talking about women, gossiping, too, let's face it, and you shoot the whole day." He swung the passenger's door wide, and turned away.

"Listen," Bernhardt said, "I want to thank you guys. A lot."

"No problem, friend." Clinton got in behind the truck's steering wheel. "Anything I can do to stick it to that stuffed shirt Preston Daniels, I'm your man."

"Appreciate it." Bernhardt stepped back, smiled, waved the pickup out of the parking lot.

4:30 P.M., EDT

"What I'm wondering," Bernhardt said, "is whether there's any way I can get the name of a passenger that arrived here the weekend of July fourteenth on Preston Daniels's airplane. She's supposed to be a very good-looking blonde, and she and Daniels probably came in together.

They probably came from New York. Or, anyhow, the New York area."

The airport manager leaned forward, picked up Bernhardt's identification plaque from the top of his desk, studied the plaque, then looked across the desk at Bernhardt.

"San Francisco . . ." In appreciation, the manager nodded. "Great place. They say New York is where it all happens. But San Francisco—they know how to live out there."

"I agree. I grew up in New York. I loved the city. Still do. But it's a lot easier life in San Francisco. Not much cheaper. But easier."

"So you're checking up on Preston Daniels, eh?" The manager—Holloway, Bernhardt remembered—leaned back in his chair, clasped his hands behind his neck, and regarded Bernhardt with interest. Holloway was a small, muscular man with a round, hard belly, vivid blue eyes and a quick, mischievous smile. His thick brown hair was crew-cut. He wore a wrinkled summer suit and a garish silk tie. His steel-rimmed glasses sparkled when they caught the light.

"I'm checking up on the woman, really. I need a name. And an address, too, if I could get it. But mostly the name."

"It sounds like Preston Daniels is headed for a divorce court," Holloway said cheerfully.

Bernhardt decided on a sly, coconspirator's smile. "No comment."

"This lady—had she come here for maybe two or three weekends previously, with Daniels? Is she the one?"

Bernhardt nodded. "She's the one."

"But she hasn't been up to the Cape for two, three weeks since. Is that right?"

"That sounds right, Mr. Holloway."

"Yeah—well—we're talking about the same lady, probably. A great-looking blonde, like you said. She's not the first, you know. 'Daniels's blondes' we call them. They're part of the show hereabouts."

"The Preston Daniels sex sideshow, you mean."

Holloway's ruddy face broke into another broad smile. "You got it."

"So how would you say I should get a line on her?"

"Best thing would be to ask Bruce Kane, I'd say. He's Daniels's pilot. At least once, I remember, Kane and the blonde flew in together, just the two of them. So I'd think he'd know her name. That time, I remember, the weather was bad. Real bad. Time they got here, she was probably reciting her rosary to Kane."

"I understand Daniels and his wife are coming to the Cape, maybe today or tomorrow. Would you know about that?"

"I have no idea."

"Do they have to file a flight plan, or anything?"

"They probably do, in New York, or wherever their flight originates. But the first we know, we're getting a handoff from approach control. So—" On the desk, Holloway's phone warbled. He picked up the phone, said something cryptic, then covered the mouthpiece as he spoke to Bernhardt: "I've got to take this. Find Kane, like I say. There's a big house out on Sycamore Street, where Daniels's staff lives. When he's here, Kane lives in that house. You can get his phone number from the girl at the reception desk. Tell her I said it was okay."

Bernhardt quickly rose, extended his hand. "I will. Thanks, Mr. Holloway. Thanks very much."

FRIDAY,
August 10th

6 P.M., EDT

"Better buckle up." Daniels reached across the narrow aisle, handed her one of her seat-belt straps. Without looking at him, Millicent found the other strap, snapped the buckle.

"Did you make dinner reservations?"

She swiveled her chair to face the rear and locked the chair, the approved landing sequence. "No. I don't want to eat out. I phoned Bessie. She's left everything out. Squab." Her voice was expressionless; her violet eyes had gone cold and dead. Stranger's eyes.

An enemy's eyes?

Would the weekend reveal the truth, friend or enemy?

"Ah—squab. Good."

"Everyone buckled up?" It was Kane's voice on the intercom's loudspeaker.

Daniels spoke into his microphone. "All set."

"We'll be on the ground in about five minutes."

"Is your car at the airport?"

"That's affirmative." Always, when they were in the air, Kane's language was laced with the flyer's patois.

"Okay. We'll take the Cherokee." He paused, glanced briefly at Millicent's frozen profile, then said, "Stay close to the phone. Stay in touch."

"Roger. Gotta get off."

"Yes . . ." Still with his eyes on his wife, speculating, Daniels replaced the microphone in its rack.

6:20 P.M., EDT

"What I need to have done," Kane said, "is have a mechanic check the shimmy damper on the nose wheel. And I need to have him do it tomorrow. You know where to get me. Let me know."

"I'll do my best," Holloway said. "But I've only got two mechanics this weekend."

"Well, call me tomorrow, before noon. I'm not doing another landing with that shimmy. If you guys can't fix it, I'll have to take a shot at it. So I'll want to know, one way or the other, before noon."

"Right." Holloway waited until the other man got to the door of the office. Then, partial payback for Kane's scowling bad manners, the airport manager said, "By the way, there's a guy named Bernhardt looking for you." He glanced at Bernhardt's card, still on his desktop. "Alan Bernhardt. He's a private detective, from San Francisco."

6:30 P.M., EDT

On the third ring he heard Daniels pick up the phone, his private line.

"Yes?"

"This is Bruce."

"Yes . . ." The inflection had shifted guardedly.

"The—ah—nose wheel. It could be a problem, getting it fixed by Sunday."

"Then you'll have to find us a charter."

"All right. I'll let you know."

"Is that the reason you called?" It was a haughty question: the emperor, interrupted during his dinner hour. Unthinkable.

"There's—ah—something else."

"Something else?" Another change of inflection, this one plainly apprehensive. The emperor, faltering.

"I'm at the airport. I talked to Holloway. He's the manager. He said that a private detective wants to talk to me. His name is Bernhardt."

"Bernhardt?"

"Alan Bernhardt. And he—he comes from San Francisco."

"San Francisco . . ."

"Right."

"What's he after?"

"It's about . . ." Should he say it? Was the line secure? He was in a phone booth at the airport parking lot. But Daniels's line could be—

"It's all right."

Always, Daniels knew what he was thinking, a mind reader.

"It's about Carolyn."

"Ah . . ." The single word was spoken very softly. The emperor, wounded. Flicked by a sword point, blood on the silken sleeve. The first wound of many.

"Does he want to talk to me?" Daniels asked.

"I don't know. All Holloway said was that Bernhardt wanted to identify Carolyn—wanted to find out her name."

"Her name . . ."

"Right. And Holloway told him that I'd probably know. So—"

A police car was turning into the parking lot, coming closer. Chief Farnsworth. Unmistakably, Joe Farnsworth behind the wheel.

"What is it?"

"It's Farnsworth."

"Looking for you?"

"I don't know."

"If he's talked to Bernhardt . . ."

"I know."

"Call me back—" A pause, for calculation. "Call me about ten-thirty."

"What about Bernhardt, though?" As he spoke, he saw Farnsworth's car stop at one of the parking lot's intersections. "Holloway knows where I live. He told Bernhardt, gave Bernhardt the phone number on Sycamore. What if—?"

"I've got to go. Call me at ten-thirty." The line went dead.

He hung up the telephone and stepped clear of the booth. His car was parked in the small licensed lot adjoining the airport's main parking lot. It was a Buick Skylark, the same car he'd driven the night he killed Jeff Weston.

To get to the Buick, or to return to the terminal, he must cross Farnsworth's line of sight. It was as if the policeman had taken up a position calculated to command two fields of fire, trapping him.

Meaning that he must walk down the aisle, pass Farnsworth's car, nod pleasantly to the fat man behind the wheel, and cheerfully continue walking to his car.

Daniels's car, really.

6:40 P.M., EDT

In the mirror, Farnsworth watched Kane come closer—closer.

Killer Kane . . . Where had he heard that name? Was it an old comic-strip character? Buck Rogers, was that it?

With his hands resting on the steering wheel, he waited for Kane to pass in front of the squad car, waited for the pilot to look at him. When it happened, Farnsworth smiled, nodded, crooked a forefinger. He saw Kane stop, stand motionless for a moment, then come to the car, bending down.

"Get in," Farnsworth said. "There're a couple of things I want to talk to you about."

"Sure . . ." Kane was nodding, putting on a smile, opening the passenger's door, sliding inside.

Farnsworth put the cruiser in gear. "Have you got a few minutes?" He let the car move ahead, toward the parking lot's exit. "Something I'd like to ask you about."

"Sure . . ." Kane spread his hands. The knuckles, Farnsworth noticed, were scarred.

"I'll drive down toward Knickerbocker's Pond."

"Fine."

"Good flight?" Farnsworth asked.

"Very good. Except for the traffic, getting into Barnstable on a Friday afternoon."

"I understand the FAA's thinking about doing something to take care of the problem."

"They're trying to limit touch-and-go's—training flights—during the summer months."

"Would that help?"

Kane nodded. "It'd help a lot. But it'll take a year, at least, to get the damn thing approved. It's got to go through channels."

Affably, Farnsworth chuckled, then stepped on the brake, brought the cruiser to a stop on the shoulder of a narrow road that led down the dunes toward Knickerbocker's Pond. He switched off the engine, set the parking brake, then laboriously levered his body until he faced the other man, who was turning toward him. "The reason I want to talk to you," he began, "has got to do with a private detective. His name is Alan Bernhardt." He waited. Then: "Does that name ring a bell?"

A frown, then a puzzled nod. "Yeah, as a matter of fact, Holloway— the airport manager—said something about that."

"Have you talked to Bernhardt?"

"No. I just landed. And I've got a mechanical problem. A shimmy in the goddamn nose wheel."

Farnsworth decided to say nothing, decided to let silence work for him as he stared at the other man. Finally: "You remember that missing-persons circular I showed you a week of so back, don't you? The woman named Carolyn Estes, who was last seen here during the weekend of July fourteenth?"

Kane's face froze as he nodded. "Sure. Carolyn. Did she ever show up?"

"No," Farnsworth answered, "she didn't."

"Hmmm."

"And in the meantime, two other people died. And they were both connected to Daniels, one way or the other."

Kane swallowed. "Two other people?"

"Yeah. His daughter died in San Francisco. She OD'd. A week ago, I think it was."

"Th—that's right. God—" Kane shook his head. "I can't say I was surprised. But . . ." He let it go somberly unfinished.

As if he hadn't heard, Farnsworth said, "And then there's Jeff Weston, the punk that Diane was apparently screwing. Jeff was killed the day after Carolyn Estes turned up missing. So you can see, they were all connected to Daniels, one way or the other."

Kane was nodding. "I thought about that, too. Of course, it could all be coincidence."

"Oh, sure." Smiling, Farnsworth spoke affably. "No question about it. No question at all." He held the smile for a moment longer. Then, gently: "Of course, that's not the way this fella Bernhardt sees it. I understand he and Diane spent some time talking, out in San Francisco. And the way Bernhardt's got it figured out, Preston Daniels killed Carolyn Estes on the night of Sunday, July fifteenth. Apparently Diane was fooling around with Jeff Weston, out on the dunes near where her father lives, and the two of them saw Daniels haul the body out of the beach house. They followed him when he drove away from the beach house and buried the body." As he said it, he saw Kane stiffen, saw his eyes suddenly sharpen. Was it surprise? Shock?

"So the next night," Farnsworth continued, "Jeff Weston gets killed while he's delivering dry cleaning for his mother. Bernhardt figures Jeff tried to blackmail Daniels, and Daniels had him killed. In fact—" Farnsworth's mouth twitched in a small, playful smile. "In fact, Bernhardt figures that you killed Jeff, on Daniels's orders. That's—"

"But—"

"That's probably because your car was seen at the scene. That Buick Skylark you drive."

"My car? But—"

"Please." Still smiling, he held up a hand. "I'm almost done. Bear with me. Okay?"

Kane made no reply.

"Still according to Bernhardt," Farnsworth said, "Diane got spooked, and ran away that night. She went out to San Francisco, where her father lives. Bernhardt thinks you followed her out to San Francisco. He thinks you tried to kill her out there. You missed your chance, but she was so shook up, the way Bernhardt figures, that she OD'd, that same night."

"But that—that's bullshit. Total bullshit. I *saw* her in San Francisco, but I sure as hell didn't try to kill her. Christ, I went out there—Daniels *sent* me out there—to get her to go back home."

"You were seen with a club—an iron pipe, maybe, just about to attack Diane Cutler. Come to think of it—" Farnsworth paused. Then he nodded reflectively, as if an idea had just occurred to him. "Come to think of it, Jeff Weston was killed by a pipe, probably."

"I don't think I have to listen to this crap." Kane's voice was harsh, defiant. Approvingly, Farnsworth saw the pilot's eyes harden, saw his hands involuntarily clenching into fists. Yes, Kane was up to the job.

Ignoring the other man's response, Farnsworth said, "This fella Bernhardt, he's been all over the Cape, yesterday and today, asking about Carolyn Estes. He's trying to find out her name, of course. If you want to find someone, pick up someone's trail, you've got to have a name. Then—" Meaningfully, Farnsworth paused. "Then, once you've got a name for the computers, then you're in business. So far, I don't think Bernhardt's got much. Everyone knows about Daniels's blondes, but no one knows them by name. Which is, I'm sure, the way Daniels arranged it. You'd fly the two of them in, and they'd go right out to his place, and have their fun. Then they got back in the airplane, and you flew them to New York, or wherever. The housekeepers didn't even know Carolyn's name. So that means—" Another meaningful pause, a final turn of the screw. "So that means that, besides me and Daniels, maybe you're the only one on the Cape who knows Carolyn Estes by name. Which means that, when Bernhardt finds you, and questions you—and if you give him the name—then it's Katie-bar-the-door. Bernhardt'll have a name. He already knows where the body's buried. So I won't have any choice but to get a crew together, and tell them to start digging around. And if they find anything, then, for sure, the state attorney is going to issue a warrant for Daniels's arrest."

After careful calculation, Kane spoke cautiously: "That's *if* I give Bernhardt a name. But suppose I don't."

"He still knows where the body's buried. He can take that to the state attorney."

A silence fell as they stared at each other, each searching, each probing. Finally Kane spoke: "You know where it's buried, too—don't you?"

Farnsworth smiled, but made no reply.

"If you think Carolyn was murdered," Kane said, "why aren't you digging for the body?"

Still smiling, mock-playfully, Farnsworth continued to eye the other man. Finally he spoke softly, gently:

"Can't you guess why, Kane? You're a smart guy. You've been around. You've even had a little trouble with the law, I understand. Can't you guess why I'm not looking?"

No reply. Only Kane's eyes, boring into his.

As if to prompt a reluctant student, Farnsworth said, "You got well paid, I'm sure, for killing Jeff Weston and trying to kill Diane Cutler." He let the words linger between them for a final moment. Then: "And if you're smart, you're still getting paid—to keep your mouth shut."

"Jesus . . ." Incredulously, Kane shook his head. "You, too?"

"There's so much money there," Farnsworth said. "What's a million or two, compared to Daniels's neck? He pays that much every year just to keep up his goddamn yacht. I read that in one of those magazines. You know, the ones on the checkout stands, at the supermarket."

"Jesus . . ." Contemptuously, Kane snorted. "I should've known."

"Well," Farnsworth answered, speaking more briskly. "Well, now you *do* know. So let's get on with this."

"Yeah . . ." Another incredulous shake of the head. Then, more assertively, partners now: "Yeah. Right."

"You're the cutout," Farnsworth said. "The messenger boy, in other words. You go to Daniels, and you tell him that I want a million dollars to keep quiet."

"*A million dollars?* Are you serious?"

As if he hadn't heard, Farnsworth said, "It'll be in two parts. A half-million now, up front, and a half-million exactly a year from now, when there's no chance of anything going wrong. Daniels and I don't see each other from now on. That's important. You carry the money. You take messages back and forth. Got that?"

Silently, Kane nodded.

"There's also the problem with Bernhardt." He waited for Kane to nod again. Then: "As far as I know, Bernhardt and I are the only two people who know where Carolyn Estes is buried. Maybe Jeff Weston left a letter, or something, but if he did, I haven't heard about it."

Kane frowned. "Is Bernhardt a one-man operation?"

"I think so. He hires people, probably. But he's the principal."

"What if Bernhardt goes to the state attorney? What then?"

"Ah." As if he were encouraging a promising student, Farnsworth nodded. "You've put your finger on it, you see. Bernhardt came to me yesterday. I stalled him. Private eyes're used to that. But sooner or later he's going to find out Carolyn Estes's identity. And that'll be that. He'll get a missing-persons circular, and he'll find a dozen people who saw her at Carter's Landing. And then he'll start pounding my desk. And if I don't start looking for the body, then he's going to go to Boston. And that'll be the end of everything. Daniels goes to trial, and we lose our meal ticket."

"So what'll we do? Bribe Bernhardt?"

Regretfully, Farnsworth shook his head. "I don't think so. Daniels might try it, if and when Bernhardt talks to him. But, sure as hell, Bernhardt'd take that as an admission of guilt."

"So what's the answer?"

"The answer," Farnsworth said, "is that you've got to get rid of Bernhardt. And you've got to do it soon. You've got to do it tonight."

"But—Christ—you're talking like I'm a—a contract killer. I— Christ—I hit that Weston kid too hard, that's all I've done. And now you—"

"So far, Bernhardt hasn't gone any further than me, and I was able to stall him. But by tomorrow, I figure he'll be on the phone to Boston. And when that happens, and my phone rings, the first thing I'm going to do is arrest you for the murder of Jeff Weston. Then I'll start working on Daniels. Hell—" Suddenly Farnsworth guffawed: a wet, clotted laugh that ended in a long, racking cough. Recovering, he said, "Hell, I'll be a hero. I'll be on TV. Nationwide. I'll be famous. '*The straight-arrow cop who arrested Preston Daniels.*' " Pleased, Farnsworth nodded. "Yeah, I can dig it, as the kids say."

"You're fucking crazy, Farnsworth. You know that?"

Farnsworth shrugged. "Everyone to his own opinion." He draped a fat arm over the seat back and pointed behind them. "There's a paper sack on the floor back there. Get it." He watched Kane obey, saw the other man reach inside the sack, saw him withdraw a blue-steel revolver.

"In the trade," Farnsworth said, "that's called a cold gun. Meaning that it can't be traced. Use that. Use it tonight. Bernhardt's staying at The Gulls, that's a motel out on Twenty-eight. Unless I miss my guess, you won't have to go looking for Bernhardt. He'll come looking for you. That could be your chance, if you handle it right."

"Jesus . . ." As if in utter disbelief, Kane shook his head. "Jesus, this is unreal. I can't believe this is happening."

"By the way, before I forget—" Farnsworth pointed to the sack. "There's a pair of surgical gloves in there. Be damn sure you wear them. You've been arrested. Your prints are on file."

Mechanically nodding, Kane said, "How many times've you done this?"

"Three, maybe four times, over the years. But this is the first chance I've had to really score."

"I mean murder. Having someone killed."

Sunk deep in the glowing pink flesh of his cheeks, Farnsworth's small mouth curved in a prim Cupid's smile. "No comment."

"I'm going to talk to Daniels first. I'm not going to do anything until I talk to Daniels."

"No problem." Farnsworth smiled again, his china-blue eyes sparkling. "We're the Three Musketeers. Right?"

In silence, Kane returned the revolver to the brown paper sack. It was a large sack, allowing him to fold it over the gun twice, for safety. "I don't suppose," he said, "that you've got any idea how I'm supposed to pull this off."

"I've got the whole thing figured out," Farnsworth answered promptly. "I bet I didn't sleep more than a couple of hours last night. But I've got it all laid out for you. Everything."

7:15 P.M., EDT

Kane dialed the pay phone, waited through four rings.

"Yes?" Daniels's voice. Abrasive. Plainly irritated.

"This is Bruce again. I know you don't want me to call until ten-thirty. But something's come up. I've got to talk to you. Now. Right now."

"Is there a problem?"

"Definitely, there's a problem. A big problem."

"All right. I'll meet you—" A moment's calculation. "On the Bridge Road, north of Miller's Pond. You know where I mean. At eight forty-five, let's say."

"It's got to be sooner than that. It's got to be now."

"We're just sitting down to dinner."

"I promise you—you'll be sorry, every minute you put this off."

"Are you threatening me?"

"No. Not me."

Not me . . . The two words, ominously suspended, echoed. Not Kane. Someone else.

"All right. I'll leave as soon as I can."

"Good." He broke the connection.

7:30 P.M., EDT

Bernhardt found the telephone number Cutler had given him, touch-toned the number on the motel phone.

"Daniels residence."

"Yes—my name is Alan Bernhardt. I'd like to speak to Mrs. Daniels. Millicent Daniels."

"Can I tell her what it's about?" Accented with a regional twang, the woman's voice sounded weary, washed-out.

"You can tell her that it concerns her daughter. Tell her I've just come from San Francisco."

"Just a minute, please." In the background, Bernhardt heard low voices. Finally another voice came on the line: a cool, precisely calibrated voice. Millicent Daniels, without doubt.

"Mr. Bernstein?" It was a clipped, aloof question.

"Bernhardt. Alan Bernhardt."

"Sorry." The apology, too, was aloof.

"I hate to bother you, Mrs. Daniels. But I was wondering whether I could talk to you this evening. It's about your daughter."

"My daughter?" It was a closed, cautious question.

"I'm based in San Francisco, Mrs. Daniels. When Diane came to town a few weeks ago, Carley Hanks hired me to help Diane. Then—later— Mr. Cutler hired me."

"I—I don't understand." The calmly calculated cadence of her voice had roughened, lost its assurance. "You say Paul hired you. Why?"

"Mrs. Daniels, is there any way we could talk about this face to face? I talked to Diane several times. I was one of the last people to see her before she died. She told me some pretty devastating things. I want to talk to you, tell you what Diane told me. But these aren't things we should talk about over the phone. Believe me."

A silence. Then: "There's a place called The Compass Rose, in Carter's Landing. It's a restaurant, but there's a small bar in the rear. I'll meet you there at eight-thirty."

"Good. Thank you. Eight-thirty."

"How'll I know you?" she asked.

"I'll know you. I saw you at the funeral."

"You were at the funeral?"

"Yes, Mrs. Daniels. I was at the funeral."

8:30 P.M., EDT

"Diane told Bernhardt where you buried the body," Kane was saying. "And Bernhardt told Farnsworth. And now Farnsworth wants a million dollars, or he'll start digging."

They were sitting in the Cherokee, parked facing Nantucket Sound. The night sky was overcast; the surf line was fading into the mist, and would soon disappear. Seated behind the steering wheel, eyes fixed on the water, Daniels was conscious of an irrational calm. Was it possible that even death—even murder—came down to the balance sheet, his stock in trade? Emotion was unpredictable, the wild card. But greed was a constant. Greed was quantifiable, therefore negotiable. Money couldn't buy love. But people had their price.

His voice, therefore, was steady as he said, "I've got to pay him. There's no other way. For either of us."

"If you pay Farnsworth that much," Kane said, "then you've got to do the same for me."

Amused, Daniels smiled, looked at the other man quizzically. "You figured that out, did you?"

"Three people dead. How much is that worth?"

"It's like everything else, Bruce. It's what the market can bear. But then there's a certain market risk factor. You want a million dollars plus what I've already given you. That makes you a source of capital drain. You and Farnsworth, you'll cost me more than two million dollars, cash. Meaning that, if I paid someone—a real pro, not an amateur—to eliminate one or both of you, why, I'd save a lot of money. Let's say I paid someone a hundred thousand dollars to kill you, no questions asked. I'd be saving myself a bundle. And the same thing applies to Joe Farnsworth, obviously."

"If you think you can—"

"Another thing—" Daniels raised his hand, for silence. "Farnsworth knows something that, in fact, is worth a lot of money to me."

"The location of the body, you mean."

As if he were pleased, Daniels nodded deeply. "Exactly. That information, plus his badge, is a combination that could cause me real trouble. But in comparison, you really don't have much, Bruce. All you've got is that when I told you Jeff Weston was bothering me, and you undertook to rough him up a little, teach him some manners, you hit him too hard, and killed him. You might say I paid you to do it, but there's no proof. Then, when I sent you to San Francisco to talk some sense into Diane, get her to come back home, why, you tried to attack her, for unexplained reasons." He smiled. "Does that sound like a million dollars to you?"

Kane came back instantly: "You're forgetting about Bernhardt, aren't you? He's been looking for me all over town. He's trying to find out Carolyn's identity. Suppose I give it to him? Then suppose I tell him you hired me to rough up Weston—and hired me to kill your own stepdaughter? Imagine what Millicent would say, come to that."

Now Daniels's smile was contemptuously tolerant. "You'd be incriminating yourself, not me. I'd just deny everything."

"Farnsworth says we've got to kill Bernhardt. Now. Tonight, before he goes to the state attorney and tells him where the body's buried. What's that worth to you, to have Bernhardt killed?" As he spoke, Kane produced a blue-steel revolver. "He even gave me the gun. It's untraceable."

"If you kill Bernhardt, I'll pay you a half-million. That's in addition to what I've already given you."

Contemptuously, Kane shook his head. "You're a cheap bastard, aren't you? What're you worth? How many billions?"

"Most rich men are tight with money, you'll find. That's how they got to be rich."

"If I don't kill Bernhardt, and he goes to Boston over Farnsworth's head, you're fucked. I might go to jail for aggravated assault, or manslaughter—a fight that went wrong. But you killed Carolyn, and you buried the body. That's as good as admitting you killed her. So when Bernhardt starts talking you're fucked."

Daniels spoke abstractly, speculatively: "It's an interesting situation. The chief of police is soliciting you to kill a man. Meaning that you'll be acting with complete safety, complete impunity. In Carter's Landing, Farnsworth is the law. The whole process starts with him."

"It's still risky. If something goes wrong, you can bet Farnsworth'll turn on us. I've seen people like him before. They don't play unless they've got all the cards."

"I deal with people like Farnsworth every day." As he spoke, Daniels studied the other man's face, searching for something. Finally he returned his gaze to the ocean, and the line of surf beneath the lowering mists. "All right, it's a deal. A million. Same terms as Farnsworth gets. You can tell Farnsworth. A half-million for each of you by next Friday."

Kane's scarred mouth twisted into a smile. "Cash?"

"Naturally."

8:50 P.M., EDT

Seated across a small oak table, her glass of white wine untasted, Millicent Daniels shook her head incredulously. "I can't believe it. I—I just can't. I know he's had women on the side, but—" She broke off, stared down at the table. Then: "He lives like a king, you know. There's always someone in attendance, some flunky, someone to take orders. And the telephone. It's like he's the center of some gigantic electronic web that's spread out over the whole world. Push a button, and someone somewhere comes to attention. Push another button, and he's made a million dollars. Limos—airplanes—they're all there, waiting. So—" She shook her head again. "So the idea of him digging a hole in the ground and rolling a girl's body into it—I just can't conceive of it."

"But it happened, Mrs. Daniels. If you believe Diane, then you've got to believe it happened."

"She didn't actually see him burying the body, though."

"Are you familiar with the landfill? It's a few miles to the northeast of Carter's Landing. They're going to build an overpass out there."

She shook her head.

"It's about five acres, maybe less. And it's entirely fenced. There's

249

only one gate. Which, as it turns out, is never locked. Diane was too cautious to get trapped inside."

"And you say Preston hired Kane to kill the boy Diane was with that night."

"I think so. There's no real proof of that, though. Chief Farnsworth might have proof. But I don't."

"Does Chief Farnsworth know about the dead girl?"

"I've told him everything I know. He hasn't told me everything he knows, though. I'm sure of that."

"Does he know the girl's name?"

"I think he does. But he hasn't told me."

"Does he know where she's buried?"

"I told him Diane said the body is in the landfill. But, as I said, it covers a lot of ground. And there aren't any landmarks. Or, at least, very few."

She sat silently for a moment, searching Bernhardt's face for something she couldn't define. Then: "You think Preston sent Kane to San Francisco to kill Diane."

"Yes, I do. I had someone there, on guard. She saw it happen—saw Kane, with a weapon."

"And then Diane OD'd. Because of the shock."

Deeply regretful, Bernhardt nodded. "Within an hour or two. Carley Hanks was in the apartment when it happened."

"Carley . . ." As she said it, she was suddenly overwhelmed by the images: Carley, age seven or eight, the noisy, bright-eyed, lively one, always underfoot. Carley, a teenager, she and Diane in Diane's room on the third floor, door locked, whispering, giggling. Who lived in that wonderfully gabled room now, with its sweeping view of San Francisco Bay? Another teenager—a girl who could laugh one moment and cry the next?

At the thought, she suddenly felt the center of herself give way, felt the tears begin. Four years ago, before the divorce, Diane was a giddy, unpredictable teenager. Now she was dead. She'd hurt so badly that finally she'd killed herself.

"Oh, Jesus . . ." The table was so small that she'd put her purse on the floor beside her chair, something she hated to do. Should the wife of Preston Daniels have to put her purse on the floor? Eyes streaming, she found her purse, put it in her lap, found a Kleenex, wiped at her eyes, blew her nose.

The wife of Preston Daniels . . .

That's how it had all begun. First there was the fragment of the thought that Daniels might marry her. Then came the fantasy. And with the fantasy, she'd felt herself begin to change. She'd been riding in his limo—one of his limos—when it had happened. She'd been alone, just she and the driver. She'd never ridden in a limo before she met Preston Daniels. She'd never bought anything she'd wanted, without regard to price.

Anything she'd wanted . . .

Anything was derived from *thing*. And things were inanimate, without life. Just things.

Like Diane, now. A thing, without life.

She tried to speak, failed, tried again, her eyes cast down in a rush of remorse. "Jesus, I—I'm sorry. I—I was just—" She broke off, turned her head away from the other patrons of The Compass Rose, away from anyone who could see her. The wife of Preston Daniels, crying in public. Running her mascara. It was unacceptable.

Making it, suddenly, all the more important that she finish the sentence: "I was just remembering how it was when they were just kids. Carley and Diane, I mean."

"I hate to put you through all this, Mrs. Daniels. But I—well—the truth is I guess I feel guilty. If there's something that I could've said to Diane, something I could've done, it might not've happened the way it did."

She laughed: a harsh, bitter sound, the sound of illusions shattering. The sound of her life coming apart. "*You* feel guilty. Jesus." As she said it, an image flashed across her consciousness: Preston Daniels, judged guilty of murder. Daniels, on trial. Headlines on the front page . . .

And headlines on the financial page: *Daniels Empire Topples.*

Everything, gone.

Once again her mouth twisted into a bitter smile. "Living with Preston is a little like living with a very powerful engine that's always running at full throttle. He never really relaxes. When he plays tennis, it's to release energy, so he'll be able to function more efficiently in the boardroom. Making love—" Eloquently, she shrugged. "It's the same thing."

Bernhardt decided not to respond.

"More than anyone I've ever known," she said, "he controls his brain, not the opposite. But still, it's hard to imagine him killing someone, and burying the body, and not letting it bother him."

"It's got to bother him."

She shrugged. "Subconsciously, probably."

"What about Kane? Do you see him as a murderer?"

"Kane . . ." Her eyes hardened. "I very seldom talk to him. But I've never liked him."

"Can you imagine him killing someone?"

She nodded. "Definitely. Preston, no, not really. But Kane, yes."

"Do you think it's credible that Daniels would hire Kane to kill the Weston boy, and then kill Diane? Do you think it could've happened that way?"

She considered the question carefully, then said, "When you first told me this, I didn't think any of it was credible. I couldn't imagine Preston with a shovel in his hand, digging. I simply couldn't. But then I ask myself who Preston could hire to dig the grave. Who does he trust that much? And the answer, of course, is that he doesn't have anyone. Absolutely no one. He doesn't have a single close friend. He has a brother, but they quarreled over a business deal, years ago. They haven't spoken since."

"So he's left with Kane."

"Who, I'm sure, did it for the money."

Across the table, Bernhardt looked at his watch, then took a business card from an inside pocket and wrote on the back. "That's where I'm staying, Mrs. Daniels. The Gulls, on Route Twenty-eight. Do you want me to keep in touch with you, tell you how it goes?"

"You'd better let me call you, Mr. Bernhardt."

He nodded. "That's probably best."

"I think so."

"I'd better go. I'm still trying to locate Kane."

"Preston got a call just before he left the house tonight. He left in a hurry. I had the feeling it was Kane who called."

Again, he nodded. "Thanks. I'll remember that." He put some money on the table, and they rose in unison. "I'll see you to your car."

"Thank you." She nodded, began walking toward the door, pausing long enough for Bernhardt to open it. Outside, the fog was rolling in from the ocean, making halos around each of the parking lot's lights. As they walked, she spoke softly: "You're a nice man, Mr. Bernhardt. Are you married?"

"I was married. My wife got killed, in New York. It was a mugging."

"Oh, God . . ."

He made no reply.

"Did you have children?"

"No. We were just going to, when Jennie died."

She gestured to her car, a Mercedes. Silently she went to the driver's door, inserted the key. As she swung the door open she said, "The last time I saw Diane, it was in New York. We had a terrible fight." Without looking at him, she got in the car and started the engine.

"I'm sorry. I'm very sorry."

She nodded. "Yes, I know you are."

9:40 P.M., EDT

Bernhardt saw the car parked at the curb: a blue Buick Skylark, Kane's car. The car was parked in front of the two-story frame house on Sycamore Street used by members of Daniels's staff. Since yesterday, Bernhardt had called three times at the Sycamore Street house. Twice the house had been deserted. Once a weary, resigned, middle-aged woman had told him that he'd just missed Kane, who had probably gone to the airport.

Paula had described Kane as "a man in his middle forties who looked like a middleweight." Amused, he'd asked her how many middleweights she'd ever seen in action. They'd been in bed, and her reply had been a forefinger dug into his short ribs.

A vicious man, a man who'd murdered once, and tried to murder again. How would the conversation go? *"Hello. My name is Alan*

Bernhardt. I'm looking for evidence that'll send you to prison, maybe the death house."

Or, *"Hello. I'm Alan Bernhardt. If you'll just be kind enough to confess, therefore incriminate your boss, I'll use my influence to get you off with a slap on the wrist."*

He leaned across the seat, unlocked the glove compartment, withdrew the .357 Ruger in its soft leather holster, shut the glove compartment. The revolver was stainless steel, Ruger's top-of-the-line Magnum. Herbert Dancer, his former employer and all-around amoral son of a bitch, had given him the automatic as a token of his esteem. Translation: of all Dancer's investigators, Bernhardt had been the only one who'd consistently questioned Dancer's motives. Most megalomaniacs, he'd discovered, need one honest man close to them. And Dancer had chosen him.

He swung out the Ruger's cylinder, checked the load, carefully returned the cylinder with the hammer and the one chamber left empty. He holstered the gun, slipped the holster inside his trousers on the left side, clipped the flat steel spring over his belt. It had taken him more than an hour at Airport Security in San Francisco, filling out forms and submitting to a long, petty interrogation, before they'd taken the gun, emptied it, packaged it, tagged it, and consigned it to the cockpit crew for the trip to Boston.

He drew a long, deep breath, swung open the Escort's door, and began walking across Sycamore Street.

9:45 P.M., EDT

Seated behind the steering wheel of his own car, a green Taurus sedan, Farnsworth smiled as he saw Bernhardt lock his rental car and begin angling across Sycamore toward the house where he'd find Kane. Did Bernhardt realize how easily he'd fallen into the trap? It was as if Farnsworth were the director and Bernhardt, Kane, and even Daniels were the actors. A gesture from the director, and they went where they'd been told to go, did what they'd been told to do.

Until, when the last scene was played and the floodlights were shut down, he would pick up his prize, and smile, and walk away—and disappear.

9:50 P.M., EDT

When she'd begun, he'd immediately gone to the door of the study and closed it. When she'd finished—finally exhausted by her own emotions—he asked quietly, "Is there anyone else in the house? Any servants?"

"As soon as I got back," Millicent answered, "I sent them home." Adding bitterly: "I know how you hate for anyone to witness our periodic little scenes."

"Okay. Now, can I say something? Will you listen to me, while I say something?" Daniels spoke quietly, trying to calm her with his voice, trying to steady her with his eyes. Arms folded, at bay, still breathing deeply, raggedly, she stood with her back to the wall of books that were the backdrop for his desk. Selected by a renowned bibliophile, the books were old and valuable and beautifully bound. His father's study had been lined with books like these—most of them read.

Surprised by the wayward thought, the instant's image of his father's study flashing across his consciousness, he frowned. All day—all week, all month—random images had materialized, fragments of the past, many of them centered on his father, that stern, silent man, that disapproving stranger who stood so tall and imposing, arms folded, his eyes slightly narrowed: the eternal judge, looking down, passing sentence.

But the images were a distraction, therefore dangerous. Requiring that he now refocus his thoughts as he ventured a single step closer to her. Saying: "I'm terribly sorry about Diane, Millicent. And I won't pretend that I don't feel guilty. I never gave her a chance. Never. I—I always saw her as the price I had to pay, to get you. And I—"

"Don't, Preston." As if to push him away, defend herself against him, she raised her hands. "Don't patronize me. Don't insult me. I—I'll call Chief Farnsworth, I swear I will, before I'll let you patronize me."

"Millicent, you should recognize that—"

"I blame myself, Preston. I don't blame you. You laid it all out for me. You wanted me, and you'd take Diane, too, if that's what it took to make the deal. But you asked me to leave Diane in San Francisco. I refused, of course. I thought—I actually thought—that I was a loving mother. I believed—really deluded myself into believing—that Diane would be better off in New York, with me. After all, how many teenagers were driven to school by chauffeurs? How many—" Suddenly her voice caught. Eyes closed, blindly, she shook her head.

"Millicent—" He advanced another step.

"Don't touch me. I'm warning you, Preston. Don't touch me." She was gasping for breath. Her eyes were blazing, filled with hatred. But, God, she was beautiful. Never had she aroused him more than at this moment. If he could touch her, he could calm her. As if he were approaching a dangerous animal, he extended his hand, to make contact.

"Preston—" It was a shriek: Millicent, suddenly gone wild. Involuntarily, he stepped back.

"I'll call Chief Farnsworth."

Once more, she'd said it. Signifying fixation, determination. Bernhardt had talked to Millicent, and Millicent would talk to Farnsworth. Sooner or later, Millicent would talk to Farnsworth. He could see it in her eyes, hear it in her voice.

"Millicent, you—you've got to listen to me. You've got to listen to reason." As he spoke, he watched her carefully. The next moments—the next words—would decide everything. With a few words, a sentence, she could bring it all down, destroy everything. The female, aroused. The mother, avenging the death of her young. This was the power that drove her, that had lit the manic fire in her eyes. An irresistible force. Implacable.

Yet, ultimately, controllable. His specialty. His particular gift.

But time was required. He must have time to calm her, time to regain control, to bring her back from the edge.

Time and money, the two constants, the eternal verities. For himself, for Millicent, nothing more mattered. If he could bring her back, he could—

"—next, Preston?" she was asking. "Who'll die next? Is it Bernhardt? Is he next?"

Bernhardt.

The faceless presence, suddenly the ultimate threat.

Bernhardt alive represented danger.

But Bernhardt dead could represent disaster. Because Millicent, when she learned of Bernhardt's death, would go to Farnsworth. She would tell Farnsworth that Paul Cutler, attorney at law, officer of the court, father of Diane, had hired Bernhardt to come to the Cape.

And Farnsworth, that obscene, corrupted guardian of the law, would put in the call to Boston. Farnsworth would save his own oversize skin.

And then the jackals, always out there, would begin to circle. Reporters at their keyboards. Editors holding the presses.

"Millicent—" With the single word he tried to reach her, this one last time. "Millicent, I've—there's something I've got to do. It's—it's about this, all this. Can I—I've got to—" He broke off, shook his head, began again: "Will you stay here, until I come back? Will you do that?"

Her face was expressionless now, as if hatred had frozen it forever. An endless moment passed—and another, her eyes locked with his, a wordless, soundless struggle. Finally, very deliberately, she nodded. Then, without speaking, she turned, went to the door, opened it, walked out of the room. Behind her, the door closed with a single click.

Instantly, he took his keys from his pocket, unlocked the desk, opened the right-hand top drawer—the drawer that held his revolver and ammunition, nothing else.

10:55 P.M., EDT

"Assuming that you're telling the truth," Bernhardt said, "then if I were you, I'd make a deal."

"Is that so?" Kane's smile was mocking. "What kind of a deal would that be?"

"You're telling me that you didn't have any part in the girlfriend's murder. Based on my information, I'd say that's probably the truth."

Watching the other man carefully, Kane made no reply. The living room of his apartment in the Sycamore Street house was tiny, furnished with one brown plastic sofa, a matching armchair and two straight-backed wooden chairs that badly needed refinishing. There were three lamps, each one with a skewed shade. Bernhardt sat in the center of the sofa, Kane sat in the armchair. Less than ten feet separated them.

"You also say you didn't kill Jeff Weston. And when my associate saw you about to attack Diane, in San Francisco, you say you just wanted to talk to her. You say you were carrying a rolled-up newspaper, which Pau—which my associate thought was a club. Well—" Trying for a cheerfully objective cynicism, hoping to keep the other man off balance, Bernhardt shrugged affably. "Well, I've got to tell you, Kane, that I don't believe you on either count."

"Listen, Bernhardt, you—"

"According to Diane's story," Bernhardt cut in, "she and Jeff saw Daniels disposing of his blonde friend's body. That connects the three incidents—the two murders and the attempted murder. Then there's the MO in two of the incidents. A club. So I've got to figure that—"

"I'm not going to listen to any more of this shit, Bernhardt. We've been at this for an hour. And in about two minutes, I'm going to throw your ass out of here. I'm going to—"

"However," Bernhardt went on, "neither one of those two incidents—the murder of Weston and the attempt on Diane's life—are what this case is all about. You know that, and so do I. And, unless I'm very much mistaken, Farnsworth knows that, too. You're a very little fish, Kane. But Daniels is a very big fish. Which, I believe, could give you a lot of leverage, if you're smart."

Kane's eyes were smoldering. Beneath the T-shirt he wore, the muscles of his neck and shoulders were drawing tight. But he said nothing. Watchfully, he waited: the predator, gathering himself.

Surreptitiously, Bernhardt shifted slightly on the sofa, at the same time unbuttoning the corduroy jacket that concealed the Ruger, holstered beneath his belt on the left side. "What this case is all about," Bernhardt said, "is the murder of that girl. Daniels's blonde. That's where it all starts. And I'm betting that Daniels called on you for help—hired you—after that murder was committed, after he'd buried the body. Isn't that right?"

Now Kane's icily mocking smile returned as he said, "You don't expect me to answer that, do you?"

Bernhardt's answering smile was cat-and-mouse cheerful as he said, "Let's go back to the deal I was talking about. Let's construct a hypothetical scenario. Let's say that you look around, and you realize that you could be getting into real trouble. You decide you want to cut your losses, you want to get out. So what's the best way to proceed? How do you protect yourself? If you make a deal with Farnsworth that'll incriminate Daniels, how do you know Farnsworth'll keep his word and go easy on you? The answer is, you don't know. So you need a third person, for protection. A lawyer, let's say. Except that a lawyer who's good enough to help you is going to want a lot of money—up front. He'll want twenty-five thousand, probably, just to get started. So let's say you decide not to hire a lawyer. And let's say Farnsworth is really starting to lean on you. What do you do? The way I see it, you've got three ways to go. You can hang tough, and hope Daniels doesn't fall. Or else you can make a deal with Farnsworth, which I think would be pretty risky business."

As he said it, Bernhardt saw something behind Kane's clear gray eyes shift, saw the lines around his mouth tighten. Had Farnsworth already offered a deal to Kane?

"Which brings us to the third alternative." Bernhardt smiled, spread his hands. "Me."

Kane snorted contemptuously. "You?"

"You flew Daniels and his blonde girlfriend to the Cape the day before she died. You flew him back to New York the day after she died. You know her name. You can connect her to Daniels. If you'll make a statement to that effect, and if you'll testify that Daniels paid you to shut up both Jeff Weston and Diane Cutler—if you'll do all that, and I add to it what I know, and I take the whole package to the state attorney in Boston, I can guarantee that he'll make you a deal. He'd do anything to get your testimony."

For the first time, Kane's eyes shifted tentatively. "You wouldn't go to Farnsworth?"

Promptly, Bernhardt shook his head. "No way. I don't trust him."

For a long, speculative moment Kane made no reply as his gaze wandered thoughtfully away. This, Bernhardt knew, was the decisive moment, make-or-break time. Was Kane about to give in? So easily? So quickly? Moments ago, he'd been hostile, belligerent. What unknown nerve had Bernhardt pressed? Was it something to do with Farnsworth?

Finally, speculatively, Kane said, "What if I can do all that—tell you all that? What've you got to go with it?"

"I've got what Diane told me. She laid out the whole thing, what she and Jeff saw, and when they saw it."

"She knew where the body's buried, then."

Bernhardt nodded.

"And she told you."

"Yes."

"Where'd she say it was buried?"

"Ah-ah—" Bernhardt raised an admonishing forefinger. "First you. Then me."

Now Kane's belligerence was fading, replaced by transparent calculation. Holding eye contact, boring in, everything at risk now, he said, "Her name was Carolyn Estes. She lived in Manhattan. Greenwich Village. But she's not—she wasn't—in the book."

Aware that he was exhaling, a spontaneous release of tension, Bernhardt nodded. "Okay. Good. Now I've got something I can take to Boston. Tomorrow. First thing tomorrow. How do you spell her last name?"

"Wait. I gave you something. What about me? What've you got for me? You know where she's buried. Where is it?"

Aware that he was gambling against long odds, aware that a vital piece of the puzzle was still missing, Bernhardt spoke softly, reluctantly: "He buried her in the landfill. The one about five miles northeast of town. He took her there in his Cherokee, wrapped in a blanket, or a tarp. Sunday night. About midnight. He buried her himself."

"The landfill . . ." Slowly, Kane nodded. When he spoke, it was in a different voice, an enigmatic voice: "Yeah . . ." He nodded again. "That's right. The landfill . . ." He continued to hold Bernhardt's eyes as he asked softly, "But where in the landfill? That's the question."

Watching the other man, conscious of unknown crosscurrents, a presence unseen, therefore dangerous, Bernhardt also spoke very softly: "Are you asking me?" A last definitive pause. "Or are you going to tell me?"

Kane smiled: a confident smile, subtly superior, gently mocking: "I can do better than that, Bernhardt. I can show you."

11:15 P.M., EDT

He heard the latch click, saw the door open a cautious crack to reveal Bessie's pale, pinched face. Then came the predictable exclamation: "Mr. Daniels. Why—" Then, fretfully agonized: "Just a minute, Mr. Daniels. Just a second." The door closed, the night chain rattled, then the door opened to reveal Bessie Nichols, wrapped in a chenille robe. Her hair was in curlers, her eyes were round and anxious. Of all his domestic help, Bessie was the most loyal, the most dependable—and the mousiest.

"Mr. Daniels," she repeated, anxious now. "Is anything wrong?"

He was ready with a reassuring smile. "Nothing's wrong, Bessie. I'm just looking for Bruce. Something's come up. Is he here?"

"Oh, Mr. Daniels—" Agitated, she spoke with deep regret: "You just missed him. Ten minutes, maybe even less, you missed him by. I was letting Foxy in for the night. Foxy, that's my cat. And I saw Bruce leave."

"But—" Daniels half turned toward the street. "His car—"

"He was with someone. A man."

"A man? Who? Did you recognize the man?"

She frowned. "How do you mean? Do you mean did I know him, know his name? Because I don't. But I recognized him from yesterday, when he came by looking for Bruce."

"Can you describe him?"

"He was about forty, forty-five. Tall and skinny. Six foot, at least. He had those aviator glasses, I remember that, and a lot of hair and a long nose. He seemed to be dark-complected, too. Not Negro or Mexican, not like that. Just dark."

"How was he dressed?"

"A light-colored sports jacket," she answered promptly, "and no tie. And he walked kind of slouched, it seemed like. The way a lot of tall men walk."

"Did they take his car, he and Bruce?"

She nodded. "Yes, sir." She pointed toward the street. "The car was parked on the other side of the street, under that streetlight, so I got a real good look at it. And it was red. Small, too. A Japanese car, maybe."

"You're sure it was red."

"Absolutely. Red. No question. And small."

"Okay." He nodded, stepped back, smiled. "Sorry to bother you, Bessie."

"No bother at all, Mr. Daniels."

11:30 P.M., EDT

"Have you been to the landfill?" Kane asked.

Behind the steering wheel of the Escort, Bernhardt nodded. "Certainly."

"The whole thing is fenced. There's only one entrance."

"I know."

"They're building the approach to a bridge—a causeway, really—across a chain of saltwater ponds. It'll relieve the congestion on Route Twenty-eight." Kane pointed. "Turn right here."

Bernhardt slowed, made the right-angle turn that put them on a narrow two-lane blacktop road leading north, away from Route 28. The blacktop road was deserted; the night sky was overcast. To the east, the lights of Hyannis were fading in the fog. Bernhardt glanced at Kane's dimly defined profile, then returned his gaze to the road ahead. What could account for Kane's abrupt turnabout, his sudden decision to cooperate? They'd talked for a little more than an hour. From the first, Kane had been hostile, defiant, sometimes belligerent. But then, when Bernhardt had said he'd deal with the state attorney, not Farnsworth, Kane had suddenly caved in, begun to cooperate.

Why? What had suddenly turned the tough, perpetually angry pilot around? Behind his street-fighter's persona, was Kane scared?

Or was he pretending, faking it, running a scam? Once more, silently, Bernhardt glanced at the man beside him. Since they'd gotten into the car together, they hadn't talked about the Estes murder; Daniels hadn't been mentioned.

The landfill covered acres. The terrain changed with every dump-truck load, every bulldozer pass. A crew using probes could work for days before they found Carolyn Estes's body. Perhaps weeks. Perhaps months.

Until an hour ago it had been Bernhardt's belief, his working premise, that only the murderer knew the exact location of the grave. Only Daniels.

Yet, in minutes, Kane would point out the grave.

Signifying what?

In exchange for murdering Jeff Weston, had Kane demanded that Daniels point out the grave site? Somehow the scenario didn't scan: the swaggering, bad-tempered pilot, dictating terms to Preston Daniels.

Was there another scenario? Was it possible that—

"There." Kane pointed ahead. "Turn right. This is it."

As, yes, Bernhardt recognized the sandy, rutted dirt road that led to the gates of the landfill, just over the next rise.

11:40 P.M., EDT

Crouched on his knees in the trough between two ridges of sand and cut grass, Farnsworth saw the Escort turn into the entrance of the landfill. Once inside, the car's headlights went out as the small sedan slowed to a crawl, making its way along the narrow track compacted by the dump trucks on their daily rounds. In seconds, the Escort disappeared among the mounds of earth and debris outlined against the night sky: slabs of concrete and twisted claws of reinforcing rods and shards of broken pipe and splintered metal. Earlier in the day, the landfill's foreman had told Farnsworth that, once since July fifteenth, the trucks had been held while the bulldozers had come to level the site. Soon, the foreman said, the bulldozers would come again. Eventually the ready-mix concrete trucks would arrive—and Daniels's secret would be safe.

Until now, safe.

11:42 P.M., EDT

Driving slowly in second gear, lights out, Daniels brought the Cherokee up to the top of the last rise in the road just as—yes—the Escort turned into the landfill's entrance and disappeared from view behind a hillock. Was this the beginning, the first incarnation of his worst fears, his most persistent nightmare: the body of Carolyn Estes, a worm-eaten cadaver, exhumed?

Or was it the prelude to salvation: only one murder more?

11:45 P.M., EDT

"Here." Kane pointed. "Go to the left, here."

Guiding the Escort slowly and cautiously between the mounds of dirt and debris, running without lights, in low gear, Bernhardt winced as the car's right front wheel struck an obstruction, a metal-racking sound.

"Jesus, how much farther?"

Looking straight ahead, his body rigid, Kane's voice was expressionless as he said, "Just a hundred feet more. Maybe a hundred fifty."

"I'm getting the feeling," Bernhardt said, "that we could be trapped in here. It's a goddamn maze." As he spoke, Bernhardt glanced in the mirror. Nothing. On all sides, the surreal terrain was closing in. When he was in the tenth grade, because his grandfather had insisted, almost the only demand the old gentleman had ever made on him, he'd taken Latin, a year of torture. A phrase from Julius Caesar had somehow lingered in his memory: *closed in by the nature of the place.* It was one secret of Caesar's military success: he never allowed himself to be closed in by the nature of the place.

A killer beside him, face strangely frozen, directing him through a labyrinth of unnatural shapes that, foot by foot, left the real world far behind. Suddenly too far behind. In this place, this dark, deserted place, reality was shifting, falling away. Leaving him unmoored.

Unmoored, and—yes—suddenly afraid.

The Ruger was holstered on his left side at the belt, positioned for the cross-body draw favored by most detectives, recommended by most police-academy instructors. But his jacket was buttoned. Concealed by the jacket, the Ruger rode only inches—only an inch—beneath the steering wheel.

Suddenly the time for judgment was gone; only instinct remained. Survival.

He lifted his foot from the accelerator, stepped on the brake as he brought his right hand down from the steering wheel to the single button that secured his sports jacket.

Instantly, the man beside him reacted. For Kane, too, only instinct remained: "Don't. Don't do it."

The car jerked to a full stop. Still with his hand at his belt, Bernhardt turned to face the other man. Kane was smiling. It was the first time Bernhardt had seen him smile.

In his right hand, Kane held a short-barreled blue-steel revolver. To maximize the distance between them, Kane sat with his back pressed against the door, facing him.

"Surprise."

"Not really."

"You've got a gun."

Bernhardt sighed. "Yes, I've got a gun."

"Okay—you know how it goes. Use two fingers. Take out the gun. Put it on the seat. Do it slowly. Very slowly."

Twisted behind the steering wheel in an effort to face the other man squarely, another instinct, Bernhardt unbuttoned his jacket, took the Ruger from its holster, put the pistol on the seat. Cautiously, Kane grasped the Ruger, thrust it into his belt. "Okay—" Kane jerked his head, gesturing with his revolver. "Go ahead. Drive."

"Drive where?"

"Just drive. I'll show you."

"Where's the girl's body?"

"You'll find out." The muzzle of the revolver moved again. "Now drive."

Bernhardt put the gear selector in low—and pulled out the headlight switch.

"*Hey!*" The revolver came up, swung in a short, vicious arc, struck him high on the shoulder.

11:48 P.M., EDT

Slowly, cautiously, Farnsworth rose from a crouch to stand erect, his head and torso above the ridge of cut grass that fringed the top of the low-lying dune. How long had it been since the Escort, running without lights, had entered the landfill and disappeared among the mounds of debris? Two minutes? Three? Earlier, making his plans, he'd considered giving Kane a miniature walkie to carry in his pocket, a monitor, a bug. But if the police-issued walkie-talkie were found in Kane's possession afterward it would—

From the landfill came a sudden flare of headlights, quickly gone.

A signal?

No, not a signal. If anything went wrong, their prearranged signal was the car horn: two quick blasts, then two more.

"Make him turn off his headlights," he'd warned Kane. *"In these dunes, you can see lights for a mile, even in the fog."*

Eyes fixed on the spot where he'd seen the instant's flash of headlights, he glanced at his watch. He would allow exactly two minutes to elapse. Then he would decide.

11:49 P.M., EDT

Through the Cherokee's windshield Daniels saw an instant's flash of headlights, quickly gone. Was it a signal?

Was it a powerful flashlight, not headlights? They could be hidden in the landfill: the police, warned by Bernhardt. The men from Boston, waiting and watching, their warrants in their pockets, weapons cocked, ready.

First they would take Kane into custody.

Then they would come for him.

Bernhardt—the police—finally the reporters—all of them arrayed against him. All of them, and Millicent, too.

Leaving him only one option, one choice.

Aware of the lassitude that dragged at each movement of hand and arm, suddenly debilitating, he opened the glove compartment, withdrew the .357 Magnum. God, the pistol was heavy. Why, suddenly, was it so heavy?

11:52 P.M., EDT

"Here it is. Stop the car." Once more the revolver moved. "That big slab of concrete. That's it."

Looking to the right, just ahead, Bernhardt saw the skeletal shapes of twisted reinforcing rods protruding from the huge concrete slab outlined against the sky, an evocation of no-man's-land in the First World War, the landscape of hell. It was as if the slab had been part of a blown-up artillery bunker.

Or was it the headstone of the dead woman's grave?

"Stop here."

Bernhardt braked the Escort to a stop, switched off the engine, once more turned to face the other man.

"What's it all about, Kane?" As he spoke, he rubbed his aching shoulder. "What're you scared of? Is it the law? Or is it me?"

"Give me the keys. Slow and easy."

As insolently as he could manage, an actor's imitation of a fearless tough guy, Bernhardt took the keys from the ignition, handed them over.

"I'm going to get out of the car," Kane said. "When I'm out, then you slide across and get out."

"I want to know what's happening. I want to know why the gun." It was the tough guy's lines again. What else could he do?

Kane smiled: a small, malicious smile. For Kane, the tough-guy role was a natural, perfect typecasting. "You want to find Carolyn's body, you've got to dig for it." Once more, he gestured with the revolver. "There's a shovel near that slab. I'll show you where, when you get out. The dirt where you'll be digging is loose. Very loose."

"A shovel?"

"Get out. *Now.*"

"I'm not going to dig. That's bullshit. Digging is for the police, not for me." As he said it, Bernhardt could hear the tremor in his own voice, could clearly hear the false bravado, could clearly hear the fear. Soon, he knew, the physical manifestations would begin: first the dryness of the throat, then the weakness at the knees, finally the countless small visceral spasms, the beginning of shock. Fear was a state of mind; shock was a physical condition. The antidote for both was adrenaline, the animal kingdom's connection to modern man. Get angry enough, pump enough adrenaline, and meek men became heroes.

Get scared enough, and the meek died where they fell.

A gun—a shovel, concealed—a thug with flat, vicious eyes. A murderer, about to earn his murderer's wage. And on his paymaster's tally sheet, Preston Daniels would make one more entry: debit one stack of gold, credit another accuser killed.

Jeff Weston, dead. Diane Cutler, dead.

And Alan Bernhardt. Dead.

He realized that words were all that were left, his only hope. Once an actor, always an actor. Sing for his supper, beg for his life.

No. Not beg.

Instead, fight. Bluster.

Only fear could save him now. Kane's fear.

"Oh, yes," Kane said softly. "Oh, yes, you'll dig. Do you know why you'll dig?"

If he answered the question, he went on the defensive. Frank Hastings had taught him that. And Pete Friedman, the squad-room fox, had taught Hastings: never—never—answer a suspect's hostile question, one of the first rules. Requiring him, therefore, to accept the gambler's gambit, go for the tough talker's bluff:

"You're making a stupid mistake, Kane. You're thinking the way a loser thinks, don't you see that? Daniels hires you to do his killing for him, and then you take the fall. You don't know where Carolyn Estes is buried, not precisely. We're—" He broke off, gathered himself for another bluster, another bluff. But the brave words were unconvincing, at least to his ear: "We're here to bury me, isn't that it? I'm going to dig my own grave, and then you'll shoot me." Momentarily he broke off, searched Kane's face in the dim light for some sign of uncertainty, of fear. "You don't want to shoot me first, because someone might hear the shot. Someone might come before you get the grave dug. That's the problem with shooting off guns in a place like Cape Cod. You got it right, using a club on Jeff Weston. But you should've—"

"Get out of the car, you bastard. Now. Right now. Or I'll shoot you there, in the car."

"I don't think Hertz would like that, Kane. All that blood—" Pantomiming dismay at the other man's dilemma, Bernhardt shook his head.

"I'm going to count three. When I count three, I'm going to shoot. I swear to God, I'll shoot." Slowly, Kane drew back the revolver's hammer: one click, two clicks.

"Diane's father knows I'm here, Kane. He hired me. I report to him twice a day. He knows I'm here, right now. He knows I'm here with you."

"You're lying."

"I have an assistant. She—" Suddenly his throat closed, the grip of fear. His whole body was trembling. The revolver—the muzzle—had grown enormously, the center of everything. "She expects me to—"

"One."

Was Kane's voice unsteady? Was there uncertainty in the pale eyes? Fear?

"And Farnsworth. He knows, too."

"Now I know you're lying." The revolver came closer; the muzzle expanded again with the movement, a round black abyss. Death.

"I'm not lying. My assistant, she saw you in San Francisco. She recognized you. She—"

"Two."

11:54 P.M., EDT

Yes, he could clearly see it now: the Escort. Inside the car he saw the shape of a figure braced behind the steering wheel, facing the open passenger's door. Bernhardt, facing Kane. Kane, beginning his murderer's countdown. Kane, holding a pistol Wild West style, arm straight out. Kane, about to kill again.

He began moving toward the Escort. Was he close enough? Was there time to move closer?

"Two."

Using both hands, he raised his revolver, drew back the hammer, steadied the sights on Kane's torso, began squeezing the trigger.

11:55 P.M., EDT

Muscles locked, racked by spasms of terror, helpless, his whole body rigid, braced against death, Bernhardt realized that his eyes were closed. An instant's image of his mother appeared. She was reading to him from a child's picture book, smiling as she turned the pages. She—

An explosion. A shot.

Instantly, his whole body unlocked, began to quiver. His eyes were open, searching for the face of death, the final vision.

Vision?

Was he alive? Had he been wounded, the pain masked by shock? Had he soiled himself—shamed himself?

The car—he was still in the Escort, his body wedged behind the steering wheel; the Escort's door was still standing open.

"Ah—" It was a low, muffled moan.

Kane?

Aware that he could move, he was pushing himself away from the steering wheel. His feet were sliding across the seat, out the door. Then his legs. Sitting erect, he saw him: Kane, lying on his face, his hand still clutching the blue-steel revolver with the two-inch barrel.

Without conscious thought, suddenly energized, he sprang to the body, twisting the revolver from fingers that still twitched.

Was it suicide?

He raised the gun to his nostrils. No, there was no smell or cordite. Meaning that someone had—

To his right, there was movement. A figure. A man, crouching. Instantly, Bernhardt dropped to the ground, brought the revolver up, trained it on the intruder.

"*Bernhardt.*"

A stranger's voice. The figure was tall and slim. Not thick and gross, therefore not Farnsworth.

But if it wasn't Farnsworth, then—

"It's Preston Daniels. Don't shoot."

11:56 P.M., EDT

Standing on top of the low sand ridge, Farnsworth blinked, refocused his gaze on the entrance to the landfill. First he'd seen the quick flare of headlights from inside the fence. Then, moments ago, he'd seen a figure slip through the entrance and disappear behind the first mound of earth inside the landfill.

Someone had tracked the Escort, someone whose car was concealed among the dunes.

Someone who was stalking Bernhardt and Kane.

Or did Bernhardt have backup, someone who'd kept out of sight for the last two days, kept in reserve for this moment?

Or had Bernhardt called Boston? Had the state attorney sent help? At the thought, Farnsworth shook his head. No, it couldn't be the law. The law would never send a single man into danger. It was the first rule of survival. Never look for trouble alone.

Daniels? Could it be Daniels? Could Daniels—

A shot.

One shot, then silence. No second shot. No screams. A good, clean kill. Yes, Kane was a killer. The proof was in his cold gray eyes; killer's eyes.

272

But was there a witness? Had the intruder—the third man inside the fence—seen Kane do it?

The third man . . . It had been a movie. Orson Welles. Joseph Cotten.

Fifteen minutes, he'd calculated, would elapse while Kane filled the shallow grave, got rid of the shovel, escaped in the Escort.

Fifteen minutes for the third man to track the sounds of earth being shoveled into the grave.

Crouching low enough to keep his head below the line of the dune, Farnsworth went to the Taurus, took the flashlight from its clip beneath the dash, took the Walther PPK from beneath the front seat. The Walther was a cold gun, untraceable. He held the gun up to catch the pale light and slid back the slide enough to confirm that, yes, there was a cartridge in the chamber. Making it necessary only to cock the gun's hammer and fire. Seven shots, semiautomatic fire. Plenty.

11:57 P.M., EDT

With the .357 tucked in his belt, with his hands held wide from his body, palms forward, Daniels walked slowly toward Bernhardt.

"Is he dead?"

Bernhardt looked down at Kane. The hands and feet were still twitching, but the spasms were weaker now. "He's dying, I think." As he spoke, Bernhardt thrust the revolver he'd taken from Kane into the pocket of his jacket, then turned to face Daniels.

"Christ, you saved my life."

"Yes . . ."

"Why?"

Daniels was ready with a puzzled frown. "Why?"

"I'm trying to get you for murder. Kane was doing your work for you."

Daniels smiled. Like the frown, the smile was calculated, part of the moment-to-moment improvisation that began when Millicent confronted him, told him that Bernhardt had gotten to her, told her everything. As he'd listened to her, watched her closely, felt the imapct of her raw, ungoverned hatred, he'd realized that, just as Bernhardt had accused him of Carolyn's death, so Millicent would accuse him of Bernhardt's death.

Yet Millicent's hostility, driven by grief and guilt, could be managed. Time, and patience—and money, the three would wear Millicent down.

But Kane, grown greedy, the blackmailer, would always be dangerous.

How had he missed it, failed to realize the danger Kane represented? Farnsworth, the pro, that was a straight business deal, both of them with something significant to lose—and gain.

Therefore, kill Kane—one more death—and he was safe. Finally safe.

Except for the bones, finally safe.

"I've got to sit down," Bernhardt said, moving to the Escort. The passenger door was standing open; the interior light illuminated the scene. Kane's body was still now, no longer twitching. In delayed shock, trembling, Bernhardt sat on the passenger seat, his feet resting on the ground. He watched Daniels come to stand between him and Kane's body.

Daniels spoke in a quiet, measured voice: "It was Kane, you know. You understand that, don't you?" Waiting for a response, some sign that the words had registered, he watched Bernhardt's eyes. Yes, the eyes were quickening. Signifying that the time had come. With one body lying beside him and another body buried somewhere close by, the time had come.

"It must've happened when Kane drove Carolyn to the airport, that Sunday night. He could never keep his eyes off her. He was obsessed by her. I always knew he was, and I should never have allowed them to be together. But she had to get back to New York that night, and I couldn't leave the beach house, because of a call I had to take. I think Kane pulled off on a side road not far from the airport. He—" Daniels shook his head. "He must've gone crazy, probably because of cocaine. And she resisted, I'm sure of that. And that's all it took. She resisted, and he lost control. I think he blacked out. But when he came around, he knew just what to do. Maybe, subconsciously, he'd planned the whole thing. I wouldn't doubt it. In any case, he came here, and buried her. He didn't know that Diane and her boyfriend witnessed the whole thing. So then he had to—"

"You're lying." Bernhardt spoke in a low, exhausted voice.

Once more, Daniels frowned. "What?" It was an expertly delivered monosyllable, projecting a regal surprise. "What did you say?"

"I said you're lying." Bernhardt drew a long, deep, weary breath. "You killed her, Daniels. And you sent Kane to kill Diane, to shut her up."

"You've got everything twisted, Bernhardt." Projecting both pity and perplexity, Daniels shook his head. "You've had a bad scare, and you aren't thinking straight. You say you're out to get me for Carolyn's murder. And, in fact, Millicent told me the same thing, tonight. Now—" Pantomiming long-suffering patience, he spread his hands and smiled. "Now if that's all true, then why wouldn't I have let Kane kill you just now?"

"Because people know why I'm here. Your wife, and Farnsworth, and people in San Francisco. Besides, with Kane dead, you thought you'd be safe. God—" Projecting a bone-weary exhaustion, a disarming tactic, he shook his head, at the same time gathering himself. "God, I aged ten years, just before you shot him." As he spoke, Bernhardt used his left hand to grip the frame of the door, ready to pull himself to his feet—while, one movement masking the other, a momentary distraction, he drew Kane's revolver from his jacket pocket, aimed at Daniels's chest.

"Step back, Daniels. Two paces. No more."

"Bernhardt, you—"

"Do it now, Daniels. Or I'll shoot you." Using both hands, the approved grip, he raised the revolver to eye level, drew back the hammer to full-cock, carefully sighted. "I won't kill you. That could get me in a lot of trouble. But I'll sure as hell put one in your shoulder. Then, when you're down, I'll come in close, shoot out your kneecaps. Both of them. So you'll never walk again."

"You're bluffing."

"You sent Kane to kill me, you son of a bitch. He was counting to three." Bernhardt settled himself, gripped the revolver more firmly.

"One."

"Listen, Bernhardt, let's talk about—"

"Two."

"*Shit.*" Daniels stepped back. One pace. Another pace.

"Okay. Now the gun. Take it out, lay it on the ground. Carefully. Very carefully. Use two fingers. Then, when you're—"

"Okay, Bernhardt—" The voice came out of the darkness behind the car. "Let's both of you lay your pieces on the ground. First you, Bernhardt. Then you, Daniels."

"Me?" Daniels asked.

"Oh, yes," Farnsworth answered. "Oh, yes, Mr. Daniels. You, too. Especially you."

2:20 A.M., EDT

Millicent's eyes widened incredulously. "Preston is in jail? Locked up? *Preston?*"

"He killed Kane," Bernhardt answered. "He killed him in cold blood. I saw him do it. And so did Farnsworth."

They were standing in the entryway of the Daniels beach house, with the outside door closed behind them. The entryway was lighted by overhead mini-floodlights set in the ceiling. Standing in the cone of one of the floodlights, wearing a high-collared robe that swept the floor, her hair loose, hands clasped at her waist, face pale without makeup, Millicent could have been acting the part of a queen in a Shakespearean tragedy. Instead of speaking, Bernhardt stood silently, watching her as she stared past him. What were her thoughts? Would she stand by her husband, the source of enormous wealth? The trial would center on Daniels's dead mistress. How much was Millicent's pride worth to her? What was the market price?

Daniels's ego was a known quantity.

What about Millicent's ego?

Now, almost dreamily, she turned away. "Come in," she said. "Sit down."

"Thank you." He followed her into a large, dramatically furnished living room that faced out on the ocean. The room was furnished around a huge slate-topped coffee table. They sat facing each other across the table. After a long moment, finally meeting his gaze, she said, "What happens now?" Her voice was dulled; her eyes shifted uncertainly.

"I can't tell you exactly what'll happen," he answered. "He'll get in touch with his lawyers, I'm sure of that. In a few hours, they'll start coming down on Massachusetts' law enforcement like a pack of lions. And his flacks, I'm sure, will come down on the media. Hard."

Numbly, she nodded. She was staring down at her hands, tightly clasped in her lap. The muscles of her throat were cruelly corded. This, Bernhardt reflected, was not Millicent Daniels's most flattering pose. Finally she began shaking her head.

"That's the part I hate," she said. "The reporters and photographers. The tabloids. It's so—so tacky."

Tacky? Was that where it ended, for Millicent Daniels? With her child dead, was tacky the ultimate judgment?

"If I were you, Mrs. Daniels, I'd hire a lawyer. I'd hire a good lawyer, and I'd follow his advice."

"Yes . . ." Irresolutely, she nodded. "Yes, I'm sure you're right."

"I wouldn't use any of your husband's lawyers if I were you. You should get your own. Someone who's only concerned with your best interests."

"Yes . . ."

"I'd do that as soon as possible. I'm almost sure Daniels will be out on bail by this afternoon."

Startled, she raised her head; her eyes came into sharp focus. "But— but this is murder. Is there bail, for murder?"

"I'm not a lawyer. But I believe the court's free to grant bail whenever it wants. One consideration is whether the suspect is a flight risk. And, obviously, Daniels isn't going to disappear. Besides, he'll obviously try to make Kane the villain of the piece, so he'll be posing as the perfect citizen. He's going to say that Kane killed Carolyn. Then Kane killed Jeff Weston, he'll say, to shut Weston up. He'll also say that

Kane tried to kill Diane and me, for the same reason. And, of course, he'll say that he killed Kane to save my life. Which, in a sense, is true. Thank God."

"Will they find the girl's body, do you think?"

He shrugged. "It's not a certainty. As I understand it, that landfill's been bulldozed flat at least once since the murder. If she didn't show up then, maybe she'll never show up. Even Daniels probably couldn't pick out the spot where she's buried."

"He'll go free. If the body isn't found, he'll go free." Her voice was a low, uninflected monotone, the voice of utter resignation, of utter defeat. She began to slowly shake her head. "He'll be a hero. By the time his lawyers and his flacks get finished, all anyone will remember is that he saved your life. He'll use you, just like he uses everyone else."

"I don't intend to let that happen."

Her smile was grim. "You might not have a choice. Most people don't, when they go against Preston."

"Does that include you?"

She raised her eyes, studied his face—and made no reply.

THURSDAY,
August 16th

6:30 P.M., PDT

As Bernhardt's key turned in the lock Crusher began to bark clamorously, that unfailing ritual of greeting. With the lock free but the front door still closed, Bernhardt shifted the bag of groceries to the crook of his left arm and used his right hand to push the door open, bracing himself for the inevitable collision as, still barking, furiously wagging his tail, the Airedale jumped on him—once, twice, three times.

"Get the ball, Crusher. Find the ball."

Instantly, the dog turned away and began frantically sniffing as he searched in all the usual places for one of his tennis balls. Quickly closing the door, Bernhardt retreated down the long hallway to the kitchen. He deposited the sack of groceries and the briefcase on the kitchen table just as Crusher came prancing down the hallway with a tennis ball in his mouth. Bernhardt unlocked the rear door behind the kitchen, pried the ball out of the dog's mouth, and threw the ball out into the rear garden, where Crusher caught it on the first bounce. Bernhardt closed the door and walked back down the hallway to his office, once the flat's front bedroom. The message machine's counter showed four calls, about average for the hour and a half he'd been out of touch. He sat at the desk, selected a pen, turned to a fresh page in his notepad, and pressed the recall button.

"You were right," Paula's voice acknowledged, "surveillance is dull. But I'm tuned in on this guy, and I'm going to catch him dirty, isn't that the phrase? Anyhow, I'll give it until his wife comes home, which is usually about six-fifteen. So I should see you about seven. I'll get some fish. Salmon, if it isn't too expensive. 'Bye."

The second message was from the credit bureau, and the third was a blind call from a harassed-sounding woman who said she'd call back tomorrow—maybe.

The fourth caller was a man: "Yeah—Bernhardt. This is Chief Farnsworth calling, from Carter's Landing. I just thought I should tell you that a couple of hours ago we found a woman's body out at that landfill. It's Carolyn Estes, probably. There's no identification, but who else could it be? We've had about twenty-five guys working with probes for three days, a real workout, I don't mind telling you. Working those probes, you know, it's tricky. You got to know what a body feels like. But, anyhow, when they finally turned her up, there was less than a foot covering her. I have an idea the state attorney's going to be in touch with you about the preliminary hearing. Meanwhile, I'm going to be on TV tomorrow, nationwide. How about that?"

—Collin Wilcox

San Francisco, 1991